scarred

scarlett finn

<u>Also by Scarlett Finn</u>

<u>NOTHING TO...</u>
NOTHING TO HIDE
NOTHING TO LOSE
NOTHING IN BETWEEN: ONE
NOTHING TO DECLARE
NOTHING TO US
NOTHING IN BETWEEN: TWO
NOTHING TO SAY
NOTHING TO GAIN
NOTHING IN BETWEEN: THREE
NOTHING TO YOU
NOTHING TO THIS PREQUEL: ONE WILD NIGHT
NOTHING TO THIS
NOTHING IN BETWEEN: FOUR
NOTHING TO DO
NOTHING TO FEAR
NOTHING IN BETWEEN: FIVE
NOTHING TO DENY

<u>GO NOVELS</u>
GO WITH IT
GO IT ALONE
GO ALL OUT
GO ALL IN
GO FULL CIRCLE

<u>KINDRED SERIES</u>
RAVEN
SWALLOW
CUCKOO
SWIFT
FALCON
FINCH

<u>EXILE</u>
HIDE & SEEK
KISS CHASE

<u>THE EXPLICIT SERIES</u>
EXPLICIT INSTRUCTION
EXPLICIT DETAIL
EXPLICIT MEMORY

<u>THE FORBIDDEN NOVELS</u>
FORBIDDEN DESIRE
FORBIDDEN WANT
FORBIDDEN WISH
FORBIDDEN NEED
FORBIDDEN BOND

<u>WRECK & RUIN</u>
RUIN ME
RUIN HIM

<u>MISTAKE DUET</u>
MISTAKE ME NOT
SLEIGHT MISTAKE

<u>THE BRANDED SERIES</u>
BRANDED
SCARRED
MARKED

<u>TO DIE FOR...</u>
TO DIE FOR TRUTH
TO DIE FOR HONOR
TO DIE FOR VIRTUE
TO DIE FOR DUTY
TO DIE FOR LOVE

<u>RISQUÉ & HARROW INTERTWINED</u>
TAKE A RISK
FIGHTING FATE
RISK IT ALL
FIGHTING BACK
GAME OF RISK

<u>FORBIDDEN PREQUEL DUET</u>
ALL. ONLY.
ONLY YOURS

<u>LOVE AGAINST THE ODDS STANDALONE COLLECTION</u>
SWEET SEAS
HEIR'S AFFAIR
RESCUED
MAESTRO'S MUSE
GETTING TRICKY
THIRTEEN
REMEMBER WHEN...
RELUCTANT SUSPICION
XY FACTOR

<u>LOST & FOUND</u>
LOST
FOUND

ONE

"THERE'S A TERRIFYING GUY at the end of the bar glaring at you. Should I call security?"

Nya Yorke smiled at her new server's words and finished pouring the draught beer for her customer. She hadn't seen the "terrifying guy" arrive at Sizzle, the club she managed, didn't mean she didn't know him.

"He vetted security," Nya explained. "Don't think they'd toss him out on his ass."

Even if they tried, they'd find themselves knocked down flat in a pool of their own blood.

"You know him?" Jada hissed in her ear.

She handed the customer his drink and accepted payment with a smile. "Unfortunately, I do." Nya put the money in the register. Only when it was closed did she twist toward her new waitress to fixate on the man. "He's my boyfriend."

Leaving Jada to gape, she strutted up the bar and came to a stop opposite Archer. The music was loud so she didn't bother with a traditional hello. Slapping her forearm on the bar, she leaped up and grabbed his jacket to pull him down for a kiss.

When he gifted her his tongue, she smiled at her

body's the instant carnal reaction.

"When I said call me if you need anything," he shouted over the bass of the music. "This isn't what I meant."

"I know," she said. "There's a guy standing two-thirds of the way down the bar."

Tracing her finger down Archer's sternum, she batted her eyes like they were flirting.

"Did he touch you?"

Shaking her head, she nuzzled her cheek on his hand when he caressed her face. "No."

"You called me to cut a guy who flirted with you?" he asked but didn't hesitate. "I'm on it."

Without further question, Archer intended to hurt the guy. Except she couldn't let him. Catching his arm to press his hand to her face, she twisted her wrist, silently asking him to kiss her brand, which he did.

"Fella," she mouthed, drugged by the cloud of their attraction.

Archer wasn't as distracted. "I'm curious, what the fuck did he say? I say all kinds of nasty shit to you and you never get offended. He must be a real pro."

His almost impressed gaze wandered toward the guy.

She boosted up to steal his mouth before it could get far. "He's wearing your mark and he's asking questions."

Zeroing in on her, he snatched her chin. "You've got skills, Squirm." His interest grew more acute. "What's he asking?"

"If you'll be in. He heard you'd been seen here."

"Does he know who you are?"

"To you?" she asked. "If he saw us kissing, he does now."

His gaze fell to her mouth. "That's why you should learn to keep those lips to yourself until you clue me in. Still so much to teach you."

"You mean you wouldn't have kissed me if I'd talked first?" she asked, pushing out her breasts.

His brief moment of admiration cooled, he reached over to fasten a button on her shirt.

"Those are for private viewing only."

"These babies pay Mama's bills," she said, unbuttoning it again.

He lunged over the bar and seized a handful of her shirt to yank her against the bar. "That's what Daddy is for, baby, and those belong to him."

A mean-looking security guard, Robbo, stepped into a pool of light at the corner of the bar. Once he registered the identity of the guy holding her, and exchanged a nod with him, he melted away.

Archer did up two of her shirt buttons this time.

Tucking her hair behind her ears, she didn't fight him. "Letting you handle Sizzle security gave you ownership of the place," she said, but wasn't really complaining. The club had never been safer. Because Archer hired all her new security guys, they were more loyal to her boyfriend than her. "I have more résumés in the office for you to filter."

Running his hands over her breasts, he checked out the patron who'd been asking about him. "Let me deal with him first."

Taking his hand, she held him back. "Don't get hurt... I might need your body later."

Kissing her brand once more, he wandered off without reassuring her or pandering. Taking a deep breath, she tried to be subtle about observing first contact. No punches were thrown, no knives bared, so she relaxed and went about serving her customers.

It was almost closing time. Archer wouldn't start a fight with so many drunk idiots ready to brawl in the vicinity. As often as their schedules allowed, her man took her home at the end of a shift. Given he was there anyway, she imagined he'd hang around and give her a ride. She'd get the skinny then... if he was forthcoming. With Archer, that was hit and miss.

Though he could be secretive, he was thorough. Especially when it came to her safety. A new security system had been installed. They were recruiting security guards with the aim of hiring three times as many as before.

Archer handled all of it. She'd known he would from the moment he'd sat in her office chair and picked up the first stack of résumés. One by one, he scoffed and discarded anyone unsuitable in a heartbeat. Her man knew something about almost everyone. Those not on his radar weren't immune from his scrutiny. He quickly gathered whole life histories on those he didn't know.

They hadn't planned for Sizzle to become his base, he'd never had a regular one before. Except word was seeping out about their relationship. He'd been spotted there so much, people often asked for him.

Most of the time, she played dumb, but this guy wore Archer's mark, revealing the two men had history. Good or bad, Archer needed to know he was there. If the stranger wanted help, her guy could decide whether or not to give it. If the visitor wanted to hurt her lover, Archer would handle that in his usual swift, final way.

TWO

IT USED TO BE at the end of a Sizzle shift, all she could think about was sleep. Bed was still on her mind, but slumber was far from it. The customers had been ushered out while she completed the usual task of cashing-out the registers.

Archer's hands landed on her shoulders just as she finished bagging up the last of the takings. "Are we far from take-off?" he asked, burying his lips in the hair at her crown.

"No," she said, putting a rubber band around the bag. "I just have to take this to the office."

"Nya!" The voice of her newest server attracted her attention left. "Can I head out?" Jada asked, side-eyeing the unfamiliar man behind the bar with them. "We've finished cleaning up."

Without knowing Archer, he probably intimidated the crap out of the twenty-two-year-old. He was there so regularly that Jada would get used to him.

"Jada, this is Archer," Nya said. "He's part of the furniture… not that you should sit on him… that's my job."

Some of the server's wariness waned, but it didn't dwindle altogether. "Your boyfriend?" Jada asked. "He doesn't work here?"

"No," Nya said. "Not officially." Since they'd got

together, he'd spent so much time watching over her that she'd considered giving him a paycheck more than once. Packing the money bags into a cloth pouch, she closed over the register. "You can't leave on your own, we all leave together."

Jada wasn't happy but didn't complain. Instead, she wandered off to join the other employees gathered around one of the tables opposite the bar.

Security had tasks and continued to do sweeps, but they kept doors locked after the last customers left. The staff did the cleaning up and sometimes griped when bored and wanted to go home. Nya did her work fast and they were paid for every minute they spent there. Maybe it wasn't fair, she just couldn't take the risk of letting anyone go out into the street alone and vulnerable. Losing one member of staff was enough; Jamie's death hadn't been for nothing.

The only exception to her rule was Archer. When Archer was at the club and the staff finished their work, they were allowed to leave together as a group. With her guy watching over her, she could finish her work with only him for company and he'd take her home after.

That night he'd been ensconced in his conversation with the stranger, even after closing. The now-absent-stranger.

"Where's your friend?" she asked him, moving down the bar toward the office with the takings.

Her man followed. "Gone. I kicked him out, don't worry. There won't be any trouble."

Only when they were both in the office, with the door closed behind them, did she ask another question. "Who was he?"

With an absent gaze, Archer scanned the room he'd been in dozens of times, a sure sign she was about to be dismissed.

"Don't worry about it."

Grumbling to herself, she went to the safe and input the combination to open it. "He came to my club, I have a right to know," she said, dumping the takings inside.

"You did the right thing, you called me," he said. "I'm

taking care of it."

He wasn't going to tell her who the guy was or what he wanted. Fine. If it became a regular thing that this same stranger showed up, she'd push harder. For now, she moved on.

"And the job?" she asked, locking the safe. "The one you left to come here tonight, how's that going?"

For the last three days, someone had been resident in his apartment. Some might use the word "imprisoned," others maybe, "captive." Potato, potatho. She could handle what he did and understood he hurt people to get information. And that he did it for money. His motives weren't altruistic or benevolent, but he didn't hurt anyone innocent. Those he stole into his custody deserved whatever fate befell them. In another room, those "victims" often handed out unjust punishments themselves.

"Getting there," he said, sliding his hands into his pockets.

His eyes roamed over the documents in her in-tray and those scattered on her desk.

Always looking for an angle, always seeking secrets, even in her boring office where he had permission to look at everything, her guy wouldn't switch off.

Telling him she was capable of handling what he did seemed straightforward at the time. What she hadn't factored in, and what ended up being more difficult, was not the pain he inflicted on others, no, but the sexual deprivation he inflicted on her.

"Can you come over?" she asked, sauntering toward him, sliding her arms under his to loop them around him.

Tucking her thumbs into his waistband at the back of his jeans, she curled her fingers around the horizontal sheath containing his always-present knife and squashed herself into him. He was the only guy allowed to carry a weapon in Sizzle.

"Tomorrow," he said. "I'll come over tomorrow."

Nearing the end of her rope, she exhaled and stuck out her bottom lip, stopping just short of stamping her foot.

"This is crazy, Fella, I never see you. I want you to come over. I want to be with you."

"It's been three days, Squirm. You knew the script when we hooked up."

"But we're *not* hooking up!"

Having gorged herself on his body at any time of her choosing for weeks, she'd been spoiled with his attention. That over-indulgence had switched to an extreme famine that pinched from the very first night.

That her sulk entertained him only frustrated her further. Still, she didn't pull away when his fingers scooped under her chin.

"It's temporary, Squirm."

Unsatisfied, she enjoyed his touch despite her remaining disappointment. "Until the next job," she muttered.

His amusement reached its limit and his temper soured. "Yeah, until the next one. What do you want me to do? Stop working?"

His job wasn't what bothered her, it was their separation.

"No," she said. "But you could let me come over."

"No." His firm voice startled her. Once his mind was made up, his decisions were final. "Not while I have a source in my place. No way. Not a chance."

To an extent, his need to protect her was flattering. But, boy, was he taking it too far.

"What harm can an hour do?" she asked. "I'm not talking about moving in."

Another sore point. After a casual comment about what it would be like living with him, during one of their lazy days, he'd shut her down on the prospect of them ever staying together full-time.

All she'd said was it would be a breeze to room with him because he was always tidying up after her. The implication being she'd never have to lift a finger again; except to do about seventy percent of the cooking. The other thirty percent, he sought flesh, and she hadn't succeeded in cooking that for him yet.

He strung together some patience. "I've left him alone too long already. If I come to your place, you know I'll end up spending the night. We suck at leaving each other once we're lying together."

With no persuasive argument in her arsenal, she stayed silent, and he turned as if to go.

She wasn't ready to lose him yet so grabbed his arm. "I'm sorry," she said. "I don't want to fight."

Their time alone these last few days had been scarce, she didn't want to waste their precious seconds on negativity.

"Squirm—"

"I know," she murmured, stroking his rough jaw. "I'm sorry."

Continuing her caress as she whispered her apology, she pulled him down and pushed up until, eventually, she got what she wanted: his kiss. While he had other responsibilities demanding his attention, he avoided kissing her for the same reason he couldn't lie with her—he'd never want to leave her.

Right then, she wanted to distract him.

Without shame, she'd admit to not being as adept at the self-control thing. She had no desire to be. Her desire was focused on this pillar of a man. When he snatched his arms around her waist, the power in them squeezed the air from her lungs, increasing the pace of their battling tongues.

Fervor came out in a moan. She was already off her feet with her toes dangling. In full control, he stormed forward and pushed her down. Whatever his plan, she didn't care, she trusted him. When his hard, heavy body settled down on hers, details ceased to matter. Nothing mattered but him.

Buttons flew left and right when he ripped open her shirt, her bra was next to go, and then his mouth was on her breasts. Driving her fingers into her hair, she whimpered his name on a gasp, delighting in the sensations she'd missed. That buzz, that breeze, only he could make her shiver in a heatwave.

Screwing in the club, with so many employees right on the other side of the door, was a terrible idea. But, hey, good sense never stopped her making bad decisions.

Clawing her way up under his tee shirt, she scratched his chest, delivering him a pain he returned by sucking hard on the nipple between his teeth. Her yelp got him up, not to his feet, just enough to clamp his mouth over hers, pinning her head, and the rest of her, to the unyielding wood of the desk.

She didn't hear him unbuckling his belt but the mass of his hand tugging up her skirt had clear motive. Yes, motive, she wanted motive. His fingers scooped her underwear aside to allow two to drive into her. Pumping his digits hard and fast, they scouted and prepared the path his cock planned to travel. In a practiced move, he pressed his thumb against her clit and circled hard, massaging it against the bone behind.

All the while his mouth stayed on hers, she increased the movement of her hips against his hand. His possessive lips parted and closed in a persistent rhythm. Her guy's tongue demanded submission in the speed and insistence of his kiss. He had it. Had anything he wanted. All of her.

As one of his hands stirred her juices, the other grasped her breast to flick and pinch her nipple, rubbing the tender peak with his rough fingertips.

Withdrawing from their kiss until they barely made contact, he knew exactly how to torment her.

Her tongue searched for his when it slipped from its mate. "Archer," she said his name into his mouth.

Protest fled when the hot, hard head of his entitled cock kissed the opening his fingers departed. This was a bad idea.

Their eyes collided.

"This is wrong," she mumbled.

Instead of cooling their desire, the words inflamed it. Mm, he wasn't the only one with tricks.

Pushing deeper, unrelenting in his pursuit, nothing dissuaded him. "I know," he breathed in a gruff exhale. "I fucking love it."

That was all it took for her hips to rise, and her pussy to swallow more of him.

"You're so bad."

"You're so wet," he said, fucking her fast.

She met every advance. "Because of you."

"I like it. I missed it. I need this right here." Each of his sentences came after a long, fast plunge into her. "Your hot fucking body's all I think about. You should be in my bed.

You think I don't fucking want that? You spending the night alone, that's fucking wrong."

"This is wrong," she said. Clutching at his shoulders, tiring as orgasm approached, she ran her hands up his neck, into his hair, down his back, consumed by their union. "Oh, this is wrong. This is bad. We're in charge. We shouldn't be doing this. We should stop. It's so wrong!"

After his hoarse laugh warmed her, he dropped his head beneath her chin and sucked hard on the front of her neck by her pulse point.

"You are bad," he said, his breath moistening her ear. "You want it bad, horny one. You've wanted to ride my cock from the minute I walked in here."

Pathetic, maybe, but completely true. Yelling out, she froze in the grip of climax. His pelvis still worked; his cock drove in and slid out as he galloped toward his own reward. She shouldn't have shouted; she shouldn't have screamed. The staff would know for sure what was going on.

Oh, hell.

Grabbing his head, she forced him to kiss her. If his tongue was in her mouth, she shouldn't be able to call out again. Except at that crucial moment when their bodies reached bliss once more, he whipped his mouth away and growled at her.

"Scream," he demanded, ordering her to surrender. "Scream, damn it!"

His need fueled the pressure in her body. Her head snapped back as she bucked and relented, unable to stop herself screaming out his name.

Still shaking, her body damp, her abdomen quaked when his dick slid out of her. She didn't even try to move, just blinked through the stars he'd put in her eyes and listened to him buckling his belt.

"You're a bad influence on me," she panted, eventually finding the strength to lift her head. "Did you come here just to do that?"

He didn't answer her, not with words, his sly half-smile spoke for him. "I had business," he said. "There's nothing wrong with mixing in a little pleasure."

Pulling his tee-shirt from his jeans, he grabbed his jacket from the chair. She hadn't even noticed he'd discarded it. Tossing it over his shoulder, he turned to swagger from the room, leaving her on the desk, legs still akimbo, breasts bared, and mind in complete chaos.

Her head hit the desk with a thud. The office was trashed, she'd have to tidy up and face her staff.

They shouldn't have screwed on the desk at this hour when everyone was desperate to get home to their loved ones. All that waited for her in her studio apartment was a cold shower and an empty bed. Covering her face with her hands, she laughed. Being bad with Archer was the best "bad" she'd ever known.

THREE

RUNNING UP THE STAIRS of Tag's apartment building, she let herself in through the front door, then locked it behind her. Once again, he was living alone in a place far more suited to his personality.

Forcing herself to have at least one full day off from Sizzle per week, she usually spent her down time with Archer. But, grr, he was still occupied by his guest.

It was fine. She wanted to update Tag on how things were going with the new security measures and staff. Sizzle was technically owned by him after all; it was only right he be kept in the loop.

The small entry hallway opened into a vast living space with high ceilings, sash windows, and hardwood floors. The place was flashy, just like the Tag she knew. Except this time, when she went inside, with her purse hung over her body and a grocery bag under her arm, she came up short.

Standing in the middle of the room, wearing nothing more than a bedsheet, was a ravishing brunette; one she recognized.

"Oh," the brunette said, wearing contrite shame, clutching the sheet tighter to her chest. "Oh my God, he's married. I knew it. Why wouldn't he be? A guy like him, of course he's married. I'm sorry—"

"No, I—he—no—I…" Nya hurried to calm the woman on her way to a meltdown. Except she was too surprised to do it well. Shock prevented her from putting together a coherent sentence for another five beats. "I'm not his wife."

The brunette glanced toward the glass shelving unit near the kitchen, then strode over with an outstretched arm. "This is you. The, the picture, this is you."

The one photograph Tag had in his whole apartment was of her. It was sort of an inside joke, a tease, because she hated having her picture taken. She hated it being displayed even more. Funny that this woman should think she was a girlfriend because of that mocking picture, ha, served Tag right.

Her actual boyfriend would balk at the idea of putting up her picture. He didn't bother with superfluous items, he used the barest minimum of furniture. Not because he was trying to save the world or going for a particular style of décor, oh, no, but because knick-knacks gathered dust and dust was Archer's natural prey.

"Yes, that's me," Nya said before the brunette could pick up the picture to examine it too closely. "But I'm not his girlfriend. I'm not his wife. I'm… I'm just a friend."

The brunette relaxed, she stopped walking, and her stuttering ceased too. "Oh, thank God."

Okay, quick reminder, it wasn't her place to sling accusations. Polite questions weren't accusations, right? Had she been with Archer too long?

"And who are you?"

"Oh, I'm…" The brunette averted a smile as a sort of coquettish glimpse at the floor. Oh, this beauty was smitten with her oldest friend. "Farrah Hexam."

Not news. No. IDing the woman was easy because she'd seen her before. Someone might then wonder at her shock. That didn't come at the *who*, no, it came from *how* she knew the woman.

To get himself out of a mess with Farrah's villainous brother, Brett Hexam, Tag had been tasked with meeting the beauty. To shoot the breeze? No, it was a con. Their meeting was supposed to be by accident, everyone but Farrah was in on it. Tag's goal? To flirt and tempt her away from a boyfriend her brother deemed unsuitable. Guaranteed Brett Hexam wasn't declaring open season on the young woman's vagina.

Hexam was a scary guy, a gangster many levels above Tag on the street. The clash over the original mess almost ended her life, and Tag's. Solving Hexam's personal problem was supposed to zero the clock.

And until that moment, right there in Tag's living room, she'd believed that was exactly what happened.

The play finished weeks ago. In the diary according to everyone except Tag, apparently.

Farrah dumped the boyfriend, so Hexam cleared Tag's debt and her friend was freed from his self-exile. Life was supposed to return to normal with all that in their rearview. The last thing she'd expected to find was this woman naked in Tag's apartment.

Just to be clear, naked was never part of the original deal.

"Have you been seeing him long?" Nya asked, moving into the kitchen with her brown paper grocery bag.

Archer had to have rubbed off on her. These questions should be aimed at Tag. She shouldn't be probing this random, apparently naïve woman, while her guard was down. Still, getting information from Farrah's side, since serendipity gave her access anyway, would be a good benchmark to ultimately decipher Tag's honesty when asked the same questions.

This relationship was such a bad idea, Tag would have to lie and make excuses. He couldn't possibly tell the truth. There was no justifiable reason for him to be screwing around with the sister of the man who'd wanted to hurt him not that long ago. His excuse would be—though he wouldn't phrase it in this way—that his cock was making decisions likely to get him killed.

"We met about six weeks ago," Farrah said, coming over to lean on the counter between the kitchen and living room. "I was seeing someone at the time, we couldn't… you know…"

There was that girlish smile again. Nya was crazy in love with Archer. When she thought about him, molten carnal awareness infused her. Had she ever giggled when someone mentioned his name or asked a question about him? Giggling, okay. She'd try harder to nail that.

"You're not seeing that guy anymore?" Nya asked, unpacking Tag's treats from the bag and the pastries she'd bought for them to share with coffee from his swanky machine.

Except he wasn't here, so she'd share them with Farrah instead. Maybe the bribe would succeed in persuading the beauty to share details.

"No, that ended," Farrah said. "I finished it and… I should've been sad, I really cared about him, but… I couldn't stop thinking about Tag."

"So you contacted him?"

Tag should've let Farrah down gently. The point was never to get into a relationship with her, never to sleep with her. The point was to separate the Hexam sister from her ex. And that had happened, she'd pestered Archer until he allowed her to watch the final confrontation, when the boyfriend caught Tag and Farrah kissing on the street. She'd seen it with her own eyes.

Gio, Tag's right-hand guy, had set it up to ensure the boyfriend witnessed that first kiss. Everyone involved, except Farrah and the ex, knew when it was going to happen. Hence her opportunity to convince Archer to let her sit in his car with him and watch from afar. The altercation was loud and emotional, but no blows were exchanged. That was the first and last time she'd laid eyes on Farrah. It was supposed to be the last time Tag saw her as well.

The end. Credits roll. Over.

How the hell had her friend walked himself into another mess?

Archer would blow a gasket. He'd cashed in favors and pulled strings to get Tag out of the last mess. This time wouldn't be so easy.

"Maybe I shouldn't have," Farrah said. "But, yes, I

did. I was upset. I called Tag and he was so nice to me. He invited me over for a drink."

"Last night?"

If this was a short-lived affair, it wouldn't be public, and there shouldn't be deep feelings involved. Maybe it could be nipped in the bud before there was any permanent damage.

"No," Farrah said, displaying her glowing white teeth. "I'm not quite that easy. This was two weeks ago. We've been keeping it quiet."

Yes, well one would have to be wary of publicizing a boyfriend when your brother was a torture-loving maniac gangster. Was Tag looking for trouble these days? In the past, he'd been the sensible one, but this was off the charts stupid. What was wrong with him? Maybe this was some kind of premature mid-life crisis. At only thirty-four, that was wishful thinking.

Oh, or maybe he'd been given news of a terminal disease! If he was too scared to be decisive in ending his life, could be he wanted Hexam to do it for him. Something had to be going on for him to be inviting bodily harm like this.

"Why?" Nya played it cool while making the absent Archer proud. "Why would you keep it quiet?"

"It was Tag's idea," Farrah said, tapping a manicured fingernail on the marble kitchen counter. "I don't know, I guess it makes sense. I'm not long out of a relationship, it wasn't long-term, but maybe it's a respect thing."

Respect for others wasn't Tag's primary motivation in life. Keeping his head was, or it should be. That wouldn't be much of a problem if he followed the one on his shoulders as opposed to the one dangling between his legs.

"Is he around?"

"He went to take a call in the bedroom."

She retrieved two plates and put a pastry on each one before carrying them over to the table. "Share with me," she said, pushing a plate toward Farrah.

"Oh no, I couldn't, I…" She glanced at the door, at the plate, and back at the door as if Tag might be horrified to catch her eating. Although the sheet covered her figure now, on that street corner, there was no denying Farrah's svelte form. Yes, she had noticed when watching the woman crying on the street, standing between two men hell-bent on screaming bloody murder.

"Tag likes a girl who can eat," Nya said. "Trust me. I won't steer you wrong with him."

Except she probably should.

Tag had a habit of disliking her boyfriends and doing everything he could to drive a wedge into her relationships. Her approach had always been the opposite, maybe because she enjoyed being contrary. She encouraged his girlfriends, nurtured them, tutored them on Tag, and listened to them cry when he eventually broke their hearts.

Bonding with his women was habit. Usually. This relationship was a terrible idea; Hexam would go ballistic. Nya should be doing everything she could to discourage it if she wanted to save Tag's skin. Again.

Farrah came over, balanced on her dainty little tiptoes and perched on the corner of the perpendicular seat. "You sure you're not the crazy ex-girlfriend trying to kill me?"

"No, not ex either," Nya said, tearing off a piece of her pastry and popping it onto her tongue.

Peering closer, Farrah tilted. "You're not the potential girlfriend with designs on him who wants to claw out my eyes because I've been with him?" she asked, touching a fingertip to the pastry before licking the invisible taste with her delicate pink tongue.

Wow, Hexam hadn't only sheltered his sister, he'd made her paranoid about every potential threat.

"Not potential, no. You don't have to worry about me. Tag and I are just friends, have been for years. I have my own man to worry about, I don't need another taking up my time."

"You're seeing someone?" Farrah asked like this was the best news she'd ever heard.

"Yes." Nya elongated the word and pulled off another piece of pastry to gobble it up as she brushed her hands together to rid them of crumbs. "Enough about me, I want to hear about you and Tag. You've been seeing each other for two weeks?" Farrah nodded. "Has he been treating you right? Taking you to dinner and movies…?"

Farrah was already shaking her head. Good. If they hadn't been seen out in public, there was a chance Hexam didn't know this was going on. Archer had said Hexam was planning to leave the country, she'd never followed up to find out if he actually went.

There had been no need to ask questions when, as far as she was concerned, Tag's debt was settled and Hexam was in their past.

"Do you live around here?" she asked. "Have a place of your own?"

With a fingertip, Farrah pressed a tiny flake of pastry from her plate and forced herself to slip it past her lips. "I live with my brother."

Damn, she lived with her brother, which meant every time Farrah went out, Hexam knew it. Every time she came back, he knew it. Every time she didn't bother to shower after having sex with Tag, her brother would smell the stench of it when she got back to his pad. Hexam had gotten rid of one boyfriend and would want to get rid of another, especially one he had such a fraught history with.

She didn't know much about the previous boyfriend, just what she'd managed to finagle from Archer. Hexam's greatest worry was that the man wanted to wheedle his way into the Hexam operation. Tag was one of Hexam's competitors; he would have to suspect the same, or industrial espionage, when he found out what was going on.

"Your brother, is he a nice guy? Have he and Tag met?"

"I don't think so," she said, scooting even closer to the edge of the chair.

Impressive, there couldn't be much keeping the tall, slight woman balanced. What prevented Farrah from using the chair as others did? Maybe her brother didn't let her sit at the grown-ups' table.

"No?"

"No, they haven't met," Farrah said with more confidence. "Brett isn't kind to my boyfriends. I think he'd prefer to keep me locked up all the time. He doesn't understand I'm a woman, I'm not thirteen anymore."

A woman of twenty-three if she wasn't mistaken. Young, even by Tag's standards. Her interrogation wasn't even close to over, but a door at the opposite end of the room opened and Tag came marching in.

"I'm sorry, I—" Halting, he took in the scene and dropped his hand to his side, still holding the phone he'd been scrolling through. "Yorkie," he said with an uncomfortable shift.

Raising her brows, she wasn't going to make this easy for him. He didn't deserve easy when he was making such a dumb decision.

"Taggy," she drawled, leaning back in her chair, taking one heel to the crossbar. "I'm just getting acquainted with the new woman in your life."

"I thought she was your girlfriend," Farrah said on a giggle.

"Isn't that funny?" Nya asked, pinning her unimpressed glare on him.

She expected him to give her an explanation, one that he could give in front of Farrah. In fact, she wouldn't have put it past him to flat out deny there was anything going on. No doubt later, he'd concoct some ridiculous excuse that he'd backpedal with Farrah when they were alone again.

"She's not my girlfriend," Tag said to Farrah while narrowing his eyes on Nya. "She's a nuisance, butting in where she doesn't belong."

So he was going with anger?

She bobbed her head in acceptance of the interesting tack. "At least you're not denying it. I'm surprised you didn't tell me about her," she said, lightening her tone. "Usually you let me know when you hook up with someone new."

He didn't take out a full-page ad, but he'd never gone out of his way to conceal his relationships from her before. His keeping this a secret proved he knew exactly how stupid he was being.

Instead of shame, he got infuriated. "You shouldn't be here. Sailing in without invitation is rude."

She scoffed. "I have a key! You can't give someone a

key, then expect them not to use it."

"For emergencies," Tag said, coming toward them. "You have a key for emergencies, and so you can get in if I'm not here when you fight with your lug-head of a boyfriend."

"Is that why you're not denying this?" she asked. "Because you know you can tell me it isn't what it looks like now, but the minute I walk out of here and tell Archer what I saw, he'd find out the truth in a minute."

"Archer?" Farrah asked. "You know Archer?"

"Yes, she does," Tag said, folding his arms. "He's the lug-head."

Nya spread her hands on the table edge. "When did this become a game of tear down Archer? He's keeping it in his pants, he's not doing anything wrong."

"Last I heard you were at it like rabbits," Tag said, holding onto his anger. "Or is that why you're here? To tell me he's lost interest in screwing you?"

For a moment, she considered taking a leaf from Farrah's book and doing the silly smile thing when thinking about what they'd done at Sizzle the previous night, but she didn't. She got to her feet and rounded the table.

"I meant he's screwing only who he's allowed to screw. He makes sensible decisions about who he sleeps with."

"Sensible?" Tag said, puffing himself up as she came to a stop in front of him. He was already much larger than her, he didn't need more bulk to intimidate; it had to be habit. "I don't think you're a sensible choice for any guy to screw."

It was like fighting with a brother, at least that was her guess.

"Why?" Nya waded in with full-on sarcasm. "Because I'm so easy to fall in love with and will only break their hearts when I realize they're not good enough for me?"

She almost wished Archer was there to witness her triumph because he'd enjoy it. All that spunk he'd been pumping into her had to be seeping into her blood. She was managing a beginner's level of condescension he'd be proud of.

"Because you root around, root around with that little

nose of yours until you find dirt. You roll around covering yourself in muck, then wonder how everybody knows you were the one digging in a place you shouldn't have been."

"That's rich," she said and understood why he was being snide.

He'd been caught with his hand in the cookie jar. He'd been caught screwing his enemy's sister and it was clear the sister had no idea.

"Why shouldn't he be with me?" Farrah asked.

Nya didn't answer her. "You haven't been out of trouble for two months and you're already in it again." Her focus stayed on Tag, it was her place to judge him. Farrah was a stranger, Nya didn't give a crap about her safety, Hexam would take care of that. "What is this, some kind of attention seeking? Are we not giving you enough?"

When she patted his chest, he snatched her hand. "We'll talk about this later," he said.

So he wanted to appease her but couldn't do it in front of Farrah. That made sense.

"Okay," she said, pulling her arm free from his grip. "I'll leave you to your sordid, secret affair." Going to grab her purse, she slung it across her body. "It was very nice to meet you, Farrah." Striding across the room, she acknowledged the practical stranger, but only set a glare on Tag. "Try taking a cold shower and thinking this through before you get us all tossed into a woodchipper."

Sailing from the room, she slammed out of the apartment, something she was getting used to doing. The only way Archer knew to close a door was to throw them back into their frames with great force. Under his influence, she'd started doing the same.

So much for a pastry and a catch up with her best buddy. The rest of the day was her own and she didn't know what to do with it. No, actually, she did. It wasn't like she could sit on this news now she had it.

Okay, so she wasn't supposed to be casually visiting his off-limits apartment, but her guy just loved to be in the know. With valuable information like this, she might just be forgiven for breaking his rules.

FOUR

TAG'S NEW APARTMENT was closer to Archer's than it was to hers. That made it easier to justify stopping in to see how he was doing. The cab ride was thankfully short. She was desperate to talk about the repercussions of Tag's ill-judged actions and the inevitable devastating shockwaves that would follow. Not only for Tag, but for Archer as well. Her guy had staked his own reputation on cleaning up Tag's mess with Brett Hexam.

Passing the graffitied walls of Archer's apartment building, the place might be messy, but it was a palace compared to where she lived. She hopped over the soda cans, ignored the rotting banister and kept on going until she reached his floor.

She had a key for his apartment too. Just like she'd said to Tag, he couldn't give her it and then not expect her to use it. Going inside, she anticipated finding him standing behind the couch reading subtitles on the silent TV, except he wasn't. There was a man seated at the central kitchen table. A shaking, sniveling, crying man who wasn't wearing a shirt.

Closing the door, she dropped the keys into her purse then ducked sideways to look under the table to confirm he was chained to the solid eyebolt Archer had driven into the floor beneath it.

"Please," the man said like she was rescue incarnate. "Please help me."

Choosing not to respond, she felt sorry for this guy, but not enough to undermine Archer. When they talked about her facing what her guy did, she hadn't predicted addressing it quite this directly.

Finding herself there, like this, was curious. She'd sat in that chair, chained to that bolt, begging Archer not to hurt her. Now she was on the opposite side of the equation; it was strange how powerful she felt.

"He's got me chained up," the guy said with exasperated desperation. "I've been here for weeks."

That was an exaggeration.

She crooked a brow. "You've been here four days," she said, surprised how normal her voice came out when this man was so frantic.

Shock silenced him for a beat. "You have to help me. You have to let me go."

Honesty was better than ignorance. "That ain't gonna happen," she said, lifting her purse over her head and going to dump it on the breakfast bar. "Has he fed you? Probably not." She responded to her own question. "I could make you a salad… though I haven't been here in a few days; I haven't stocked up his groceries. Let's see what we've got."

"Who?" the guy hooted. "Who are you? Please, won't you help me?"

"I could," she said, opening the fridge to find nothing but soda, beer, and steak. "Eurgh." Although she grumbled, she hadn't expected to find anything else, and slammed the fridge to go looking in his cabinets. "If you tell him what he wants to know, he'll let you go."

"I… I can't…"

When she found nothing of interest, she went to the freezer to retrieve one of her popsicles. They were the one thing she didn't mind keeping indefinitely and their expiry date wasn't short like her other purchases.

One of her favorite snacks, she loved the sweet, frozen water, and her appreciation for them had grown since she and Archer started to play with them. For now, they'd serve to hydrate her. She didn't like beer or soda and there was nothing else lying around that appealed to her taste buds.

The victim was whispering, hmm, suggested Archer wasn't far away.

"He didn't just leave you here," she said, trashing the popsicle packet and skirting the breakfast bar to return to the body of the room, ensuring to leave distance between herself and the captive.

Sauntering to the opposite end of the table, she took one long suck of her popsicle before holding it away from her body.

"I… I don't know where he is."

"Fella!" she called out.

Less than a second later, he leaned backwards out of the bedroom.

"You've got to be fucking kidding me," Archer said.

Returning to the bedroom, he was only gone for a second before he reappeared. Marching out of the room, he stomped up the hall to the side of the table and dumped the leather roll filled with his blades.

Eyeing the package on the table, she speculated on what was to come. "Oh, it's about to get interesting," she said, taking another slurp of her popsicle.

She rolled her tongue around the tip, maintaining wide, innocent eye contact with him as she curled her lips around the top.

"You shouldn't be here," he said, fixated on her mouth, as stern as she'd expect him to be given her disregard of his order.

Letting the popsicle slide from her mouth with a satisfying pop, she smiled. "You're not the first man to tell me that today," she said. "I have news." Extending a hand, she drew her fingertip along the back of the chair in front of her. "Very interesting, but equally terrible, news."

She had him. She knew it! He didn't register interest, but it beat from him. Licking the popsicle from base to tip, she circled her tongue around the top once, twice, and then tickled the tip down to the base of the first ridge, right where the edge of his head would be if she was sampling something more intimate.

His thought must have been the same because he snatched her hand and ripped the popsicle from her mouth.

"Calm it," he growled, yanking her so hard that she fell into him. "What news?"

"I can't tell you here," she said, side-eyeing the man still at the table. "You have to get rid of him first."

"He's not gonna tell anyone. I'll cut out his tongue before I set him free."

"That won't do," she said, tracing the outline of his lips with her fingertips. "He could still write something down. You'll have to slit his throat."

It came off as flirtation, as foreplay; she was trying to do her bit and he knew it. Archer read her signals and played along. This moment was hot, but not for the reason their audience would think.

"Would you like that, baby? Like to watch me work, spilling his blood for you? Would that make your pussy drip?"

"Mm hmm," she purred, enjoying her role as simpering Archer-devotee.

"I can't do that if he tells me what I want to know. You know the rules. He tells me the truth, he gets to go free."

She sagged like an impudent child being refused a treat. "He's had you four whole days," she said. "How many chances does he get? How long until you're mine again?" Dragging her fingernail down over his chin to his tee-shirt-covered chest, she parted her lips. "I think four days is enough. I think you should do it now."

"No!" the captive exclaimed.

They ignored him. "How many more days does he get?" she asked again. "Come on, Fella, get rid of him and you can put me in your chains."

"He gets one more day," Archer said.

She reversed and because he still had hold of her hand, he came with her. When she sat on the corner of the table, opposite the chained captive, Archer guided the popsicle back to her lips. She accepted it into her mouth letting him pull and push the cold, wet mass over the heat of her melting tongue.

"You don't get that long," he said, pushing it further into her mouth. "You tell me what I want to know right here."

Holding the popsicle on the threshold of her throat for a few more seconds, he then withdrew it from her lips. Grabbing her hair at the back of her skull, he yanked her head back hard and, with the popsicle, drew a wet line from her chin, down the column of her throat into her cleavage. The tingling shivers the ice left in its wake vibrated throughout her body. That was nothing compared to what happened when Archer bent his knees to kiss the spot the popsicle occupied before lapping his tongue up over her damp skin to erase the sweet, wet, vertical trail he'd drawn.

Seizing her lips in an open-mouthed, all-consuming kiss, his powerful tongue proved its superiority over hers. She loved his palpable dominance when he demanded what was rightfully his.

Popsicle forgotten, his hand closed over her breast. He had to have cast the sweet treat aside, though she didn't give a crap what he'd done with it. Both her hands looped around his neck, locked to pull herself tighter to him, her legs climbed higher around his waist. Attaching herself to the man towering over her, ensconcing her in his power, consuming her with his dominance, she was weak, vulnerable. Helpless under the weight of his need.

His entitled grip on her hair tightened, he tugged and pulled the strands, propelling spikes of pain into her skull. Ripping his kiss from hers, he bit her bottom lip. Overwhelmed tears sprung to her eyes, but it was awareness that quaked through her. Writhing on the spot, her breasts swelled until they felt heavy on her lungs and constricted by the fabric she wished he'd rip from her body.

Her mind was swimming, awash with ideas of passion and bliss. Her core grew slick in anticipation of the invasion she prayed he'd mount on her.

"Sex," she breathed. "I'll tell you what you want to know in exchange for sex."

Lunging forward, he forced her body to slant back to support her weight on her hands. "Here?" he grunted, slamming both hands down hard over hers, pinning her to the spot. "In front of this scumbag? Is that what will get you off? Letting him watch as I fuck you? You'll tell me what I need to know now, and maybe, if you're lucky and I'm happy, I'll let you suck your reward from my balls."

"And if you're not?" she asked, her pants becoming shallower.

Taking one hand away, he unbuckled his belt. Instead of pulling himself out, he stole her hand, yanked it forward and forced it into his underwear. Coiling her fingers around his engorged shaft, he coerced her to stroke him.

"It won't matter how much you beg," he said, working her hand over his dick, tightening his overlying grip. "I'll fuck myself inside you, take you to that sweet spot, and leave you hanging. I'll shower those tits in my hot spunk and never let you have a taste. You know the rules. I get what I want, and you beg for scraps."

The speed of his movement betrayed his need. He wanted her, and with every tug, her desire grew too. Unable to reject his will, her body surrendered to his. She let him move her soft palm in his chosen rhythm, up and down the silken sheath wrapped around the dynamite she wanted to explode within her.

Sucking her tongue from her mouth, he released it only when it was coated in his taste.

"Fella," she moaned, trying to return to their kiss.

He resisted. "If what you tell me isn't good enough, if it isn't worthy, I'll fuck my way up your hot, tight ass, take what I want, and make sure you never sit down again. I'll watch you cry for release and it won't make a damned bit of difference. There's only one cock you're allowed to ride and if I'm not satisfied, you'll never get off again."

The pressure created by his words on her center, on her heart, on her head, forced her to clamor for every heaving breath. Trying again to kiss him, she was thwarted when he eased back to talk again.

"What have you got? Is it worth it?"

"Yes," she exhaled. "I promise."

Sweeping an arm around her hips, he yanked her

forward, clamping their interlinked fingers around his cock, locking their bodies together.

"Then I think we better warm you up," he said. "'Cause you've got a lot of talking to do."

Hauling her up, he stormed through the apartment, ignoring the distraught, speechless captive. Striding to the bedroom, he tossed her onto the bed and dropped too. Beneath the bulk of his body, she wriggled and writhed, stroking, scratching, desperate to stimulate him to the summit she approached. Accepting the intensity of his demanding kiss, his lips quickly leaped to her jaw, to mark her neck, only releasing her to pull her top off, leaving it tangled in her hands.

When she bit his shoulder, the open door came into view. She didn't care. She wrapped her legs around his hips and sought his mouth, but it was occupied by her responsive breasts, aching in need of his devotion.

"Arch," she gasped. "I need to tell you—"

His mouth silenced hers, driving his tongue in deep stemming her words.

With a satisfying slurp, he broke the connection. "I don't give a fuck about your information, Squirm," he murmured and kissed her again.

Thrusting both hands beneath her skirt, he scooped them under her ass, then he was pumping into her. Just like that; just that fast. She'd never heard him say he didn't care about her information, any information. He always needed to be in the know.

Hmm, this was a sign. He'd been deprived of her body, struggled with their separation as she had. Damn, it felt good to want and be wanted. Typical man couldn't be honest until he was balls deep inside her, unable to control his body's need.

As his shaft stroked her inside, she didn't care about the news. When he withheld his kiss again, she dragged her teeth through his stubble. He growled and pinched her nipple hard, forcing a yelp from her throat.

His satisfaction came with a slow withdrawal and a hard advance. He slammed into her another half a dozen times, but she was too raw and couldn't handle it. Couldn't handle the intensity of his need. Couldn't hold her own back. Calling out his name, she screamed until her throat burned and her lungs were empty.

Her whole body seized around his, her arms, her legs, her pussy, all of her was desperate to hold him in place.

"Squirm," he ground out the word through gritted teeth and pinned her to the mattress with the authority of his urgent kiss.

She squealed when he poured himself inside of her and she yelled for him again. Devoured by their passion, she'd never felt so full, so content, so alive. He flopped away from her onto his back and they panted while locked in a tangle of limbs.

"When you disobey me, you do it right," he said.

Her lips spread in a grin. Adjusting onto her side, she tucked herself in close to him and rubbed her face on his cheek. Kissing his stubble, she licked the corner of his lips before relaxing to align her mouth with his ear.

"You bring it out in me. I think I'm going to like this," she said. "Coming to you while you work."

He shifted onto his side, forcing their bodies flush together and held her in his arms. "Now," he said. "Talk."

FIVE

THE DOOR WAS OPEN, and he caught her checking it out. That guy was still out there. Sound didn't carry well when doors were closed; that knowledge came from experience. She didn't want anyone but Archer to hear what she was about to share.

"One second," he said, bumping his forehead on hers before vaulting off the bed.

Yanking on his jeans as he left the room, he closed the door, either to conceal her nakedness from his captive or to save her from witnessing her guy manhandling him into the bathroom again. When she'd been captive there, Archer hadn't shown her any more of the apartment than she absolutely had to see, which could be another reason for him hiding the bedroom.

It didn't matter either way. There were some grunts and shouts and scuffles from beyond the room. Ignoring them, she stretched before getting to her feet. It was warm, so she folded the blanket to the bottom of the bed, then went to the dresser, figuring she didn't want to be naked during a serious conversation.

The drawer was only ajar an inch when the bedroom door opened.

"What are you doing?" Archer asked, closing the

door behind himself.

"Grabbing a tee shirt," she said and continued to open the drawer.

Archer had other ideas and came over to slam it shut again.

"I don't think so," he said, snagging her waist to back her away from the dresser and guide her down on the bed.

"I'm not allowed to wear your clothes?" she asked. "Since when?"

"Since I've been living without this sight for too long," he said, lying down with her.

Staying on his side, he put her on her back and flattened his palm on her throat. He slid it down over her breast to her abdomen and kept going to cup between her thighs. He brought it back up over her hip to her cleavage.

"I never thought of myself as a tit man," he said, squeezing one breast, then the other.

"An ass man?"

Angling his body to reach her knee, he skimmed his hand up her inner thigh. "A leg man."

"I don't have nice legs," she said, pointing her toes.

His gaze leaped to hers. "Who told you that?"

"No one."

She was short and her legs were proportionate to her body, nothing to the towering pins she'd seen wrapped in micro-minis strutting around the club.

"What's your best feature?"

"My charming personality," she said, grinning.

He mirrored her amusement. "Sure it is, Squirm."

"You don't think so?"

"That's not my favorite part of you."

"So what is?" she asked, insinuating an arm beneath him to curl it around his shoulder from behind.

"My favorite part of you…?"

Three of his fingers curled into his own palm and the fourth, his middle finger, slid inside her tender passage.

"Hey!" she said on a half-gasp, half-laugh, smacking his upper arm. "I came here to talk to you, not for more of that."

"You came here because I told you not to; you wanted to piss me off."

That hadn't been her primary reason… though it may have slipped into her decision-making process by mistake.

"Pissing you off does come with benefits," she said, rolling to her side to kiss his chest. "Lying naked in bed with you doesn't go with talking."

"Sure it does," he said, nuzzling her hair and kissing her brow.

On instinct, her head tipped back and linked her mouth with his. It was nice to just be together. With a contented sigh, she flopped onto her back and admired the now-familiar ceiling.

"Spill," he said, tweaking her nipple and returning his head to his hand supported by his elbow. "What did you come to tell me?"

"It's about Tag."

"There's a surprise." Archer dropped onto his back, they lay side-by-side, staring upward. "What shit's he into now?"

Saying it fast was easier than aiming for a gentler approach. "He's having sex with Farrah Hexam."

In an instant, he was on his side again, looming over the top of her. "For real?"

"You think I would make something like that up? Just to have an excuse to see you maybe," she said. "No, I promise, it's true."

Archer was suspicious, but of what?

"He told you?"

"I walked in on her naked in his living room."

"She hot?"

She gaped and smacked his chest. "Archer!"

"What?" he asked with an innocent shrug. "She's stacked, I'm curious."

Narrowing her eyes, she saw through his ploy to make her jealous. "No, you're not. You're trying to pay me back for disobeying you."

Visiting while he had someone chained up was against every rule he'd laid out for her. She'd be paying for her defiance for a while.

Lowering to burrow his mouth in her hair at her ear, he murmured, "If you like what you saw, invite her over to visit with you. We can have a little two on one action, that might solve our problem."

"I don't think so," she sneered, giving his chest a hard enough shunt he was forced to retreat. He flattened a hand on his pec like she'd hurt him, though there was no way she did. "I'd rather watch Hexam take Tag apart than watch you pleasure another woman."

He peered at her like she'd just revealed something intriguing. "Really?"

This wasn't a time to play games, so she softened. "Archer," she said, stroking her hand over his. "I'm scared. This is serious."

Exhaling, with his indifference, she didn't know if he was pissed or choosing to humor her.

"Okay, tell me what happened."

She took a deep breath. "We talked. Farrah filled in the blanks and when Tag joined us, he didn't deny the relationship... not that he could."

Archer grumbled something she didn't hear, then he was getting up off the bed. "That guy's a piece of work. I don't have a fucking clue how you managed to hold onto your friendship with such a fucking idiot for so long."

He wasn't angry, which was an improvement on the reaction she'd expected. Though given what he spent most of his life doing—collecting information—he'd probably heard it all and then some. During his years of practice, he must have learned how to temper his emotions, even when hearing the most shocking news.

"You know why we're friends," she said, bending her knees to then straighten her legs, tucking her feet under the blanket she'd folded across the width of the bed. "And he's not an idiot."

"Sure he is," Archer said, sliding open his closet door. "The guy does nothing but make stupid choices. He's screwing the sister of the guy who wanted to kill him not long ago. Screwing Farrah was never the deal; Hexam will go crazy when he finds out. It's spite, he can't be in love with her."

Considering it for a second, it was the only plausible explanation for throwing caution to the wind.

"He might be."

Archer turned around quick. "Did he tell you that?"

"No."

"No, he didn't," Archer said, coming to the end of the bed. "He didn't tell you he loved her. He didn't even tell you he was fucking her. How can there be feelings involved when he's ashamed to be with her? You can't be ashamed to be with someone and love them, it doesn't work that way."

"Says the world's authority," she said, sitting up in the middle of the bed, crossing her legs. "When we got together you told me we couldn't go public."

But he wouldn't be cornered. "No, I didn't," he said. "I told you I had to talk to you before word got out because we had to lay ground rules, because I know what you're like. Taking on causes, sticking your nose in—"

"*I* stick my nose in?" she asked, almost unable to believe he was laying that accusation against her. "You can't overhear someone got a toy in their breakfast cereal without strapping the guy down and waterboarding him until he reveals what it was. You need to know everything."

"I know what I'm doing. You jump in without thinking about consequences. I stay neutral. You get emotional."

"So damn neutral that when I told you six weeks ago I was ready to go after Jamie's killers you ignored me, and you've ignored it ever since. When are we going to do something about that, or do you plan to let me down?"

Loosening, he wasn't so keen on being called out. "I'm working on it," he said, going back to his closet.

She was sick of that response. "You're working on it, that's what you say about everything. It's an excuse. You're doing nothing."

"You don't trust me?"

They shouldn't really fight, not while there was a captive in the other room. Did he have to be so high-handed all the time? Still, she calmed down, determined to prove she didn't lead with emotion.

"You say Tag makes bad decisions but can only come up with one example. That doesn't prove your point."

He turned his chin to his shoulder. "You interrupted me after one example," he said. "That's not the only one I've got. Ripping off Hexam was a bad idea. Ripping off anyone is a bad idea and Taggert makes a habit of it. He creates nothing but bad feeling everywhere he goes. He chose to stiff me, and that could've caused all kinds of shit for him…" She assumed he was done and stroked her hands over the sheet beneath her. Those were good examples of bad decisions, and they happened in a short space of time. If her guy was going to look at it like that… yeah, maybe he had a point. "And then there's you…"

She stopped stroking to raise her head. "Me? What about me? Tag doesn't make bad decisions with me."

Slowly, he turned, ever nonchalant, while perpetually confident he was right because the damn bastard usually was.

"For fifteen years he's been running around after your ass, protecting you and bailing you out." His deliberate words edged into condescension. "How many times has he made a move on you, huh?"

Back to this. Archer didn't like her friendship with Tag, but she sensed that was because he didn't understand it, not because of any inherent jealousy.

"He doesn't make moves on me," she said. "He doesn't think of me like that."

"Trust me, no guy runs around after a pussy like yours without wondering what it tastes like."

"Archer!" she chastised him and screwed up her face.

Tag and her pussy being subjects of the same sentence grossed her out.

Non-apologetic, he spread his arms. "I tell it like it is."

"And you think that was a bad decision? That Tag has never tried to have sex with me proves that he makes bad decisions? You don't know him as well as you think you do."

"I don't think I know him at all," Archer said, almost cutting her off.

Pivoting back to his closet, he was more interested in completing his task than finishing their conversation.

His interest made her curious. "What are you doing in there?" she asked, leaning to the side, trying to see what he was doing. She saw nothing but shadow beyond him. His body filled the width of space meant for the closet door.

"I need to call a guy."

"Call a guy?" she asked. "Who do you need to call?"

"I need to find out when Hexam's coming back into the country."

"So he did leave," she asked, inspired by relief.

"Yeah, he did, a couple of weeks ago."

That would've been around the time Farrah called Tag. "Farrah knows you. When I said your name—"

He whirled around. "You used my name in front of her?"

Despite his obvious anger, she couldn't be apologetic. "Why wouldn't I? What happened to not being able to love someone if you're ashamed of them? I'm not ashamed of you."

His jaw worked, sometimes she pushed his patience.

"I remember your little speech about being proud of your guy," Archer said. He remembered everything. "But you have to be smart, Squirm. She knows we're together?" She nodded. "Shit."

He caught his forehead in his hand.

"Why is that a bad thing?"

Should she question his interest in Farrah? No. The situation was complicated enough without trying to factor in her own dislike of the idea of Archer fantasizing about other women.

"Because now when she tells her brother she's with Tag, Hexam will find out that Tag's best bud, you, is dating me, the guy who was supposed to be neutral. The guy who set up the deal in the first place."

Humbled, she sagged. "Oh," she said. "That's a fair point."

"Hmm."

Tag only knew Farrah because Archer set up the deal

with Hexam, after assuring him Tag would do as he was told and nothing more.

"But Hexam doesn't have to know," she said, grabbing a pillow from behind her to pull it against her chest. "Does he? I mean if he's away, you can find out when he's coming back. We'll make sure the relationship is over by then."

Hope prodded him. "You told Tag to dump her and he agreed?"

She couldn't lie. "I couldn't do it while she was sitting right there," she said. He deflated into a scowl again. "But he knows I'm not happy."

"How does he know that? No, wait," Archer said before she got the chance to take a breath. "Scratch that stupid question. I've never met a person so bad at hiding how she feels."

She was proud of her honesty and her emotions, even if that meant displaying more feeling than her guy would like.

"Farrah seems nice. It's a shame. I think she really likes Tag." Recalling how Farrah reacted to the mention of Tag spurred her next query. "Should I giggle when I hear your name?"

His wandering thoughts snapped back to her.

He frowned. "Should you what?"

"Never mind," she said. They had other things to worry about. "The next time I get a chance to talk to Tag alone, I'll tell him this is a bad idea and that he has to break up with her. I don't know how it will go down, he can be stubborn."

"Bullheaded," Archer said. "You've told me that before."

She couldn't let him come up with a war plan because they were on the same side.

"Usually if I make it clear something means enough to me, he'll do whatever I ask."

"The game's changed, Squirm," Archer said, seating himself on the end of the bed. "You're competing with another woman now. One he has to care about or he wouldn't have taken the risk of screwing over Hexam… again. Unless he really does have a death wish. This could be some sort of power play, and Tag's using this sister to show Hexam he's superior."

"Tag wouldn't be that petty," she said, although not completely confident in that statement. "He wouldn't use an innocent woman just to make a point."

"Then you're in serious trouble," Archer said. "Because if he was using her, you could use those big doe eyes of yours and appeal to his ego and he'd do whatever made you happy. But if he really cares about this gal and you go in telling him to break up with her, just because it makes our lives easier…" He shook his head. "I don't see it happening."

"You don't know him like I do," she said, secure in their friendship if nothing else.

Progressing up the bed, he sat in front of her. "And you don't know what lengths a guy will go to, to keep the woman he loves."

Taking hold of his shoulders, she climbed into his lap. "Implying, I suppose," she said, looping her legs around him as he rested back on his hands. "That you would do anything to keep me."

Narrowing one eye, he exuded suspicion. "I smell manipulation. If it's more sex you want, you got it. Ask for anything else and I'll tell you to call back later."

"I want Jonno," she said, massaging his shoulders. "I was watching Jada in the bar last night and I kept seeing flashes of Jamie. It feels like we've forgotten about her. I get these vivid images in my mind of what she went through… It's not right."

"What is it you want to do?" he asked. "There were seven of them. Do you plan to kill seven men? Is that what will make you happy?"

Murder seemed too easy. Yes, if a man put up a fight and it became necessary, she certainly wouldn't weep over the loss of any of them. But she wanted more than just a bullet in the back of their heads.

"I want to hurt them," she said. "It's not enough to simply take their lives. I want them to suffer like she did."

It seemed there were no limits to what she could say

to her guy, nothing shocked him, and she never felt judged for honesty.

"Every man has a pressure point," Archer said. "I can make them suffer. We'll hit them one at a time." That was more of a promise than she'd had from him before. "Let me get rid of this guy, then we'll take out the trash."

"This guy," she said. "This job. How much are you making for him?"

Scooping his hand under her chin, he pulled her in for a kiss. "Not a cent."

That upset her, but she wouldn't jump to conclusions.

"Then why?" she begged, desperate to understand.

"He knows where the first guy is."

Gaping, disbelief seized her. He'd said he knew the identities of four of the men at Sizzle on the night Jamie died. She'd asked for them to start planning how to take those men down. Archer hadn't confirmed anything, he'd said nothing about it at all, now she found out he'd been working on it all along.

Her smile was automatic. "I love you," she said, taking hold of his face to smudge her lips on his.

"There isn't a minute that goes by I'm not thinking of you," he said. "You think I don't care, you think I forget, but I don't. I know how to bide my time and be patient. This is important to you, I don't plan to let you down."

Kissing him, she couldn't stop smiling. "I love you."

"Good. 'Cause since you're here and you don't have Sizzle, I'll let you stay a while."

"Thank you," she said, kissing him again presuming more sex was on the agenda.

"Are you hungry?" he asked. "I'm hungry."

Which had become synonymous for him asking her to cook.

"I'll see what you have in there," she said. "But you have to let me wear something."

"Only 'cause there's another guy in the apartment," he said, standing up, keeping her form twined around his. "I'll let you cover up, but my hands get to go anywhere they want."

"Like every other day of the week," she said. "Your hands belong on my body."

"And your body deserves attention, lots and lots of attention."

Sitting her on the dresser forced her to straighten her legs on either side of him when he opened the drawer to pull out a tee shirt. White. She should've known. He preferred her in white, it allowed him to see the outline of her nipples.

"It's a compromise," she said, pulling it on when she'd usually object. "I want to see what you have that might fill me up."

"I got something real special for you, girl."

When he tried to step deeper into the vee of her thighs, she put a hand on his chest to ease him back.

"In the kitchen, Fella," she said in a sultry tone, drawing her eyes away as she hopped down off the furniture to sashay toward the door. "There's a mess to clear up in there. That will keep you distracted while I cook, and if you plan to kick me out before bedtime, I see a foot rub in my future."

Opening the door before he could argue, she went to follow through. When her guy had a captive, he didn't like to leave his apartment for long, but he'd never let her go home alone. He'd walk her to her front door, kiss her goodnight, then put her inside and listen until the lock clicked. He'd risk losing the captive, risk exposing himself, risk his possessions, his livelihood, his reputation, all to make sure she got home safely. Never mind she'd got herself home for years before he came into her life, but she didn't resent it.

Sometimes his sense of responsibility dwarfed her. These acts, his superiority, his heavy-handed nature, it was all his way of proving his love and she welcomed that every day.

SIX

"WHERE ARE WE GOING?"

"Hush," Archer replied.

Although her guy appearing at Sizzle after her shift was a surprise, she wasn't complaining. Her assumption was he'd picked her up to take her home. Turned out that was a miss. As they continued to drive, it became obvious their destination wasn't her place or his.

"It's late," she whined. "If you have ideas about kinky sex in some weird place, if outside is your thing, I'm okay with that. What's wrong with right here?"

Looking around, the dilapidated area was even lower rent than her neighborhood—quite an achievement. Most of the industrial buildings seemed abandoned. They appeared to be forgotten factories and warehouses in a deserted district she'd never had reason to visit.

Archer wasn't forthcoming, so she filled the silence.

"What are we doing out here?" she asked. "You're not going to cut me into little pieces, are you?" A joke… that he didn't laugh at, he kept his eyes on the road ahead and didn't react. Frustrated, she unclicked her seatbelt and began to unbutton her shirt. "If you won't explain yourself, I'll get the show started on my own."

Finally, she provoked a response. One of his hands left the steering wheel to cover hers over her breasts, stalling her unbuttoning.

"We're not out here for that."

"Why are we out here?" she asked, not seeing any other reason for the excursion. "Are we picking up one of your marks?"

Wild theory. Why would he bring her with him for that?

"Nope."

Glancing back, the coupe didn't have much of a backseat. If they were picking someone up, no doubt she'd be the one shoehorned in there.

Her eye caught on the back window, above the trunk. "Wait a second, we're not... We're not getting rid of a body or something, are we?" Exciting as that may be, she'd be more of a liability than an asset. "Why do you need me for that?" What he did was just fine, she didn't mind being on the periphery of it. Specifically coming to pick her up from work to drag her along while he dumped a body seemed excessive and unnecessary. "I'm not digging," she said. "I just got my nails done. One of the girls needed models to practice on for school."

As she wiggled her manicure in front of his face, he caught her hand and pressed it down against his thigh.

"No one dumps bodies out here," he said.

Although the statement was shocking, she suppressed an urge to laugh. There was something utterly ludicrous about the fact he knew that to be fact, not speculation.

"Where do they dump the bodies?" she asked, slouching in her seat though he didn't release her hand. "Wait, no, I don't want to know." He didn't respond or give any clue he'd intended to. Huh, curious... "Would you tell me things?"

"What things?"

She shrugged. "Anything. If I asked you, would you tell me?"

"If you asked me something specific, I might. I can't gift you all the knowledge in my head."

Ah, he was in one of those moods. "My question wasn't about volume," she said, twisting to slide her hand out from under his to prop her elbow on the shoulder of her chair.

"I know," he said. "Your question was about trust."

"So answer it."

"I'm about to."

Turning the car into a narrow alleyway, no artificial or moonlight broke through into the claustrophobic space. The end opened out enough for him to spin around in the crossroads formed by intersecting alleys. When he was confident the car was shrouded in shadow, he put it in park, killed the engine, then took off his seatbelt.

"There's something about you, Squirm," he said. "From that first night when I saw you arguing with Jonno, I knew you weren't like other women. It's not your fire or your loyalty, there's something else."

Self-conscious and suspicious, her eyes rolled left then right. "What's going on?"

Her lips curled. Maybe he was playing with her and she didn't get the joke yet.

This was not a typical location for a romantic declaration of love; he wasn't the type of guy to wax lyrical about their relationship anyway. If he was about to whip out a ring, she was missing something major about his intended point. They were in what amounted to an abandoned industrial slum. If not about sex...

He was solemn, not smirking. "The memory of holding you in that parking lot imprinted itself on me," he said. "You never talk about it, and I know you don't want me to bring it up. You hate that you were so vulnerable you couldn't conceal it from me, a man you probably hated."

Because he was partly right, she wriggled in her chair, knowing that, to him, she was an open book.

Clearing her throat, she got serious. "At the time, I hated that I couldn't pull it together, but it was your fault."

"My fault?"

"When I hung up that phone and turned around, the first thing you asked about was Jamie. Not your money, not Tag, you cared about a girl who lost her life in a horrific way.

Somehow, I saw your humanity and I wasn't the only vulnerable one there. That was why I let myself go."

"Other women have tried to manipulate me with sex, tears, their big innocent eyes, fluttering their eye lashes. I see through most things. While you were in my arms, your fire scalded me. You needed me and I'd have promised you anything."

Wary, she withdrew in a frown. "Did you bring me out here to let me down thinking I wouldn't scream at you?" she asked. "So I couldn't walk away? Are you about to tell me something I don't want to hear?" He tried to take her hand, but she snatched it away. "No, 'cause I'll scream bloody murder. Are you backing out of our deal? You want to tell me you were fucked up that night? Now you've had the chance to think about it, it's not a good idea? Is that what this is about? 'Cause I'll fight with you, Archer. I don't care where we are."

Poking one of her manicured nails into his hand on the edge of her seat, she kept going. "Don't think I won't do it, I will. I'll shout at you and storm away and make you follow me all the way home at two miles an hour, because you won't drive away from me out here—"

"I hooked one."

Silenced and perplexed, she straightened. "You what?"

"I brought you out here…" He exhaled. By the way his jaw clenched, and his gaze shifted toward the windshield, his hesitancy was obvious. "I gift wrapped one for you, that's why I brought you out here."

Infused with excitement, she was beside herself. "He's here? One of Jamie's killers is here?"

"No," Archer said. Not giving her a choice this time, he slanted over the car to grab both her hands. "I got one of the guys on lookout. The guy who came in just before me."

Okay, so they weren't starting with the grand prize. She was okay with that. Initial disappointment evaporated; this was actually for the best. It would give her a chance to test her limits and push her boundaries.

"Who is he? What did you do to him?"

"They call him Tulio, he works for anyone who'll pay

his bar bill. He wasn't after Tag, but he was one of Hexam's men."

Hexam's man. The situation was getting complicated. She didn't mind going after the men who hurt Jamie, she didn't care what happened to them, they deserved everything they got. Except now Tag was sleeping with Hexam's sister, they could need all the goodwill they could gather.

"Is he still working for Hexam?"

"Hexam's out of the country, remember?" Archer said, pulling her hands to his thighs until she had to angle herself over the center console. In a deliberate act, he wrenched her further over to force her breasts together, giving him an enhanced view of her cleavage. "Anyone not directly involved in the operation, the sub-contractors, I guess you could say, are off Hexam's books at the moment."

"He was there that night as a Hexam agent?"

"Far as I know, Hexam doesn't give a fuck about the guy. He was hired to work security, which he did as long as Hexam needed him. Now he doesn't need him. Guys like Tulio are easy to replace. But if you don't want to do this, we'll drive away now."

"And just leave him inside?" she asked.

Four buildings stood around them. Which one was Tulio in? To find him in the factories would take a lone person hours, which was probably exactly Archer's reason for selecting the location, far away from the city in this labyrinth of desolation.

"I'll take care of him tomorrow, he'll last the night," Archer said, nonchalant about leaving a man tethered, and no doubt terrified. That Archer had taken this risk for her was humbling. Tulio could have friends. Her guy could have been caught kidnapping the man who probably fought or screamed. Archer could've been hurt. He could've been killed. He could've been arrested.

"Thank you," she said. "You took a huge risk you didn't have to take."

"Sure I did," he said, picking up a tendril of her hair that escaped her ponytail. Tucking it behind her ear, his fingers trailed to her chin. "It's the only way to make you stop nipping my ear."

Overcome, she captured his quick smile in a kiss.

His intention better be to take her back to his place; showing her gratitude could last all night.

"Okay," she said, psyching herself up.

Jumping in without thinking too much was smarter than obsessing the whole night about what to do with her first prisoner. Archer had done this the right way. Shoving her inside and closing the door behind her forced her to act. No hesitation. Action. In case there was any confusion, she had zero experience with torturing a person. She'd never punished or murdered anyone and had no plan. All she could do was rely on instinct.

"Where is he?"

Archer didn't reply, he got out of the car and came around to open her door, as he had to, given the door's fault. She got out and caught his hand. Rubbing her cheek on his palm, she lowered it to her breast and lifted her brand to his lips, begging for him to kiss her there. He did.

Her heart hammered and her breathing got screwed up.

Adrenaline.

It terrified and energized her both at the same time.

"I'll show you," he said and tried to walk, except she didn't. He stopped to turn. "Second thoughts? Get back in the car, and I'll take you—"

"No, that's not it… You can't come."

His brows almost shot off his head.

He sauntered to her. "Excuse me?"

"You can't come, you're supposed to remain neutral, right? I mean, that's your thing, you're neutral. I don't want to upset your thing."

"Do you think the guy was teleported here?" he asked, in his slick, condescending tone. "He's seen my face; he knows who brought him here."

Did that mean they *had* to kill him?

"That doesn't matter," she said. "You kidnap people all the time for information. You shouldn't hurt him for me."

Almost smug, he tucked a hand in his pocket and

relaxed. "How do you plan to hurt him?"

Her plan was so fuzzy it was non-existent. "It's a process, right?" she asked, her eyes flicked toward the door Archer had headed for. "It will come to me."

"It's not as simple as that. That guy's gonna beg. You have to decide whether or not he gets to walk before you step through that door."

"Is that what you do?"

"What I do is different, I don't do it for revenge. I can play fair, there's no emotion in it for me. If someone tells me what I need to know, they walk free, if they don't…"

She didn't want him to finish the sentence. He'd never confirmed killing anyone, or denied it either.

"In front of that guy in my apartment," Archer said. "That girl who toyed with him. The confident savvy woman who drained my sanity down to my cock, that's the woman who needs to walk in there."

Yes, she could be that woman, unaffected by the pleading of another, cold, under Archer's power—she needed him present. With him, she was confident no one could hurt her. That strength meant she could say what she wanted, do what she wanted, and he'd be there to back her up.

"I want to scare him, like Jamie was scared. He thought it was okay to scare me. I want him to think twice before he struts in somewhere thinking he's entitled to touch a woman without permission."

"Scare we can do," he said. "Can I make a suggestion?"

Could he make a suggestion? She was going to be dependent on him throughout this. If anything went wrong, he'd have to think fast, he'd be the one to bail her out.

"Yes," she said. "Yes, suggest anything."

Curling a finger beneath her chin, he fixated on her eyes. "If you really want to scare the guy, take your time. Don't talk too much. Ambiguity is better than specifics. I'd say we should leave him for a few days, at least overnight."

Planning was necessary in what Archer did. He always seemed so laid back, yet he had to be constantly thinking, making plans, adjusting contingencies. He had nerves of steel.

If any of his captives got away, if they went to the cops or sought revenge, he'd be thrown into a battle he might not win.

Archer had planned this without her.

"How long has he been here?"

"I got him while you were on shift tonight. I sort of…" He hitched a shoulder up a couple of inches.

"You what?"

"I started without you," he said. "You'll see."

What did that mean? It was good this guy was aware of Archer and what he could do. It would, should, make him more compliant.

Turning and striding toward the entrance, Archer held her hand, leading her through it. They went down some stairs into a concrete passage with old, rusted pipes running the length of it. The dark factory basement didn't reveal much. In the distance, a dull green light emanated from somewhere.

"Did you put that there?" she asked, when they stopped next to the glow of the lantern by a steel door.

"Yeah," he said. "I thought the dark down here might freak you out."

"Thanks."

Claustrophobia afflicted her at times, usually in times of panic and high stress. Walking into a long dark corridor might be standard operating procedure for Archer, but there was scrabbling in the walls and creaks in the pipes that made her uneasy.

With his large hand engulfing hers, she didn't feel fear; the light might be alleviating some of her anxiety. How would she have reacted if they simply walked into an abyss toward an unknown objective?

"Okay," he said and bowed to kiss her forehead. "The floor is yours."

SEVEN

HE UNLOCKED A PADLOCK and slid back three bolts, all of which looked newer than the door handle and the rusty pipes. Either Archer had set this up specifically for her or he'd used this setup before. Picking up the lantern, he held it on two fingers.

As Archer stepped inside, she tightened her grip on his hand. She'd asked for this. She wanted this. This man couldn't hurt her while Archer was there. The vast space was filled with obsolete machines in disrepair. The grimy vents at the front didn't let in any light. Archer set the lantern on the floor. Although small, its light filled the space enough for her to make out some details.

Weeds grew through the cracks. Bat droppings covered some areas of the floor, and she could hear the winged creatures squeaking and fluttering above.

"Please," came a voice. "Please let me go."

A large pipe, about a meter in diameter, descended from the ceiling in the center of the room. It turned at a ninety-degree angle about a half-meter from the floor and carried on across the room, through a machine and into a side wall. A man was chained there, his arms stretched around it, just above where it curved. The position couldn't be comfortable because his arms were flush to it and didn't seem to have much room to move.

His back was to her, she couldn't see his hands. No, the view was reserved for his pasty-white behind reflecting the lantern light.

"Tulio!" Archer declared like he was talking to a friend he hadn't seen for a long time. He sauntered further into the room, taking her with him. "Told you I'd be back."

Tulio couldn't see them; he struggled to look over his shoulder, maybe in an attempt to figure out if Archer's demeanor betrayed his plans or what he'd brought with him.

The guy had to be terrified.

"He's naked," she said, stating the obvious before she could contain the words.

"Yep," Archer responded.

"Who? Who's with you?"

Their prisoner sounded panicked, though she couldn't blame him. He tried to twist further to get a better look, but the angle of the pipe prohibited him from getting far. The pipe's deviation prevented him from going too far left, he could go right, or maybe couldn't, she hadn't figured out how he was attached.

"You don't want the answer to that question," Archer muttered. "All you need to know is she's savvy, sexy, and you pissed her off… which gives me a problem."

"Her?" Tulio said. "I didn't piss off no bitch."

"Hey!" Archer let her go to march over and smack the guy on the back of the head, bouncing his forehead off the pipe with a metallic twang. "No one's allowed to call her names 'cept me. You think you're smart? You're standing there with your jewels out in front of a woman you almost raped!"

"What? Me? No!" Tulio said. "No, not me. I've got a sister, man."

Archer bent to growl in Tulio's ear. "So do I."

No, he didn't. Tulio was as likely to have one as Archer. Her love's point proved anyone could say anything in these circumstances, saying them aloud didn't make them true.

"He's naked," she said with burgeoning satisfaction.

Archer had told her forced nakedness was a torture technique. The guy had to be feeling exposed. And now he knew who she was and what he'd almost done to her, his panic must be ratcheting up. "Excellent start, baby! Now I can cut off his balls and watch him bleed out."

"Yes, sweets, you can," Archer said, proud either of himself or her.

"No!" Tulio panicked. "No, she can't."

The prisoner deserved the fear and uncertainty that came with being so vulnerable. That was exactly what she and Jamie felt in those first few seconds before they got into the breakroom, when neither of them knew what was coming next.

"She can do what the fuck she wants," Archer said, abrupt and decisive.

She loved that. No equivocation in what he said or where his loyalty lay. His tone gave such clear proof. When Archer spoke to the bound man, trussed up just for her, he remained cold and unforgiving. His tone warmed when he addressed her, showing he cared and that she was the real boss here. He'd never called her "Sweets" before, and she liked that too. The zip. The zing. The thrill.

Moving around, she maintained a wide perimeter, but wanted to see the face of this man who'd been masked during the raid in Sizzle. Archer stayed in his position, closer to Tulio than her; she didn't mind having him as a guard. Something on the floor caught her eye and she paused to peer at it. What was…? She nearly gasped but stemmed the sound by clamping both hands over her mouth.

Luckily, she wasn't in Tulio's eye line, but Archer caught her reaction.

"Is that…?" she asked, lowering her hands from her lips.

"His left pinkie," Archer stated. "I told him to expect worse. He'll never forget what he did to you."

Just as she would never forget.

"Look, look, I'm sorry, okay? I'm sorry," Tulio sobbed. In his turn as attacker, he'd given no thought to his victims' terror. "What are you going to do with me? What are you going to do? Let me go, I won't tell anyone, I swear I won't."

"What makes you think we'll let you go?" Archer asked, pivoting on the spot to glare at Tulio. "You think you're gonna walk out of here? Do you?"

"I didn't do nothing, man," Tulio pleaded. "I was working under orders; you know how it is."

"Working under orders? I don't care who the fuck told me to rape a woman, I'd never do it."

"I didn't, boss! I didn't stick my dick in no whore! Didn't put it nowhere near any bitch!"

Archer walked over and instead of slapping his head this time, he took a handful of his hair and smacked his head off the solid pipe. "What the fuck did I tell you about calling her that?" Archer snarled through gritted teeth, anger radiating from him. "You disrespect my lady one more time and I'll lose my fucking patience with you, which will piss her off, 'cause she wants to have some fun. When she gets pissed off, I don't get laid, how do you think that will work out for you down there at the bottom of the food chain?"

"She's… she's your girl? No," Tulio said, maybe it was the daze, but he shook his head fast. "No, no, no one would go after your girl, Arch, no one. Hexam respects you, man, you know that."

Hexam respected Archer, everybody did. Though, she supposed, it was more out of necessity than a testament to his glowing, courteous personality. His connections ran deep. If he didn't already have dirt, and needed to protect himself, it wouldn't take him long to dig it up and use it against you.

To the right, the spread of Archer's knives lay out on a stationary conveyor belt.

"I have an idea," she said.

Archer let go of Tulio's hair to return to her side. She didn't address him and wandered toward the glinting blades. They lived in his closet, but she'd never taken the time to examine them in detail. Running a finger over their sheathed handles, which one was best?

The support of Archer's chest met her back. He ran

his hands from her elbows to her shoulders then up the sides of her neck.

"What are you thinking?" he asked, taking her ponytail, wrapping it around his fist and yanking her head sideways to kiss and nibble the pulsing artery in her neck. Moving up to her hairline behind her ear, he tormented her with his tongue, sliding it south until it met the collar of her shirt. "You tell me what you want to do, I'll tell you which one to use."

She'd never used his knives before, he was protective of them, so she doubted anyone ever had.

"You mark every man who crosses you," she said.

"That's right."

"I want you to mark him for me."

She'd do it herself, except she had absolutely no experience with knives. She'd either cut too deep, forcing the guy to make a mess as he bled out, or cut too shallow and he'd be saved the scar that would remind him of this day for the rest of his life, for as long as she let him keep it.

That reality was intoxicating. The power of that decision. In one breath, she could order another human being dead, and it would be done. His knives were there, Archer could do it, or he could tutor her. Lucky for Tulio, death wasn't what she wanted for him, definitely not yet.

Tulio was nervous and emotional for sure. Who wouldn't be, given the circumstances? But he hadn't gone into full meltdown mode and was smart enough not to fall back onto rage, as some stubborn men would.

If he worked for Hexam, as opposed to running his own operation, Tulio was a supporter, not an instigator, meaning he could be easily replaced.

"Anything you want, Squirm," Archer murmured into her hair then kissed the back of her neck, right on her spine. "Anything you want."

Breathing the words again, he brushed his lips over her skin. Was this turning him on? No, the kiss wasn't sexual. Well, it was, but it wasn't as urgent as his touch was in the grip of blind arousal. It was intimacy. It was trust. It was an appreciation for this openness without judgment.

Sharing this was not only fulfilling their deal, it elevated their relationship to a new level of full acceptance. Complicity in criminality was one thing, but now she was his accomplice, or he was hers.

There was no doubt or hesitation when he reached around her to slide a specific knife from its sheath. Pulling it out with such deliberation, she held her breath, and watched, feeling the gentle withdrawal almost as if he were sliding his cock out of her after sex. Just when he slipped away, she exhaled in a whispered moan he'd have heard in that same scenario.

He kissed the back of her head, then retreated. Closing her eyes, she could choose to keep her back to him and ignore him while he worked under her instruction. But turning a blind eye wasn't possible; she needed to face what was going to happen because she coveted it. She compelled Archer to set this up for her.

"No! No! No!" Tulio was screaming, begging, as metal scraped on metal.

Confronting the scene, she carried on in her arc. Tulio's arms were extended round the pipe with a length of chain between them, connecting his wrists with heavy metal cuffs.

"No, man! Don't do it!" Tulio screamed out.

"Doesn't feel good, does it?" she said. Tulio stopped trying to pull away and dragged his eyes from their extreme position toward Archer to land them on her. "Does it feel good to be helpless? To be weak? To have someone hurt you and take advantage of you while you can do nothing to help yourself?"

He peered at her for a second until she moved half a step closer to better witness the moment.

Clarity dawned on Tulio. "You're Taggert's girl," he said and tried to curve to see Archer, but Archer shunted his head against the pipe. "You're fucking Taggert's girl? You're doing this for Taggert's girlfriend?"

Tulio's comprehension almost took him away for a moment, away from Archer's action. When Archer's blade pierced his furthest arm, their prisoner was forced back to the present in a wailing call. Had her guy picked there because she couldn't see it? Was he shielding her from the violence of the act? Hearing Tulio's scream wasn't optional; there was no protecting her from that. It echoed through the cavernous space, intensifying the fraught moment, sending a rash of shivered goosebumps to flush her skin.

Archer had to have gone deeper with Tulio than he did with Bryant; his scream was far less potent. Marking Tulio's upper arm was better than marking his back. Although their victim's back was more accessible, Tulio wouldn't have to see the wound if it was there. With it on his arm, he'd have to see it every day.

If it was up to her, she'd have asked Archer to do it smack bang in the middle of Tulio's forehead; that might have been too obvious. They wanted to remind Tulio of what he'd done but didn't want to declare to the world what *they'd* done.

Tulio's knees buckled, the curve of the pipe held him up. Archer moseyed back to his knives. Instead of being repulsed by the pain in this man's expression, satisfaction heated her from the inside.

"You didn't hear her cry," Nya said, taking a step toward the pipe. "How many women have you heard begging for their lives, screaming for your friends to stop hurting them? How many times have you ignored them?"

"I'm not like that!" he screamed out. "I'm not!"

"You are," she said. "You were that night. Are you gonna tell me that was your first time? That you'd never worked for Hexam or those other guys before?"

"Hexam went nuts," Tulio said, panting through the pain as he crouched with his arms stretched above him. The chains holding him up forced him into the awkward position of hugging the pipe while his body wanted to give out. "When he found out what they did to that girl, he went nuts."

"Aww, your big, bad boss has a heart?"

Tulio coughed and dragged his feet across the floor attempting to support his weight. "Hexam has no heart… He was pissed because they were supposed to do it to you." She paused. Tulio laughed. "Yeah, they were supposed to make threats. They were supposed to beat down anybody they thought might get you into giving up Taggert. But you were the target, you were the one supposed to be tortured, raped, whatever... Hexam gave the go ahead for us guys to do whatever the fuck it took to get that information out of you."

"That's enough," Archer's startling voice came from behind her, terse and angry. "That's enough for tonight."

Archer stormed across the room to wrap a length of duct tape around Tulio's mouth. He wrapped it around twice, made sure his nose wasn't blocked, then went back to his knives. She was still in the stupor of processing Tulio's revelation when Archer came over and grabbed her arm to drag her toward the door.

She staggered along behind him, so dazed that she didn't see him lock up or retrieve the light. But when they got back into the alleyway, he was carrying his knives, the tape, and the light. He took them all to the trunk and dumped them inside.

After slamming the lid, he went around to open her door. "Come on."

Still numb, she remained in the entrance where he'd let her go. "I was supposed to die."

She'd known the objective was to break her and she'd known Jamie didn't deserve what happened to her. Not for a second had she ever imagined there were express orders for her to be tortured and sexually abused.

Jonno and his buddies probably thought they had all night until Archer swanned in and told them leaving the bouncers in the street had been a bad idea.

That single thing saved her life; the fact that the raiders had been stupid in committing murder in the street.

And Archer...

Fixating on him as he strode over, she was still in too much of a daze to know he intended to pick her up and carry her to the car, which was exactly what he did.

The sirens in Sizzle, she remembered those, remembered Archer telling the assailants the cops were on their way. If Archer hadn't come in and told them that, if Archer hadn't come in and taken her out of there, what would've happened? Would Jonno, Tulio and the others have panicked? Would they have killed her? Would they have taken her with them? Would they have stayed put and used her as a hostage? What would she have endured during that siege?

Archer was mumbling something to himself when she snapped out of her trance. They were already back in familiar streets.

"Thank you," she said again.

He stopped grumbling to glance at her. "You don't listen to what that fucker said. Hexam didn't order them to rape you, he ordered them to scare you. Tulio is just trying to—"

"Hexam knows who they all are," she said. "Doesn't he? Between Hexam and Jonno they'll know everyone."

Reading between the lines, he explained why it wasn't a good idea to be direct.

"I'm working other channels," Archer said. "If I come right out and ask Hexam or Jonno, they'll know what's coming next. They could warn the guys they name."

And that would screw up all their plans. That night proved she couldn't go into this half-assed. She needed to know how to take down each of the men, how to hurt them the most. She'd relied on Archer to do the digging and until now that had worked. She needed him to go deeper and needed to decide who would live and who would die.

EIGHT

"STOP THINKING ABOUT IT," Archer mumbled.

Lying in his bed, fixated on a shadow on the ceiling, she fingered the ends of her hair spread on her breast.

"I'm not."

"You are," he said.

She almost didn't hear him. "Hmm? What? No, I'm not."

"You are. Have you noticed what I'm doing right now?" His arms were coiled around her thighs, his strong hands pressing on her hips. Elevating her head from the couple of pillows it rested on, she made eye contact with the man between her legs and, oh, it sank in that his lips were on her clit. "You're thinking about what he said."

Contrary to his belief, Tulio wasn't on her mind. "I'm thinking about Tag," she murmured.

His mouth came into view a split second before he pounced over her leg and lunged up to lie on his side, his hard chest flush with her upper arm.

"We should talk about that," he said, holding his head up on his fist. "We should talk about how we're gonna pay for his funeral after I tie him to a swamp, cover him with honey, and let the insects do their work."

"Archer!" she chastised. Unimpressed and impatient, she nudged his chest with her shoulder. "Why would you say something like that?"

"You tell me you're thinking about another guy while I'm eating your pussy? You're lucky that's all I'm gonna do to him." His fist slipped higher into his hair until his lips descended to her ear. "It's a horrible way to go, Squirm. Takes a long time for a guy to die like that. It's agony."

"You've never done that," she said, forcing her eyes to the tops of their sockets, she wanted to read the truth in his. "Have you?"

Archer rubbed her taut belly. "Why are you thinking about him?"

Talking to Archer would help her make sense of what was going on and how she should handle it.

"This whole thing's complicated. It's one big mess. I don't know how to protect everyone and do what I want to do at the same time."

"Maybe you can't," he said, stroking his fingers down between her legs, he opened them and pressed them up until they reached the apex of her inner thighs. "You have to prioritize, it's what everyone else does."

His tone implied his suggestion was no big deal, but it wasn't as easy as that in her world.

"What if you're right? What if Tag loves Farrah? We can't make him dump her."

"You can't make a guy do anything. Especially when it comes to his dick. We tend to listen to our little buddy before we listen to anyone else."

She could already tell he wasn't going to be a great help. "Forget it."

Rolling away, in an attempt to move to her own side, he grabbed her hip and eased her onto her back again.

"Don't sneak away from me just 'cause I don't tell you what you want to hear."

"You asked me what was wrong," she said, exasperated. "Then you mock me for being honest."

He exhaled. "I'm not mocking you. I'm being honest too. If he wants to be with this girl, he's gonna be. I don't care who you are, nothing's gonna change his mind."

"So you've said already," she said after a sigh, resting a hand on each of her breasts. "So Hexam finds out and Tag loses his head."

"Sounds about right. But it's his decision to make, Ny, you can't make it for him."

She couldn't. Maybe that was why she was so upset. If someone told her to stop being with Archer, she wouldn't be capable of just turning off her feelings. Tag had implied leaving Archer was best for her, but she didn't regret refusing.

She loved how they could lie like this, so close, their bodies touching, pressing into each other, arms and legs twined of their own accord. Fingers found hair, and skin molded to each of their opposite grooves and ridges. They had every right to touch every part of each other and often did, even in a non-sexual way.

Like right then, while he had his hand over her sex. It had been stimulating, but he hadn't gone straight for the center, he just wanted to touch her in a place no other person could.

"Will you find out about her? About Farrah?" she asked, choosing to sway toward him, cocooning herself in his body.

When she tucked herself in close, his pride and ego compelled him to protect and comply.

"About her? What do you want to know about her?"

"Well, we're talking about Tag's feelings, but, I mean, she dumped the last guy pretty quick. I don't want Tag to fall in love with a woman, who could get him killed, only to find out she never felt the same way. She could throw him to the dogs as soon as he becomes inconvenient. You could just ask a few questions—"

"Jesus, Ny!" he exclaimed, flopping onto his back, planting both hands over his face.

"What?" she asked, clambering over to straddle his hips.

Trying to pull his hands from his face, she fought his resistance for a good thirty seconds until he eventually let his arms stretch out perpendicular to his body.

"Being with you is a fucking full-time job, you know that?" he asked. "What is it you want from me? My heart, my soul, my balls, you've got them all."

He didn't sound particularly happy about that; he wasn't pissed off, but he was certainly impatient.

"What's the problem?" she asked, rubbing both hands on his chest. "It should be pretty easy to find out about Farrah."

"I can tell you anything and everything you want to know about Farrah Hexam right now. She's the least of your worries. Whether she loves him or loathes him, whether she's using him for sex, she has no power over telling her brother what to do, personally or professionally."

"Okay." Drumming her fingernails on his pecs, this new information needed thought. "Will she go to bat for Tag—"

"Ny, it's not your problem." He grabbed her elbows. "It's not *our* problem."

More suspicious than curious, she clenched her thighs, digging her knees into him. "Is this because it's Tag? Because you want him to be hurt?"

"Because I'm sick of hearing you talk about him? Yeah. Maybe. Could be."

"He's like my brother," she said. He still had ahold of her elbows, so she couldn't go anywhere, and couldn't react physically. "You have nothing to worry about. There's nothing sexual between us."

"You keep saying that," he said. "I'm not worried about you having sex with him. You've had fifteen years to do that and never did." Pausing to look her square in the eye, he became stony. "And believe me, Ny, I didn't take your word for that. I checked."

This was why she was always suspicious. Not because she didn't trust him, but because far more went on in his life behind the scenes than she'd ever know.

"You checked up on me?" she said. "You didn't even do that before the whole Sizzle incident."

"No, because it's not my style to go after a guy's girl, I told you that. But now you're my girl."

And that warranted more interest, or less trust?

"So you're asking about me? You know, you could ask *me* about me."

He scoffed. "There's an idea. Do you know how many people are honest about their sexual history? Very few. They tell select details, the ones that make them sound good, and hide the real kinky crap. The guilty, dirty secrets don't come out easily. Sometimes it takes days for me to get that shit."

Either going for shock value or just to prove a point, she dug her nails into him and narrowed her eyes on his.

"I had sex with a college professor when I was nineteen."

And now it was his turn to be dubious. "You didn't go to college."

"I didn't say he was *my* college professor, but that's how he earned his money."

His lips quirked and he scooped his hand under her loose hair to capture her cheek. "He was number two?"

She nodded, savoring the sensation of his hot hand cradling her head. "He promised to teach me everything I'd ever need to know. I was coming off the back of my first major relationship and, well, yeah…"

"Where does Damien fit in?" Archer asked. "Was he next?" She shook her head. "Does your six include me or not?"

Narrowing her eyes, she was getting used to hearing details. "I told you five, you're trying to catch me in a lie." She huffed. "How did we get onto this? How did we segue from going medieval on Tag to the order of my sexual partners? You're good, Fella, I'll give you that." Tapping one finger on him, she was wise to his methods and brought them back to the present. "You think this is not our problem, but it is. Because in case you've forgotten, we've got one of Hexam's ex-henchmen chained up across town. When we let him go—"

"*If* we let him go," Archer said. "You wanted to do this and if we have to go all the way—"

"Not with him," she said. "Yeah, he's a bastard, and

he probably deserves to die. But I don't know that, he didn't actually touch me or Jamie. What we need from him is information on the others. We need him to tell us who the other men were and if he can't tell us…"

"If he can't tell us…" he said, repeating her words each in a short, calm blast. "Did it ever occur to you that maybe we shouldn't be looking for these guys?"

"Are you scared?" she teased, pouting.

Deadpan, he didn't blink. "Yeah," he said, completely unintimidated by her laughable suggestion. It wasn't possible for him to appear further from afraid than he did right now. "I know Jonno, I know who he was working with. We have Tulio, he's about the measure of the kinda guys Hexam hires. He's not the kinda guy Hexam would have in his inner circle, but… yeah, he works hard, and he works cheap, and he doesn't make a mess, at least, Hexam's men shouldn't make a mess. Don't underestimate how pissed Hexam was by the way things went down that night."

She recalled what Tulio said and got a chill. "I don't."

Not anymore. Hexam was pissed because evidence had been left at the scene, because men under his purview, men he'd hired, had gone overboard in prioritizing their ya-yas.

Archer must have sensed her return to the disturbed Tulio-inspired thoughts because his voice slowed.

"If those guys really wanted to hurt you, if they'd decided on raping you and Jamie before they went in, they'd have taken you both out of there. They'd have done it as soon as they put bullets in those guys. Hexam's orders were to get in and get out. No one thought you would hold out. Everyone thought you would buckle."

"Even you?"

He didn't lie. "Before I got there, sure," he said. "To me you were nothing more than…"

"A whore," she said, while he took a breath. Archer had believed her to be Taggert's girl, everybody did. With five guys bundling into her club, holding guns, and threatening their lives, she probably should have buckled. "If it had been anybody else, I would've. Back then Tag was the only one who had my loyalty like that."

His eyes narrowed. "Back then?" Archer asked, sliding his hand down to her breast. "You better not be talking about me, 'cause we've had this conversation."

"I can still be loyal to you and give you up," she said, but couldn't imagine a scenario where she'd actually do it.

Skeptical, he peered at her. "I don't know if I believe you." Archer manipulated her nipple into a tight peak. "I don't know what you thought you were achieving in Sizzle that night. I'm surprised Taggert didn't ream you out. I would've." When she pinched his nipple, he snatched her hand. "Anyone ever threatens you to get to me, and you even think about trying to protect me… You even think about it, Ny, we're through. You and me will be done. I'm serious, Ny, anyone ever asks you—"

"I know," she said, tired of the lecture. "You don't have to worry about that. Who would ever ask me?"

"People know about us now, Squirm. Why do you think they come to Sizzle?"

"They come to Sizzle because you come to Sizzle," she said. "They know that's where you are, it's become your haunt… I like having you there." With her admission came a shrug. "I've never really been the type to rely on a guy or need him around all the time. I liked being independent and being able to pick up and make my own decisions."

"You don't anymore?"

"I do," she said when he loosened his grip enough to release her hand. Bending it back as far as it would go, she rubbed the inside of her wrist, her brand, up and down on his chest. "There's something about you, Archer, that makes it okay for me to not be in control all the time. It's seductive… It turns me on when you make decisions for me, when you take control of my body."

"Okay," he said, slapping a hand onto hers to stop her rubbing. "Wriggling that hot body all over me and talking about seduction, are we done with conversation?"

The rod of his erection had been consistently jabbing at her since she'd sat like this, now he drew up his knees and took a breast in each hand. She took advantage of his support and leaned back on his thighs.

"Will Hexam be pissed at us?"

His hands dropped from her chest. "I guess we're not done talking," he grumbled. "Will Hexam be pissed we're going after his guys? Yes. Do I think I would be able to talk him around and help him see things from our point of view? Sure. He's a reasonable guy and we have history."

Sarcastic pessimism prompted her to ask, "So much history that you sold the location of his drop to Tag?"

"That was business; he knows we have our own interests. And we're not best buddies. Besides, it's never been confirmed I was the one who did that," her guy said, smirking. "No one really knows how Tag found out."

She knew. Tag knew. Archer knew. Hexam obviously hadn't paid to find out.

"Better hope he never asks."

Her man wasn't worried. "He could never afford that piece of information," Archer said, one side of his mouth curled as his head rolled to the side. "It's late, Squirm. If we're not gonna screw, let's go to sleep."

Digging her knees deeper, she bent over to prop her elbows on his shoulders. "We have to figure this out."

"I like this," he said, craning to see her breasts pressed into his chest.

Her head was too close for him to get a good view. Their foreheads touched, so she put pressure on his to force his head down, because she wasn't finished talking.

"Can you convince Hexam that what we're doing is okay?"

Inhaling, it became obvious he was getting fed up. "Providing we're not hitting anyone in his inner circle, I could. I have to do more digging to be sure. Although…"

She didn't like that tone. "Although, what?"

"Now Tag's screwing with his sister and we kind of hooked them up… it's not gonna look good. I don't know how far his goodwill will stretch. We might have to make a decision."

Exactly what she'd feared. "What kind of a decision?" she asked, clueless as to his implication.

Capturing her hair, where it draped down around their faces, between his first two fingers on each side, he gathered it into his fists.

"You might have to distance yourself is all I'm saying."

"Distance myself from what?"

"You have two options if you're backed into a corner. Either you tell Hexam you're against Tag's relationship, that you told him so, and he deserves everything that's thrown at him."

Seemed unlikely she'd turn her back on her oldest friend and allow Hexam to rip him to shreds. That was so unfathomable, she almost laughed.

"And option two?"

The more likely course given the alternative.

"Everybody knows about us, won't take Hex long to confirm it," Archer said, tucking her hair back over her shoulders and stroking his fingers through it either side of her spine.

Why was their relationship important?

"Us?" she asked and screwed up her face. "Who cares about us?"

"Option two is you tell Hexam I went after his guys, I hurt them off my own back."

Throw him to the lions? That was option two?

"Because? Why would you do that?"

"I was pissed they'd upset you, attacked you, touched you, and I wanted payback."

Slowly lifting her torso, her hands slid down his body as shock infused her.

"A decision," she said. "You meant between you and Tag."

Archer explained, calm and casual. How could he do that? All she could feel was distress.

"If Hexam gets ahold of us and pins us into corners, and he ain't feeling reasonable, you'll have to go with whichever option you think will piss him off less. He'll be pissed about Tag and Farrah; I can't see him accepting that. But if it turns out one of the guys from Sizzle that night is close to Hexam and still on the payroll, maybe been with him for a long time… If we hurt that guy, Hexam won't be happy with that either."

"Do you like bumming me out?"

How he could be unfazed by the idea she'd betray him was puzzling.

"You can't support both of us; you'll never walk out of there alive if you try. You could be seen as the instigator since you're bang in the middle of this. So either you support their love or stand up for what we're doing."

"My choice is support their love or support my vengeance?" she asked. That wasn't the most confusing part of what he'd presented. "This isn't you; none of this is you. Why would I sell you out?"

"Because the alternative is turning your back on Tag," Archer said and sealed his lips for a minute. "And I just don't see that happening, Squirm, do you?"

Sinking back onto her own side of the bed, she retreated from his body to reflect. She'd never betrayed Tag in the past, but he was making an insane decision she didn't want to be punished for. She didn't want Archer punished for it either.

They could let Tulio go, forget this ever happened and move on with their lives. What did it say about her if she was willing to give up her own objectives to support Tag in something she didn't agree with?

Her guy must've sensed her internal conflict.

"I can try a preemptive strike."

Hope shifted her onto her side. "Okay, I'm open to that," she said, squeezing her hands together.

A preemptive strike. How would that apply in this situation?

"I'll talk to him," Archer said, raising his arms to link his hands behind his head. "Get hold of Hexam, tell him what we're doing, tell him what we know about Tag—"

"No," she exclaimed. "We can't drop Tag in the shit like that."

"See," he said, shaking his head. "You had no problem when I started the sentence with, 'I'll tell Hexam what we're doing,' but the minute I mention your boy—"

"He's not my…"

She didn't even finish the sentence, she sat up, crossed her legs, and let her face sink into her palms. This was exhausting, frustrating, and so disheartening.

After a few seconds of nothing, he stroked her lower back.

"It's okay," he said. "I don't like it. I don't like that you care about another guy this much. But it's not like I didn't know it walking into this. You chose to be chained to my wall rather than give me his address. I mean that's loyalty on a whole new level. Part of the thing I love about you is that you're that fucking stubborn."

"I'm pissed off," she mumbled into her own hands. "At myself. He's a grown man. He makes his own decisions. I shouldn't… I shouldn't feel like this."

"He's been conditioning you for fifteen years to feel like this," Archer said. "Don't be so hard on yourself."

"He hasn't conditioned me."

Archer almost scoffed. "Have you ever heard anything close to negative about that man without jumping on it as if your mother was just insulted?"

"I never knew my mother."

He prodded her hip. "You have to break the cycle," he said. "It might not be deliberate, but your gratitude for what he did never went away. You're so grateful to him that you would feel guilty about not supporting him a thousand percent, like he did for you that night."

He was probably right. She couldn't picture not jumping to Tag's defense. That's what he'd done for her and she'd never been able to repay him—not to the same degree.

"He takes you for granted, but you have to make it clear you can't pick up after him, not when it's gonna cause you physical harm. If losing Jamie, staying here, taught you anything, it's that as he's moving into the bigger leagues, his life is becoming more dangerous. You can't let him take you along for the ride, you're not equipped to handle it."

Not physically. Her body was weak in comparison to those likely to threaten her. "I used to have nightmares," she said, finding it easier to look at the closet opposite the end of the bed than at him. "I used to have nightmares about what would've happened if Tag hadn't come to me that night. I think a part of me has been afraid the nightmare would come true if I didn't have him. You think I'm insane because I run around after him, look out for him and protect him with my life." Twisting, she looked at him through the budding morning light. "I've always been so scared that I'd need someone to swoop in and save me… and he was all I had."

"And if you pissed him off, he wouldn't be here," Archer said. "You would be on your own."

She nodded and he sat up. "Pathetic, isn't it?"

"It's not pathetic," he replied, driving a hand into her hair to gather a handful of it at the back of her head. "You needed someone, and he'd proved himself. It's natural you'd rely on him when you don't have family who'd put themselves on the line for you."

"I think we've taken each other for granted. He didn't even try to apologize when he knew I wasn't happy. Getting into the big leagues has changed him; he's cocky now, more assured. He doesn't need me. I think he likes it when I need him."

"A lot of guys are like that."

"But now, after Sizzle, and Jamie losing her life… How far can I go to protect him? I can't fight, I don't have the skills or the strength. But…"

In her attempt to avert her gaze, she compelled Archer to pull her closer and catch her chin in his free hand.

"But what?" he asked.

Her eyes would be wide and glazed, because admitting the truth broke her heart. "Sometimes I feel so guilty," she whispered. "How can I question him? How can I think about disagreeing with him or betraying him, when he almost killed his own brother for me? He destroyed his fraternal relationship… for me."

Archer didn't like emotional women, crying women. She kept her eyes wide, so as not to blink out any of the tears gathering on her lower lids.

"You have to let go," he said, tightening his grip to

shake her head an inch. "His brother would never have been there, in that state, if it wasn't for what went on in the garage. Tag could've kept the guy on a shorter leash. He should never have been allowed anywhere near you. What happened that night wasn't your fault."

"But I—"

"No," he said, angry in his delivery. "It wasn't your fucking fault, Ny, and I won't hear it. You don't owe the guy anything. You have to live your life."

There was another consideration, one that could cause problems not Hexam related, but related to their relationship.

"He's going to think it's because of you. He'll blame you."

"Let him," Archer said. "Let him come at me, Squirm, please, I can handle it."

"But could I?" she asked. "If you two hurt each other because of me…"

"You don't think we've been close to it? We've been a hair away from taking each other apart, and how we feel about you is the only thing that's stopped us from doing it. I don't care. I'm not asking you to shut him out. I'm not telling you we have a problem. All I want for you to do is to look out for *you*. Follow your own gut; promise me you'll do that? Instead of sacrificing yourself to protect his ass."

As sure as he was, her fear still existed. "And one day," she said. "What if the nightmare comes true?"

Releasing her, he opened both hands and shoved her hair away from her face to take it in his firm grip. "That nightmare will never come true," he said. "I never take my eyes off your ass long enough for anyone to threaten it. You've gotta trust me, Ny. You have to trust me."

And she did. Even though she trusted Archer with her life, she didn't want it to be like she hung onto Tag until a better bet came along. Her fella had protected her before, at risk to himself, and he would do it again.

Odd how talking to him, being honest with him, confessing to him, her man a vault of secrets, made her feel better. Nothing had been resolved, but she'd sleep easier. Tag was still in a relationship that could cause him physical harm. They still had Tulio tied up in a basement and Hexam was the man holding the proverbial gun.

For now, he didn't know who to aim it at because all of this was going on behind his back. Archer once told her that the truth always came out. By his reckoning, his rules, it was only a matter of time before the current truths were exposed in the light of a public arena.

NINE

"YOU HAVE TO END it," Nya said into the phone she'd dialed after jumping out of the cab outside Sizzle.

The day had gotten away from her. Because she was running behind, the call replaced a conversation that should've happened face-to-face. Though some part of her subconscious acknowledged it was harder for Tag to give her the brush off on the phone. In person, there were too many distractions he could use to avoid answering her.

"Excuse me?" Tag asked. "I thought you were coming over here for lunch, where are you?"

"Something came up." Something like a guy tied to a pipe awaiting his demise. Tulio was a dilemma she'd never thought she'd face. Having Archer around made it easier to cope. The pressure of action wasn't on her, deciding how the situation should end was on her shoulders. "I have to run errands. There's a couple of things I have to do at Sizzle, then I'm running home to pay my rent—"

"So you thought you'd squeeze me in? You know how I feel when you cancel on me."

Yes, she did, he hated it. Tag wasn't understanding about unexpected events in her life. She couldn't tell him about Tulio; he'd warned her against going after the men who'd attacked Sizzle. So, for now, she'd have to be vague.

Heading for the doorway of the club, she dug in her bag for her keys. "I know you hate being canceled on. I do. I'm sorry. I got caught up at Archer's this morning."

"So much for him not coming between us," he grumbled.

That wasn't a good reaction, Tag really didn't like her boyfriend and time wasn't building any bridges.

"He's not! I swear it to you…" Pausing in the entryway to Sizzle, she brought a hand to her hip. How could she appease her friend? "Truth is, we didn't get much sleep. I spent the morning in bed."

"With him?"

Okay, she'd just given Tag a visual that wouldn't help. She sucked at this mediator thing.

"Yes, with him… sleeping."

"No sex?"

She couldn't claim that exactly. They had been sleeping, that wasn't a lie, but when they woke up, some kissing became rubbing. Although it hadn't been the intention, there may have been some incidental penetration.

"Does that matter?" she asked. "I'm sorry I have to cancel, but we do have to talk, we can't ignore this."

His mood was still sour. "I don't get why it's your business who I'm dating."

Carrying on into the club, she looped her keys around her thumb and rested her fist on her open purse. "It's my business because your girlfriend's brother might cut off your balls when he finds out what's going on. And because my boyfriend set it up for you to tempt this girl 'cause it was what Hexam wanted. You were supposed to tempt her, Tag, not screw her. You have to end this."

"I'll end my relationship when you end yours."

Stopping dead, it hadn't occurred to her he'd make a counteroffer. Was he serious or snide?

"What has my relationship with Archer got to do with your relationship with Farrah?" Nya asked, frozen on the spot, halfway between the door and the bar.

Having Tulio as their prisoner created urgency, she

was responsible for the life of another and had no idea how long he'd hang on without them returning. She wanted to see how he was and to check that he hadn't escaped. Archer didn't seem as concerned, but he had experience in this arena.

He'd even told her she could go for lunch with Tag, that it wouldn't be a problem, an extra hour wouldn't make any difference. Instead she'd elected to come to Sizzle to do what was needed after calling one of her assistants to advise she wouldn't be working that night in contradiction to the schedule. Tulio took priority. This was the first time she'd done this abducting and torturing thing, she needed to focus. This situation would only get harder. By hitting the easiest mark first, Archer betrayed his skill.

"I'm proving a point," Tag said. "I have as much right to say that to you as you do to me."

Irritation brought her fingers to her forehead. "You have been telling me to dump him since you found out we were together. You're looking for any excuse to get—"

"See how annoyed you are? That's how I feel."

"Don't compare the relationships," she said, scowling at no one. "What Archer and I have is nothing like what you have with Farrah."

"How would you know?"

This wasn't going well. Tag had been pissed at the start of the call and now her mood matched his.

"For one thing, you've been seeing her for two weeks, you can get rid of her."

"How long had you been seeing Archer when I found out about the two of you? Days?" he asked. "Were you even together then or was it just sex? It didn't make any difference to you when I told you to dump him. You wouldn't do it."

Granted, she probably hadn't been crazy in love with Archer when Tag discovered the relationship, but they had a connection, something that started before Tag found out. Something that started during her captivity. Something that combusted in that parking lot.

That wasn't even the point, and she was sick of dancing around the truth.

"You wanted me to dump Archer because you don't

like him," she said. "There's a huge difference between that and what I'm asking."

"Tell me," he said, smug and condescending.

The latter had little effect on her now she was dating the world's greatest aficionado in that trait.

She spelled it out. "I'm telling you to dump her for your own good."

Her friend didn't budge. "You're worried about your boyfriend, you just said it yourself."

"Yeah, I'm worried about him, but I'm worried about you too. Unless you really love her and plan to be with her forever, there's no point carrying on with this. And if you do love her, you have to face her brother. Tell me, are you willing to do that?"

Her question only riled him more. "This is none of your business," he snapped. "You just can't keep your nose out. It's typical."

Tag didn't mind her being nosey when she was looking out for his interests. In the past, when she displayed concern, he'd never gotten angry. Sure, there were times he'd pat her on the head and dismiss her worries, but he'd never been irrational and irritated like this.

"Fine," she said. "You tell me you're in love with Farrah and I will support you every step of the way. I'll even drag Archer along. He won't like it, but I'll find a way to convince him to stick with us."

"Us?" Tag spat. "I don't give a fuck about Archer. He can go screw himself for all I care."

"Great," she said, once again resenting the male ego. "Yeah, I'll tell him that. I'll tell him he can go screw himself. Do you even care that by saying things like that, it puts me right in the middle of this juvenile feud between the two of you? Archer is at least willing to make the effort."

"Oh, yes, he's fantastic. I'm sure he's real agreeable while he's got his dick up your ass."

Her mouth dropped open. "Tag, what is wrong with you?"

"Maybe I'm sick of hearing it," he said. "Maybe I'm sick of hearing you say I'm never good enough, that every decision I make is somehow a basis for you to judge me."

She'd never entertained the idea he'd feel this way. Yes, they commented on each other's lives, but if she had to tally up the instances through the years, she would guess he'd cast more aspersions on her than the other way around.

Like finding herself at Sizzle. She liked the responsibility, and it was great to have a regular paycheck. But Tag, without asking her opinion, had been the one to storm into her former place of employment and put a stop to her working there. Maybe stripping was a life choice, maybe it was a dream, maybe it was something she'd always wanted to do. Okay, it wasn't, but it wasn't like she hated it. The money was good, and she needed a steady income.

"Fine then," she said. "You want me to butt out, I will. But don't expect Archer to bail you out again. Don't come to us when Hexam puts your balls in a vice."

"I won't," Tag snapped. "You live your life, Yorkie, and I'll live mine."

"Fine by me," she retorted.

"Good."

She didn't know which one of them hung up first, or if they did it simultaneously, because she didn't wait to hear another word. She took the phone from her ear, pressed disconnect, and stuffed it into her bag.

Balling her fists at her sides, she growled and contemplated calling Archer. Except he was sick of hearing Tag's name on her lips and, as she'd said to Tag, there was no love lost between the men. She didn't need to give either man extra ammunition.

Archer once commented Tag would always hate him if she told her friend about every fight. That worked both ways. Finding a balance between honesty and protection was difficult. The first step was making sure she'd cooled down before involving anyone else.

Knowing Archer's personality as she did, he'd assume her rant was some kind of call to arms. In a physical confrontation between the two men, Archer would win, hands down. His experience was greater and he used combat skills every day. Tag was more of an ideas man than an implementer.

She put the argument out of her mind and went about the Sizzle business of paying invoices and placing orders. Next was the bank run to make a Sizzle deposit, and a personal withdrawal. At home, when she tried to hand over the money to her landlord, she got the shock of her life.

It hadn't been her intention to return to Archer's so soon, but there was no other course after her landlord closed his door in her face. Not only was she embarrassed, she was downright astounded. Choosing not to use her key, she pounded on Archer's apartment door.

As always, he opened the door without checking the identity of his visitor. His relaxed expression of expectation quickly became perplexed.

"Did you lose your key already? Babe—"

"I just went to my landlord," she said, without crossing the threshold.

He frowned and bit into his apple. "What for?"

Dumb question, except it wasn't, given what she'd found out. "To pay my rent."

"Already did."

Instead of waiting for her to come in or request entry, he went back inside to, as always, stand behind the couch to watch TV. The position was central, sure, but she didn't understand why he insisted on standing up.

"Why did you do that?" she asked, coming inside because she didn't want to holler across the room.

"You told me to."

"Uh, I did not, when did I do that?"

Holding a hand toward her, he didn't take his eyes from the subtitles on the TV screen. "In the club when you got your tits out."

Growling, she refrained from tutting at him. "I didn't get my tits out," she said, discarding her purse, shoes, and jacket before going over to take his hand. Kissing her brand, he directed her around the couch to seat her in the middle. "I can't believe you paid my rent." Twisting to glance up at him, she still didn't have his attention. "Just how many months did you pay?"

"Three," he murmured. "Figured we'd have you out

of there by then. He can keep the change. You deserve better than that place."

"I like my studio," she said though it was nowhere close to being the Ritz.

Crouching behind the couch, he ruffled her hair. "Watch this play."

Grabbing his hand out of her hair, she flipped around onto her knees to look at him. "I don't care about the damn play, Fella. We have to talk about this."

"What's the big deal?" he muttered. "I pay my mom's bills."

"I'm not your mom," she said, exasperated she had to make that distinction.

"Yeah, I know that." He folded his arms. "It's my job. I pay the bills of the woman who created me and of the woman I create with, it's how it should be. I take care of you. Get used to it, Squirm."

"Create with you?" she asked. "Are you talking about kids? You want us to have kids?"

If he'd paid the rent for a quarter of a year, he had intentions of sticking around. Not that she'd planned to go anywhere. Though she hadn't begun to consider how long their relationship might last.

"I meant created sweat, and spunk, and orgasm, but I can knock you up if you want that. Still won't live with you though."

Still won't live with her. He departed from his spot to get a beer from the fridge and brought her a bottle of chilled mineral water, her favorite brand, at the same time.

"Where do you plan to put my pregnant-self if you think I'm moving out of my apartment, but not moving in here?"

"Somewhere closer to here," he said, dampening her breast with the condensation on his bottle. Moving it over the exposed swell, the skin reacted with goose bumps. While she suppressed the shiver, he pressed it to her nipple through her top, peaking it in an instant. "I'm figuring it out."

Pushing onto her hands, she couldn't believe he was so casual about relocating her without consulting her.

"You're actually doing something about it? Making plans?"

"Sure," he said. "Your guy has his ear to the ground. People owe me. We'll get you something good."

Arguing with him was pointless, so she slid down onto her back. "Makes no difference to me if you're going to pay for it anyway," she mumbled.

"That's the spirit," he said, having read her sarcasm and chosen to ignore it.

She wasn't done. "If you plan to take over my responsibilities maybe I should give up Sizzle."

"Whatever you want," he muttered.

It was infuriating how he could dismiss her and carry on watching TV. "Yeah, I can stay at home all the time, watch daytime soaps and wait for you to impregnate me."

His voice was absent; his attention was on the game. "If that's what makes you happy."

She doubted he was listening.

"Might be tough to explain to our twenty kids why Daddy doesn't live with us," she said, pretending to ponder. "I can just tell them you're married. It's better than the truth and the girls will learn a good lesson, that as long as your man pays the bills, he doesn't have to be present."

"Sounds good."

"Archer!" she exclaimed and thrust back onto her knees to grab his belt.

"What?" he asked. "You're being stupid. I have no problem with you working and I don't plan to get you pregnant. So I paid your rent, big deal, I paid off your credit card too."

She gasped and her mouth fell open. "You didn't!"

"I did," he said, opening his mouth to fill it with beer. "You shouldn't have one of those anyway, your interest rate was ridiculous, and it leaves a trail that guys like me can track."

Uh oh, she didn't like his implication. "You didn't… You didn't close it, did you?" His response was to raise his brows and drink more beer, giving her all the answer that she needed. "Archer! That was my emergency card!"

"From the balance on that thing, I'd say you have a

lot of emergencies."

Growling at him, she poked a finger into his belly button through his shirt. "Where are you getting all this money, huh?"

"I've got plenty of money," he said. "Maybe not as much as your buddy, Tag. But we'll never be in a bind. I can always take on more work or call in favors. You're not gonna have any emergencies 'cause I'll take care of that shit before it gets near you."

With his network and skills, he would probably foresee problems before she knew they were coming. Being dependent on another person had never sat well with her. She'd resisted Tag's attempts to control her life and her finances. With Archer, it felt different, like a security blanket, not a ball and chain.

Getting into a relationship with Archer meant all kinds of adjustments in her life, she couldn't fight them all.

"We should get going," she said, tracing the outline of his belt buckle. "We can't leave Tulio out there forever. We have to feed him."

Amusement slanted his lips. "Like a pet." Archer still watched TV and gulped his beer. "He'll wait a while. He hasn't even been there twenty-four hours. We can go if you want, but I have to be back here by nine and you can't stay over."

Disappointed, her shoulders fell. "What?" she asked, aware of the vague whine in her voice. "I just got you back and you're telling me you're going to take somebody else on. Isn't Tulio enough? How many guys can you keep locked up at the same time? Is that why you put Tulio further away?"

"I didn't want him in my house," Archer said. "I didn't know what you wanted to do with him. I try not to kill here when I can help it. Too much mess."

Instead of addressing the implication of murder, she asked about the location where Tulio was being held. "You've used that building before?" she asked and he nodded. That was enough about that, Nya didn't want to know too much about what he'd used it for or what had gone on there. "Who's the new guy? Another one of our seven?"

"No. He's not a mark. He's a friend. A plan B. He

knows something."

"Something you want to know?" she asked, curling her hand around his beer bottle when he rested its base on the back of the couch. "And what if he doesn't tell you? He'll become a captive?"

Archer shook his head. "He'll tell me. We're buddies."

"If you're buddies, why can't I be here?"

"You can work your shift at Sizzle."

She sighed and propped her chin on the opening of his beer bottle. "I can't work my shift, there's too much..."

"What?" he asked when her forehead fell against his abdomen. One simple action and she piqued his curiosity. "What happened today that you're not telling me?"

He reached further along the back of the couch for the remote. She didn't see him turn the television off but heard him put the remote back down and the body she was leaning on moved.

When she opened her eyes, he was crouched to her eye line, examining her expression with his mouth just an inch from hers. Hoping it would stop him retreating, she combed her fingers through his hair to bring her hand onto his shoulder.

"Tag and I had a fight," she said. Archer tensed, so she did too, to prevent him pulling away. "It doesn't matter, it's no big deal. We've fought before, but with Hexam, Tulio, and now you're telling me I can't be here... I'm worried about Hexam, what if he comes for us? Archer, what if you're wrong and he's pissed about Tulio—"

"He won't be pissed about Tulio and 'cause you're so good at sucking my cock, I'll forget you said my name and the word 'wrong' in the same sentence. I haven't figured all the other guys out, maybe he'll give a fuck about them, but we're safe with Tulio. It's not a good time for you to be fighting with Tag; we need you to stay on top of him."

Great, pressure, just what she needed. "I know," she said. "He pushed my buttons. I told him to dump her, and he got defensive."

Shaking his head, he reminded her, "I told you he

would."

"Yes," she said, losing some of her cool. "But he told me he would only dump her if I dumped you."

Now Archer did stand up and there was nothing she could do to prevent him. "That fucker."

"He wasn't serious," she called out when he retreated toward the bedroom, leaving her on her knees holding his beer bottle. "Archer, baby, come back!"

He stomped away into the other room.

She growled at herself. "Damnit."

It hadn't been her intention to share specifics, she just wanted to let Archer know that her relationship with Tag was fraught. It felt dishonest to not be upfront about the conflict in her day.

Getting information from people was what Archer did and for some reason, it spilled out of her. When he asked a question, she was more honest than she had to be, and gave more details than were required. Maybe part of her subconscious was fearful of his more enhanced techniques of interrogation, though she knew he would never use them on her.

Casting the beer bottle onto the coffee table, she clambered off the couch and followed in his wake. When she got to the bedroom, he was reaching into the closet retrieving the knives that they'd used with Tulio.

"What do you plan to do with those?" she asked on a surge of panic, quickly closing the door and plastering herself against it. Opening her arms and legs, she pinned her back against it in hope of blocking Archer's exit. "He didn't mean it. He was being facetious to point out how unreasonable the request was. He won't break up with Farrah, just like I won't leave you."

"You fucking love me," he snarled, untying the knife roll and holding one end as he whipped it out flat on top of the bed.

Archer hunkered down and pulled out two knives to examine the blades. Putting one back, he selected another to scrutinize too.

"Archer, you can't go over there brandishing a

weapon. Your knives are beautiful, and I know you're good, but you can't walk in there and hurt him."

Except he was mad. "Don't put money on that."

"I know it's easier for you to resort to violence, but you'll only be proving his point."

Archer shot to his feet and took one long stride in her direction, aiming the knife in his hand at her heart. "And what is his point, Squirm? That I'm bad for you? Out of the two of us," he said, flicking the knife backwards and forwards between himself and the absent Tag. "Since you and I have known each other, between him and me, he's got you into more trouble than I have. I've done nothing but save your ass… and his. And I'm willing to do your dirty work. You told me you wanted to take down the men who hurt your friend. Who's working on that for you? Huh? Him or me?

"I'm working every damn minute of every damn day to do it, and I don't get paid a penny for it. I'm doing it because I love you."

"I know," she said, leaving the door to cross to him. Nya swerved around the blade he still had extended in his loose grip to wrap her arms around his waist. "I know what you're doing for me and I'm sorry I can't pay you. I'm sorry if you feel burdened. You don't have to prove yourself to me. I love you. I don't listen to what he says about you."

"He shouldn't be allowed to say anything," Archer grumbled. "All he does is fuck up your life. He's lucky I haven't taken him down already."

"Let's not fight about Tag again," she said, turning her head to rest her cheek on his torso. "We have to figure out what we're going to do with Tulio. You have to be back in time for your friend."

For whatever reason his friend was coming over, it was important to Archer. Whether it was about Hexam and his men, Farrah and her relationship with Tag, or something completely different, Nya didn't ask questions. Archer did nothing but fight for her, fight her battles. He'd never done anything that would warrant her questioning his loyalty or motivation.

"Let me deal with Tulio my way," he said, stroking

one hand from her crown to her ass. "You stay here and hang out. I'll go and deal with him."

It was sweet, but unnecessary, that he felt the need to shield her. "You're trying to protect me," she said. "But I need to see these men be humiliated. I need the closure. I can't live with myself, knowing what they did to Jamie the night she died, unless I do something."

Balling his hand in her hair, he grumbled but kissed the top of her head. "Okay, get your shit together, 'cause I have a show for you."

"What does that mean?"

"You were pretty clear that physical harm wasn't the only way to hurt someone. I didn't figure you'd want to kill Tulio, though I'll do it if you want me to. Let's just say I have a surprise I think you'll like."

He didn't elaborate, he just kissed the top of her head and went back to his knives on the bed. Nya was ready to leave already. After that statement, she wanted to get there faster. Tulio was a lowlife, a scumbag opportunist who hurt women to suit himself. But he wasn't an instigator, he was a follower. He needed to be taught a lesson and shown that if all he did was trot behind a leader, they could guide him off a cliff.

TEN

SHE ASKED HIM SEVERAL times on the journey over to Tulio's prison what her surprise was and he stayed tight-lipped. Most women wanted flowers or chocolates or expensive perfumes from their boyfriends. Those who were really lucky got jewelry, lavish meals in exclusive restaurants, or dirty weekends in exotic locations.

And there she was, sitting next to the man she loved in his beat-up car, being driven to the crappiest part of town expecting, not material gifts but, something that would mean so much more. Except she had no idea what it was.

Archer parked up in the same spot they'd been in the previous night, then went to the trunk to retrieve supplies, his knives, and a length of rope that he hooked up around his shoulder. With his fingers locked between hers, he pointed his knife roll at the lantern still in the back of the truck.

"Do you need the light?" he asked.

The green light that signaled their destination yesterday helped to keep her calm. Did she need him to carry it along the pitch-dark hallway? Yes, she probably would prefer it. But that answer didn't escape her lips.

"No," she said.

He let go of her hand to grab a stash of plastic sticks,

which he stuffed into his back pocket before he picked up a roll of duct tape to loop it around her wrist.

When he joined their hands again, she squeezed. "Just don't let go of me."

Slamming the trunk, he led her through the entrance and down the stairs. As they descended into the belly of the building, the darkness grew thicker, and she began to wish they'd brought the lantern. Maybe he felt her tremble or the sweat on her palms, but he pulled their joined hands to the small of his back to flatten her forearm along his belt, above the horizontal sheathed knife on his waistband.

"This won't take long," he murmured.

Nya hadn't expected him to stop, and she couldn't see a thing. It was so black she couldn't see her own hand in front of her face, let alone his form. So when he did stop, she walked right into him. As if he'd expected it, he brought their joined arms around to position her body in front of his. Instead of opening the door and pushing her in, he turned around, which seemed stupid. It was so dark they couldn't make eye contact.

"He's been here all night," Archer said, keeping his volume low. "He'll be dirty, he'll be smelly, and he'll be desperate. I know you want to be involved. My advice is to watch and learn."

"I shouldn't speak?"

"You can speak. Just keep your distance. Nothing is expected of you here. I've got you."

Rubbing his chest, she was reassured when it slid lower, and she felt the ridges of his abdomen through his shirt. "I'd ask you to kiss me, but—"

Catching her chin in one large hand, he forced it up, and planted his mouth square on hers without hesitation. Visibility was so low his good aim might've been luck, either that or his instinct knew where her mouth was at all times, even when sight failed him.

"I've always got you, baby," he murmured, brushing his lips side to side. "Let's get this over with and go home, okay?"

He reached beyond her until the door opened. The

echoing crack of him splitting glow sticks startled her. He tossed them past her into the room containing their captive to light up the space with dull neon light.

The moldy, dirty scent from before was now joined by the fetid aroma of stale urine. Sickening. The man, now coated in his own body fluids, they'd left hanging from the pipe was still there. His knees didn't quite reach the floor and his arms were now above his head. The position wouldn't be comfortable. It wasn't nice. On a human level, she felt a twinge of compassion, but she dampened it down. Had he or his friends shown Jamie compassion?

"Still with us, Tulio?" Archer declared, slamming the door so hard behind them that the room shook. Nya inched forward, Archer strode past her, not cursed by the hesitation that swathed her. He'd seen all this before, probably many times. "Not nice, is it? When someone takes away your basic human rights." Archer kept on going and unwrapped his knives at the side, where they'd been before. "You've made a mess."

He slid out one knife and then the other. So methodical. This part of the process was as much about intimidation and psychological torture as it was about actually selecting a knife to use.

"Come on, man, speak. Are you still with us?" Archer asked the question, but it didn't sound like he cared one way or the other.

Holding the longest knife from his stash, Archer went toward Tulio wearing disgust in his expression. Touching his blade to the bottom of Tulio's chin, he forced the man's head up and around.

"Tired?" Archer asked. "Sore? How many little girls have begged you for mercy? You put them through worse shit than this."

Her compassion faded, in fact, it vanished, pouf, just like that. This wasn't a human exhausted and in pain, this was a monster. A thug who beat people for money and was complicit in rape, even if he didn't take part in the act himself.

Archer would know everything there was to know about Tulio and she was about to find out how far his knowledge extended.

"You're in a sorry state," her guy sneered, flattening the long blade against Tulio's cheek, dragging it downward to split the duct tape, freeing it from his mouth.

The man's yelp of agony confirmed he was still alive. "Let me go, man." Tulio hadn't even been there for twenty-four hours. Although hungry and thirsty, he wouldn't be on the verge of death. "Let me go. I'm sorry."

"Sorry?" Archer said, hunkering down beside Tulio, avoiding the dirty wet stain on the concrete.

Maybe this was part of the reason he'd left Tulio naked, because although he'd urinated, the bacteria-ridden fluid wouldn't be festering in fabric and creases. Tulio didn't seem like the modest type, he probably didn't see nakedness in itself as torture.

"You don't show mercy," Archer said. "Why should I?"

Moving around in a similar curved route to the one she'd gone before, Nya got closer while still maintaining enough of a distance that she could observe the scene without participating.

"Sad state, you here, trussed up like this, what would your buddies think?"

"You got me, man. Yeah, you got me. I know it. Please, you've proved your point. Let me go."

"I don't think you get my point," Archer said. "But if you've got it, man, I'm all ears. You tell me, what's my point?"

"You're pissed," Tulio said. "About the girl, the one they offed."

His casual attitude sent a surge of anger through her. "They didn't just off her," Nya snapped and took three involuntary strides toward the two men.

Even Archer hadn't expected her to speak, but he stayed in his crouch and twisted his upper body toward her.

"You tell him, Sweets, is that our point? Are we pissed about that?"

"No, that's not our point," she said, happy to clarify for him and the slime ball who seemed to think he was better than those he tortured. "Our point is that he doesn't deserve to live. He doesn't deserve to breathe. He has no compassion. No understanding of what it is to be decent to other human beings. Our point is that karma fucking works, and if he can go around treating everybody else like a piece of shit, like his own personal toys, then that's how he should be treated. Why does he think he's better than—"

"I don't!" Tulio cried out.

Archer got to his feet, and with one swift kick, got the guy in the gut. "You interrupt her again, the next one will be to your skull," Archer said, prodding the tip of his blade into Tulio's thrown back head. "Get to your feet!" Archer turned his back on the coughing and whimpering man to come over to her with that cold, blank look in his eyes. He tossed an arm around her shoulder. "Anything you want, Sweets. You want me to cut him open?"

She didn't know if he was asking her aloud to scare the guy, or if she was supposed to be the pressure valve, a failsafe, that would prevent him from doing something permanent. At that moment, Nya understood his detachment because her own compassion had fled.

"I want to know who pulled the trigger on the men outside Sizzle," she said. "I want to know how many men he's killed."

"That would be an interesting fact," Archer said, redirecting himself to face Tulio, though his arm never left her shoulders. "Answer the lady."

"I don't..." Tulio said, coughing again, trying to get to his feet to hold himself against the pipe, his only support, using his arms that had to be in agony. "I don't kill people, man, that's not my gig."

"So it's just rape you're hired for?"

"I didn't touch her. It was those other fuckers who killed her."

"Blame everybody else," Archer said. "You're just lucky, I know enough about you to know exactly what you do and who you do it with."

Archer held the knife toward her, flipping it around to present her with the handle. Nya took it, though why did she need it? Maybe Archer just wanted rid of it because he started toward Tulio again.

Clearing his throat, Archer projected his voice, "I know what your big secret is, my girl here told me there were ways to kill a man without murdering him. And the only way we let you live is if we know you get the message, you're our bitch now."

"Whatever you want," Tulio said, hope bursting into his tone. "Whatever you want." He tried to scramble around further to see Archer who stayed just out of their captive's eye line. Tulio had to twist all the way around at an awkward angle to even attempt to get a look at the couple. "You want me to work for you? I'll do it. I'll round up bastards and bring 'em to you. I'll beat 'em for you."

Her man wasn't impressed or tempted. "I do all our dirty work. It's the only way I can be sure it's done right and that my lady is protected," Archer said. "The most I'll need from you is information, which you'll give me any damn time I ask."

"Yes, yes, sure, I'll be your ears, I'll be your eyes. I'll tell you everything I see. Everything I hear."

Funny how a man's morals went out the window, how his integrity dwindled, when he feared for his life.

Nya had a gun pointed at her head once, but she'd held onto what was important to her. Archer had told her, in no uncertain terms, he'd sacrifice himself for her, and here was this sniveling fool promising to sell his soul for just the vague possibility he might be allowed to live.

"See it's not enough for me," Archer said. She was in awe of how he took everything in stride. He spoke to Tulio in his calm, condescending tone, like he could've been talking to someone in a coffeeshop or at a ballgame. Not like he was talking to a piss-covered, blood-stained cretin tethered to a metal pipe. "Letting you walk away isn't enough of a guarantee. I don't need you scared this will happen again, 'cause I know you'll be looking over your shoulder and to be honest, I can't be bothered chasing you down. You're a fucking pain in the ass, and that's how you lost your finger. Every day you see that stub, you're gonna remember what happened here."

"Yes, yes," Tulio said. "I'll remember. Please let me go."

"Usually that's enough for me," Archer said, stopping about four feet away from Tulio to link his hands at his back and widen his stance. "Usually it's enough for me to scare a guy shitless and send him on his way. They never screw me over again. They never want payback because they know they're lucky to get away."

"Yeah, lucky," Tulio said. "Lucky. Lucky. Now please..." He tried to shift around further. The chain scraped on the pipe, and he winced. The mark Archer left on him the previous day had to be chafing against the rusted metal. The bloody line on his cheek was new and blood still trickled down from his cheekbone over the stubble on his jaw.

"But we're not here for me," Archer said. "You want to know what I found out now, Sweets?" Though he called to her, he measured his gaze on Tulio. "You want your surprise? You told me there are ways to kill a guy slow, baby, and I know how to make this guy dance for us. Tulio here is married to a beautiful Italian woman who has a couple a big-ass brothers, a huge family, they're a great bunch of people who welcomed him in, a sad pathetic orphan with no family of his own. How long you been married now? Ten years? Twenty?"

"Twelve," Tulio said.

Why was he so eager to offer that information when clearly Archer wasn't about to buy him an anniversary gift?

"Twelve years is a long time. You must love her a whole lot."

"Don't threaten my wife," Tulio said. A smidgen of respect sparked for the way he jumped to his wife's defense. "You kill me now, man, before you go near her."

Is that what Archer thought she wanted? Another innocent woman hurt because of this man's mistakes?

"I wouldn't touch a hair on her head," Archer said. She breathed an internal sigh of relief. "No, I wouldn't. But I would have a conversation with her."

Tulio's chain scratched again when he dropped some tension from his arms.

"A conversation about what?"

"Anything that comes up," Archer said. She recognized his wry tone. "Maybe about that little blonde thing, way across town, you know the one I mean, Tatiana, is it?"

"You leave her alone too!"

"Defend your women?" Archer asked. "Yet others are fair game? Doesn't seem like an even playing field to me."

"You leave them the fuck alone, both of them. You don't touch either—"

"Doesn't look to me like you're a man in a position to be giving orders," Archer said. "I know plenty of guys who would do more than hurt your beautiful women. But you've missed the point again; we're not here for me. I need an ironclad guarantee for my lady, that you won't ever hurt another woman again in your life. If I hear so much as a whisper that you have, or you do anything that upsets my lady, I'll make sure to talk to both of your women, and make sure they talk to each other. Married for twelve years, do you know her brothers well? They are scary motherfuckers… I'm wondering how they'd feel finding out you've been screwing around with Tatiana for going on four years. And Tatiana doesn't even know you're married, does she?"

There were more ways to hurt a man than by putting a knife in his back. Oh, this was a good surprise. Archer's ability to ferret out information was beyond impressive. While it was nice to see this man in physical pain, what was more important, was the lesson he learned. He wasn't invincible.

Archer knew Tulio's weak point and Tulio's reaction betrayed how he cared about both of these women. If one didn't know about the other, then he'd been stringing them along, lying, cheating. He wasn't a nice human being. Tulio truly was their bitch, he cared about the women enough to offer his own life in place of theirs, even if it was just in a snap of anger. So if Tulio stepped out of line, Archer could bring these women together. Tulio's world would implode before he was confronted by his wife's formidable family.

Archer turned around and their gazes locked. "Now, honeybun, if you want me to slit him open…"

She shook her head but wouldn't make the same promise for the others they were going to track down. Tulio only got a pass because he hadn't laid hands on Jamie, and he knew now that he was on borrowed time. If the need arose later, Archer could finish him off. For now, she liked the idea of him living in fear, looking over his shoulder, aware every time he touched one of his women that they could be snatched away at her unpredictable discretion.

"Then you're in luck, Tulio."

Archer came to take the roll of duct tape from her arm. Despite Tulio's protests, Archer wrapped it around their captive's mouth and over his eyes. He taped the guy's feet together, avoiding flesh and fluid. Then her guy stood up and unlocked one wrist, sending Tulio onto the floor with a thud.

The man couldn't fight, he didn't have the strength and his arms were basically dead. So all he could do was grumble behind the duct tape gag and buck as Archer stood astride him and bent to wrap duct tape round his wrists. Her guy tossed the rope over his shoulder again, he rolled up his knives and presented the bundle to her.

"Go out the door and up the alley," he said, handing her the car keys. "Just keep going forward, the light will find you. Do you need me to—"

"No."

Getting down there, facing the unknown was difficult. All she had to do now was depart and run.

"Take everything out the trunk," he said. "And leave it open."

She nodded, understanding his meaning.

She grabbed his arm when he took a step backward. "Wait…"

The faded florescent light haunted his features. Although he was focused on what needed to be done, she could see his love for her behind the mask.

"Change your mind?" he asked. "It's not too late. I'll slit the prick stem to stern for you, it's really nothing."

"You're amazing," she said and hooked a hand around the back of his neck to pull him down and plunge her tongue into his mouth.

He hummed in surprised pleasure, which might have been for Tulio's benefit because she'd never heard it before.

Who cared if her guy was performing when he was returning her kiss like it was their first?

His splayed hands snaked around her waist and their span reached from her ribs to her hips. Sliding them down, he cupped her ass and rocked her against him.

"Save it for later, Sweets," he said after sucking his kiss away from her lower lip.

As she stood, her guy went to the wriggling Tulio and put a boot on his ass to stop him moving. He bent to tie the rope around their victim's ankles, obviously unwilling to carry the man covered in his own filth.

When he gave her the nod, she went for the door and ran up the passage, just as he'd instructed. Tulio's moans echoed through the corridor, joined by the sound of his body being dragged at quite a pace along the concrete shaft.

She kept on going, thinking only of the task Archer had given, and fulfilled it by the time her man came out of the building.

"Get in the car," he called.

She went straight to her seat, so missed seeing Tulio being dumped in the trunk. There was a thump and some kicking, then the lid went down. Archer got into the driver's seat and reached into the glove box to pull out a bottle of hand sanitizer. Rubbing some on his own hands and then on hers, he tossed it back in and took a breath as he started the car.

"Do you want me to take you home before I dump him?" Archer asked.

She shook her head. "I've never shied from going all the way with you."

Without acknowledging the statement, he accepted it and got them going. They could've turned Tulio loose right there. But if her guy used this location on a regular basis, they wouldn't want it revealed to outside parties.

Staying quiet as they drove, gratitude overwhelmed her, she couldn't stop touching him. His arm, his shoulder, his leg, she leaned over to press her lips to his bicep and appreciated him offering his hand from the wheel.

"There's still time if you want me to—"

"It was perfect," she said. "He's a prick and we

could've killed him, then he would've just been more hassle, a body to get rid of and evidence to clean up. Now he has to live with what he's done, knowing someone's watching him. You really are good at what you do."

"Don't sound surprised," he said, bringing her hand up to kiss her knuckles. "We get rid of him, then it's back to mine."

"We?" she asked. "I can come to your place? What about your friend?"

His eyes stayed on the road. "You can meet him, but you'll have to split before the business starts. He's an old-fashioned kinda guy."

As opposed to Archer, such a modern man. Even if it was just the tiniest crack of a view into his life beyond her, she would take it. After what had happened tonight, she'd be in his debt forever.

Gratitude overflowed. "I love you," she said, nuzzling his wrist. "So much, Archer, I…"

"How much?" he asked, pulling her hand to his groin to rub her palm on the thick, hard shaft nestled in his jeans.

"Threatening men turns you on?"

Continuing with the intimate massage, after both his hands went to the wheel, a little TLC was the least she could provide.

"You, like this, turns me on. You're so fucking happy right now."

Her happiness made him horny? She wasn't usually this exuberant. Adrenaline would be heightening her reaction to the emotion bubbling through her.

Maybe that was her reason for opening his belt and his fly, for climbing onto her knees on her own seat to bow over his lap.

Bending her body across the car, she took him into her mouth.

"Jesus," he exclaimed, curling his fingers into her hair. "You are fucking grateful."

Her response was to suck harder. She was exactly that. He'd put everything on the line for her. He'd trusted her to watch him work and to know another man's secrets. One man down and six more to go.

She wasn't afraid anymore. She was invigorated. That night, wherever she was, Jamie would rest a little easier all because of Archer. This wouldn't have been possible without him.

ELEVEN

"THE GUY COMING over tonight, who is he?" she asked, retrieving their food from the fridge.

"Derren's biological son."

She stopped in the middle of the kitchen. "Really?" she asked. "I didn't expect you to be that honest."

He glanced up from the pan he was heating on the stove. "You asked. You tell me to tell you shit."

True. Not that he always made a point of following through. Either way, after what he'd done for her, she'd never doubt his devotion.

"Makes sense." She handed over his food as she went to work setting out her prep area. "If Derren has a biological son, he must have seen something of this guy in you, that's why he took you under his wing."

"Maybe," Archer said, seasoning his meat and placing it in the pan.

"Thank you for letting me stay."

Swaying to the side to nudge him, she paused her slicing to lean over and peer into his pan. He slanted his body, using his strength to urge her upright again.

"I'm just curious," she said, slicing through a tomato. "You don't have to worry about me stealing it. I'm the best girlfriend ever."

"Self-titled," he muttered, turning his steak over.

"Come on," she said, continuing with her task of chopping, preparing her own meal. "I'm better than your ex-girlfriends." When he said nothing and reacted only with a twitch of his brow, her hands stalled. "Do you really compare me to your exes?"

"No more than you compare me to yours."

Finishing with her tomato, she put the pieces into a bowl and rested a hand on the next one. "I don't really," she said, considering it for the first time. "You're more serious, more dominant." She turned to rest her hip on the counter and pointed her knife at his groin. "Your cock's certainly the biggest I've handled."

He took her wrist and turned the blade back to the chopping board. Okay, okay, she returned to preparing her salad at his unspoken request. When it was done, Archer took his steak from the pan and slid it onto a board on the other side of the stove as he turned off the heat.

She cut into another tomato and somehow sliced her finger in the process. "Oh, fuck, sonofa…!" she exclaimed, dropping the knife to snatch her injured hand. Before she could look, he pulled her finger into his mouth. As he sucked the blood from the wound, she hissed. "Even your kitchen knives are sharper than sin, Fella. Do you have to be so OCD about sharpening them all the time?"

Their eyes met, lessening the pain, as his tongue slid over the wound.

"Stop that," she said, trying to withdraw. He wouldn't let go. Instead, without looking, Archer's other hand cupped her breast to skim the pad of his thumb across her erect nipple. "It's fine."

Again, she tried to yank free and failed.

All awareness centered on the spot he salved and sucked. Her tingling pussy got more than she'd bargained for. It wasn't just the motion of his tongue that stimulated her, or the strength of his grip on her hand. It wasn't the way his thumb pushed deeper, flicking over the apex of her breast either.

"Archer," she murmured because he'd snared her with his gaze. So intent on her, his focus was absolute. She couldn't look away, like a moth mesmerized by a scorching flame. She didn't mind being burned, in fact she craved it. "Stop it. We're expecting your guy to show up."

He wasn't listening, or didn't care, because he walked forward, forcing her back until her ass hit the counter.

"What are you doing?" she asked, the breathy sound desperate and aroused. Taking her injured finger from his lips, he reached beyond her to flatten it on the counter and used her hips to turn her whole body away to do the same with her other hand. "Fella, you better not be thinking about…"

What were words? His hands were already under her skirt, hooking her underwear to pull it down to her knees. Without apology or permission, he compelled her to bend with a powerful hand between her shoulder blades, forcing her chest down against the cold countertop.

Without preamble, his fingers fucked her fast.

Squeezing her eyes closed, she rolled her forehead against the surface. "Oh, that feels good," she whispered.

"I like that."

His fingers slid free too soon. She caught a glimpse over her shoulder and witnessed him licking them clean. The lingering moisture was slick against her clit when he rubbed her slow, then fast. Up and down at first and then in circles, her hips rocked in response to his every move. Pushing back, begging more, she didn't need to ask aloud for him to know what she wanted.

Sinking and sailing on the endorphin rush, his fingers ebbed, though their purpose lingered.

He slammed his cock into her.

"Oh!" she cried out and semi-rose. Stopping her, he grabbed a handful of her hair to push her torso down flat. Screwing her there in the kitchen, panties around her knees, was so dirty. Damn if that didn't only increase her need. "Faster, Arch!"

She gasped and he pulled her head back to slide his long fingers around her throat. He didn't squeeze, just held the column of her throat in one hand, while clutching a handful of her hair in the other. Cradling her windpipe, he had complete control of not only her pleasure, but her life as well.

His hips worked hard in search of climax. "I've ruined this body for every guy," he growled. "Your pussy's stretched to fit me now. It won't take any other cock. You promise me, Squirm."

"I promise!" she cried out and would probably promise him the moon and the stars or anything he wanted.

While his shaft was inside her, she was a slave to him and anything he wanted.

"She loves it. You love it. You ain't never said no to this cock." And that was true, she hadn't. "You love it."

"Yes! I love it!" she screamed. "I love your cock! I love you!"

"Fuck, yeah, horny one. You're my little Squirm, always moving, always ready to take my dick deep any time I bend you over. You drain the spunk right outta me with that tight little cunt."

Panting and yelping, she called his name. There was something primal about the way he held her in the submissive position. At any time, he could break her neck. He could pull her hair harder and cause real pain, or just squeeze his fingers around her throat and end her life in a heartbeat. Instinctive trust heightened their intimacy. She needed him. Right then. Always. She'd never survive without him.

"Archer!"

Pounding her hard, he ground out his own desire. "My pussy. My girl."

"I love it when you fuck me! Arch, fuck me! I need it!"

Seizing her hips, he thrust in hard, once, twice, again. Pushing all the air from her lungs in one long scream, she grasped her breasts through her shirt and collided with orgasm at two thousand miles an hour. It sapped every bit of her energy, stole her soul, and yet he kept on going until he threw himself into the same abyss.

Whimpering and still moving, she wriggled when he slid out of her body. He pulled up her panties, but she didn't care that her ass was on display for the world. She was happy face down on the countertop and had no intention of moving.

"You better wash up, Squirm, you've got two minutes."

She whined as she rolled over and forced herself to stand. "You can't do that to me and then ask me to be social," she whinnied.

He winked and went to wash his hands. "You know where the bed is. If you want to get naked and wait for me…"

"And how long will that take?" she asked, suspicious it had been his plan all along to satisfy her sexually so she wouldn't ask too many questions when his friend arrived.

He moved his steak onto a plate and took it over to the table. "Your call, Squirm," he said, then there was a knock at the door. "Keeping my bed warm is your job."

"Archer," she said, causing him to stop on his way to the door.

Running her hands up over her sensitive breasts, to her neck then down to her pelvis, she bit her lip. He'd left her undone. She was exposed. At his mercy. And his half-smile knew it too.

"Get a Band-Aid for that finger," he said, and carried on to answer the door.

By the time she'd been to the bathroom to wash up and fix her finger, Archer was already halfway through his steak and there was a second man at the table. Conversation stopped when she emerged from the hallway.

"Heard you had a girl," said the stranger. "Didn't know you were showing her off."

Archer used his knife over his shoulder to gesture between them. "Kristof, Nya, Nya, Kristof," he said without looking.

"It's a pleasure," Kristof said, checking out her figure, which was just fine because she did the same in return.

He was older than Archer, she couldn't tell by how much, could be five years, could be ten. They had the same sort of build and the same sort of wary look in their eyes when meeting new people. The name was unusual. She didn't know if it was his first name or his last, but she wasn't going to ask.

"Likewise," she said, wary, and maybe a little tense.

She went into the kitchen to get back to preparing her salad. As she sliced and tossed, she tried to listen in to the conversation, except no one said a word. It wasn't until she was plating her food and drizzling on the dressing that she heard any noise at all.

"Seems like the best way to handle it," Kristof said. "But you know it's risky."

"So is everything I do," Archer said, chewing as he spoke.

"You asking for back up?"

She carried the rest of the salad over to the table.

Archer leaned back to give her room and shook his head at Kristof. "No, if I get into shit, I'd rather only have my own ass to worry about."

Kristof scrutinized her act of scooping the remainder of the salad onto Archer's plate.

Her man's large hand went under her skirt to squeeze and massage her exposed ass. He loved that she wore thongs. As long as it distracted him from the piles of salad she put on his plate, she didn't mind him being possessive in front of his friend.

"I've never seen you eat that green shit," Kristof said.

Archer smacked her ass hard. "I eat the healthy crap she puts on my plate. In return, she sucks my cock. Can't argue with that."

Kristof laughed. "No, guess not. Any more of that green shit around?"

Archer exhaled a surprising semi-laugh. Kristof was implying all it took for her to get down on her knees was a guy eating a few leaves of lettuce.

"No," she said. "Archer's the only one I feed."

"And he feeds you right back," Kristof said, looking at Archer.

On her return to the kitchen, she was forgotten. The men went back to their conversation. She ate her salad, maybe, possibly keeping an ear open to their words.

"Those three guys are the ones you have to watch," Kristof said.

"I figured that," Archer said. "I just need the inside."

"And I'm on it. I'll get the four-one-one."

Listening to their conversation was infuriating, it wasn't like they were talking in code, but they were so vague, they might as well have been. She wanted specifics but imagined those must've been covered maybe on the phone or during her Band-Aid trip.

Her phone buzzed.

Archer got up to get it from the coffee table and read the screen. Instead of handing it over, he answered the call. Oh, he just had to know everything, didn't he? She couldn't argue his arrogance in front of a new person, not that it mattered when she had nothing to hide. Their trust was actually kinda sexy.

"Yep," he said into the device. She left her salad to go to the space between the breakfast bar and the fridge. "Uh huh." Archer's gaze landed on her. "Right." Shaking her head, she lifted her hands in an open shrug, but he wasn't forthcoming. "Send Robbo over to pick Nya up." Robbo was one of the security guys Archer hired, and obviously someone he trusted. This wasn't the first time her guy commanded Robbo taxi her around. He hung up the phone. "They need you at Sizzle."

"For what?"

"Some stock issue or something. Something ran out, I don't know."

He'd been only half listening, but he expected her to go down there and fix it?

"The new girl can't figure out the barrels." That could be the problem. It was too much to expect she'd get away with neglecting Sizzle. The way shift rotations worked, there were only experienced members of staff on sometimes. They'd taken on a lot of new employees, who may have exaggerated their resumes and might not know how things worked. "Okay. Let me get changed."

"Robbo will be here in five," Archer said, going back to his seat at the table. "I'll pick you up after."

Pick her up after what? A full shift or when Kristof was gone? So it was on her to fix the problem, then wait around? Hmm, how convenient. Archer hadn't wanted her there while he was talking with Kristof, and magically he'd just gotten his wish.

Where Archer was concerned, coincidences were always suspicious.

It didn't make any difference anyway. From the snippet of the kitchen table conversation, she wasn't missing anything fascinating, or even decipherable. She'd go to Sizzle, deal with the issue, then hope Archer would be honest when they got home later.

TWELVE

FIXING SIZZLE'S ORIGINAL problem was a breeze. But the basement was an absolute mess. She'd spent close to two hours reorganizing everything downstairs before sequestering herself in the office to deal with the pile of overdue paperwork. No one else had the authority to deal with it… or the inclination.

The bassy music gave her a headache, not that she could resent it. Hubbub in the club was a good sign business was booming. As long as everyone was having a good time, her job was safe.

Her staff were capable, and she wasn't supposed to be there anyway, so they'd handle whatever came up. The fewer distractions the better, she wanted to finish the invoices before Archer appeared. One thing she didn't plan to do was screw in this office… again. Nope. Nu-uh. She'd be strong… even in the face of her guy's masculine magnetism.

The door opened and she sat straighter to chastise her staff for entering without knocking, something they would never normally do.

Oh, fuck.

The man filling her doorway didn't work for her. Not even close. Gasping, she shot up from her chair.

"We haven't been introduced," her new visitor said.

It wasn't so much his identity that scared her, it was his size. Although he was under six feet, he was built wide and hard. His shoulders strained his tee shirt and the biceps that bulged beneath were covered in tattoos leaving barely an inch of untouched skin on show.

His short beard and angry glare would steal the courage of any woman sitting alone. When he strode in and closed the door, she wanted to call out and object. If it was anyone else, she might. Except who would hear her over the sound of the club? The phone was out too. Grabbing for that would betray she was rattled.

No weapon, not one she could obviously see anyway. Didn't matter, his form was capable. A full crate of beer tested her limits, if this guy got hold of her, she wouldn't stand a chance.

"I'm Brett Hexam."

The consuming weakness lowered her into her chair. "Oh," she said.

The sheer number of possibilities for his presence silenced her. If she guessed, or opened her mouth with assumptions, she could get everyone into more trouble.

This was him. Actually Brett Hexam. The last time, he sent his men. Why did she suddenly warrant a face-to-face visit from the guy at the top?

He came to a stop on the opposite side of her desk. "I've wanted to meet you for a while," he said, fingering the pencil pot next to her computer. "I've heard a lot about you."

From where? She couldn't begin to imagine. Archer wasn't much of a gossip when it came to his own life. Not in her experience. She couldn't assume her guy revealed the details of their relationship. He'd been less than happy when learning Farrah knew they were together. That unhappiness would be magnified at this level of the chain.

Quiet. Calm. Just stay calm.

Tag had been avoiding this guy and, as far as she knew, they had no other mutual acquaintances. This meeting must be related to one of them. Except Archer wasn't the only one capable of extracting information. Hexam could've asked around, had his men question staff or neighbors. Hell, they could've been watching her, going through trash, or interviewing exes for all she knew.

"What are you doing here?" she asked. "The last time you wanted something from me, you sent your messengers."

"Before I knew who you were." He descended into the chair on the other side of the desk. "We have a problem."

"Do we?" she asked, reminding herself not to say too much until he tipped his hand. "What problem?"

"Where is he?"

When his eyes landed on her, there was nothing in them. No humanity, consideration, or sympathy. Not even curiosity. Maybe a dim glimmer of expectation existed there, like he was challenging her to refuse to answer.

"Who?"

He actually smiled as he leaned forward to rest his elbows on the table and steepled his forefingers over his mouth.

"Your boyfriend."

Okay, still not a reason. She hadn't imagined facing this dilemma. Archer told her if anyone ever asked about him, she should be honest about his whereabouts. Except, she struggled to figure out how Hexam wouldn't be able to find Archer. Where the hell was he? Last she knew, he'd been at his apartment.

Maybe Hexam didn't know where that apartment was; it couldn't be that difficult to find out when lowlifes like Jonno knew.

"I don't know."

"Oh, come on, Nya," he said.

The distance between his elbows didn't change, but he straightened his arms to flatten his hands on the desk. Although nowhere near her, they were still too close for comfort. She couldn't wriggle in her seat, stay still, too much movement would betray her anxiety.

"I don't know."

"You know he's been screwing my sister."

Suddenly, his hands weren't as intimidating anymore, and neither were his eyes. It all just drained out of her in frustrated disbelief.

"Tag?" she said, her mouth incapable of closing. "Are you fucking kidding me? You're here looking for Tag? Again?"

Hexam had been looking for Tag the night Jamie died.

"Déjà vu. You pissed at him for screwing around on you?"

Doing her best not to scream, she clamped her lips together and counted to three in her head before responding.

"Tag. Is Not. My Boyfriend," she said, enunciating each sentence, saying it slowly, nice and slowly, so he would hopefully never forget again. She counted off her bullet points on fingers. "He's not my boyfriend. I know he's sleeping with Farrah. I don't know where he is."

Honesty was the best policy. There was no point insulting the man by playing dumb when there were accepted facts.

"It's a problem. A problem for all of us, you understand?"

She didn't want to be lumped in with this decision, so she shook her head. "It's not my problem," she said, and left her chair.

Hexam surged up, grabbed her wrist, and hauled her back down.

"It's your problem 'cause I say it's your problem. You're gonna track him down, and you're gonna bring him to me."

If this had been anyone else, she would've laughed, or slapped him across the face. Wouldn't be a good move there.

"I can't force Tag to do anything. I told him getting involved with Farrah would upset you. It didn't change anything. I think they like each other."

"Aww," Hexam said, without an ounce of sincerity. "And your little heart went pitter-patter as the orchestra kicked in?"

"No," she said. "I'm telling you Farrah is going to meet and fall for someone eventually. Maybe that guy is Tag."

His grip on her wrist tightened; she hid her wince of pain. "Not if I have anything to say about it."

As he examined the red welts forming on her arm, his sneer seemed pleased. When he shifted his grip to get a better look at the bruises, he noticed her brand.

"You're a girl who knows how to work what she's got," he muttered, glaring at the scar on her wrist. What did that mean? "Archer's a good guy to get in bed with."

"I didn't realize we'd both enjoyed the pleasure."

His smirk wasn't amused, he ignored her quip. "Good for you and your buddy."

She didn't know if he meant there was something Archer could do to prevent anyone getting hurt, or if the words were Hexam's veiled threat.

"You should update your records," she said. "So next time you or one of your boys comes in here you'll know, I'm Archer's property. He's the only man in my heart and my bed. Any beef you have with me, you have with him as well."

He circled his lips. "Helluva declaration," he said, touching the mark she loved, forcing her to attempt another yank for freedom. "Shh… don't flip." Hexam pinned her wrist to the desk again. "You want to keep Archer safe? Don't tell him I was here."

Lying to Archer would be impossible at the best of times. With all the different strands of drama running through their lives, she couldn't take the risk of being dishonest with her lover.

"Are you afraid of him?"

"No. But if you've got him good, he'll sacrifice your boy, Tag, to save your ass and his."

"You don't know what you're talking about—"

"I don't give a fuck about your relationship with Archer. I give a fuck about your ex's relationship with my little sister and you're gonna put a stop to it. You're gonna tell him it's over, he's gonna break her heart and then you're gonna bring him to me on a platter."

She'd been right about his strength; her whole arm throbbed, right up to her shoulder. "And if I don't?" she asked, wincing at the pain of his tightening grip.

"Let's just say you're a valuable source of information. That value drops to zero if you don't give me what I want. I don't waste my time with trash. I toss it out."

So much for veiling his threats.

"Is that the real reason you don't want me to tell Archer? 'Cause if he finds out you were here, I'll bet he knows a couple of things about you and your business that could stir up all kinds of shit for you."

The force of his gaze winded her. "Let me worry about my association with Archer. You just worry about opening your legs for him."

Being crude wouldn't upset her. "If you leave bruises on me, he'll know," she said. Though the truth was her arm was already bruising, there was no way to stop it. "And he won't be happy about it."

"I'm sure he loves putting it in your pussy or up your ass… doubt he gives a fuck about the rest of you."

"Think again." The voice from the door was unexpected. When she turned to see her man just inside the room, she almost didn't recognize him wearing the hate and anger that twisted his features. "Take your fucking hands off her, Hex, or we're gonna have a problem."

The last thing she wanted was for them to fight at all, let alone there. The place was swarming with security guards who would back up Archer. She didn't want to start a war in a place she was trying to clean up.

"Archer," Hexam said.

Hexam's grip loosened and when he let her go, she snatched her arm to her chest and pushed her chair away from her desk, letting it roll back as far as it would go.

"You okay, Sweets?" her man asked, still fixated on their guest.

"You weren't supposed to see this," Hexam said, rising from his chair. "But now you're here, you've saved me a trip. She says she's your property, is that right?"

"That's right."

"Your girlie and I have an understanding. I expect you'll help her hold up her end of the deal and if she doesn't… you know what happens."

"Don't come near her again," Archer snarled. "Any shit you have connected to her, you bring to me."

Hexam glanced at her, then took his dubious eyes to Archer. "She said that too."

"I've got her well trained," Archer muttered.

If only that were true. But, for the purpose of the moment, she let it go. Hexam nodded once and sauntered toward the door.

"I've made my point," Hexam said, drawing his eyes from Archer to leer at her one more time. "I'll give you to the end of the week. Get some ice on that arm."

Archer didn't give Hexam any space to get out the door, meaning the man had to shuffle out sideways. Instead of looking awkward, he managed to maintain his dangerous edge, though it wasn't half as dangerous as Archer's look when he put a hand on the door to throw it into the frame.

"What the fuck was that?" he demanded.

He was angry with her? How the hell did he get to that?

"I don't know."

"You don't know? What the fuck is this understanding? You don't make deals, with anyone, under any circumstances. Period. Understand? If you've got a problem, you let me handle it."

This seemed to be the night for men to infuriate her by stating the obvious.

"Well, duh!" she snapped. "He spoke, I listened. I didn't agree to anything."

"What did he want? Is this about Tulio?"

So Archer wasn't clear on Hexam's motivation either. Misery did love company.

"No," she said, shaking her head. "He didn't mention him at all. I don't think he knows about our plans… He knows about Tag and Farrah."

"I know," Archer said, coming to loom over her desk. "Kristof told me Hexam was back in town, and he'd found out about Farrah. Taggert's been lying low. Your friend seems to be good at that, running and hiding."

The last thing she needed right now was to listen to

snide comments about her friend.

Reaching beneath the desk, she picked up her purse and jacket. "He scared me, you know," she said after she tugged on her jacket and threw the strap of her bag over her head to straighten it diagonally across her body between her breasts. "You could give me a hug, and make me feel better, be a good boyfriend and all that."

"I'll do that when I stop seeing red," he said. "I'll squeeze the life out of you if I get my hands on you now. That fucker should never have come near you. I can't believe he had the balls—"

"Like he said, he was making a point."

"And I heard it loud and clear," Archer said, grabbing her arm to tow her out of the office.

She recounted the conversation in the car on the way home, telling him everything Hexam said and how she'd refused to bow to his threats.

When Archer tossed her into his apartment, Kristof wasn't anywhere in sight.

"This isn't finished," he said.

Was she hungry? Should she eat? He seized her arm again and dragged her through the apartment. So much for food. She couldn't imagine he'd want to have sex. Except he tugged her past the dinner table, the couch, and down the hall. So sex it was, though... Instead of taking her into the bedroom, the bathroom was their destination.

Alarm slammed into her. "What are you doing?"

He still had hold of her arm. Maybe he was planning to treat the bruises left by Hexam. Please let that be it.

He opened the closet, perpendicular to the bathroom door and fumbled for something. She wasn't paying much attention, or thinking about what it might be, until the metallic jangle piqued her ears.

Immediately tensing, she pulled at her arm. "No!" she screamed and tried to get away, but he wouldn't let go. Using his body to block her, he crowded her into the corner and forced her onto the floor. "You've got to be kidding me. Archer, you can't do this to me. This is me. Look at me. Look at me!" He was already winding the chain around the pipe.

"Archer, please don't do this to me, Fella. Why are you doing this to me? I didn't do anything wrong! I'll tell you anything you want to know! Anything!"

"This isn't about information," he said, stopping to grab her chin, coercing their gazes to clash. "This is about your safety now. He's seen you. He knows you. Any of his men could come for you. Any minute. You're gonna pay the price for Tag's dick sniffing around pussy it shouldn't. I won't let you be taken down for that. I'm gonna keep you safe."

"Okay," she said, so desperate to be free she'd probably say anything. "So keep me safe. You don't have to put me here. I'll stay in the apartment. I promise. I won't leave."

He shook his head. "I can't take that chance. If you think it's okay just to run out to the store—"

"I won't! I'll stay."

"No," he said. "I can't know that unless I make damn sure you can't move."

"You don't trust me? I'm your girl! You love me."

His fingers dug in so deep her jaw ached under their bruising force. "And that's why I won't take the risk."

"You don't have to leave me in here," she said. "Haven't these last few months meant anything to you? Haven't I earned the right to have a place better than your bathroom floor?"

That got through. After a second of his eyes flicking back and forth between hers, he yanked her to her feet. Almost sagging in relief, her appeal ended his crazy moment of whatever that was. She intended to kiss him in thanks and to calm him down—

He wasn't done.

Pulling her from the bathroom, straight across the hall into the bedroom, he threw her on the bed and grabbed hold of her wrists. Coiling the bathroom chain around them, he padlocked her wrists to his headboard.

Her protests were ignored. Although she shook her hands, she couldn't free them.

"Please don't do this! Archer, just get into bed and we'll go to sleep. You'll feel better in the morning, Fella."

"No," he said and stormed to his closet. Throwing it open, he retrieved two individual knives she hadn't seen before. One he clipped to his belt, in addition to the one he always carried. The other he put in his pocket. "I'm not done and I'm not waiting for him to ambush us. I'm gonna get this cleared up tonight."

Panic about her own situation evaporated on learning he planned to walk into danger alone.

"You're going after him? Please, Archer, you don't have to do this. Let him think he's won! What harm is there in that for one night?"

"One night too many," he snarled.

He was so angry, he wouldn't be thinking straight; he wouldn't be concentrating on being smart.

"Please don't go confront him! If you leave me here, then go get yourself killed—"

"I'm not the one who'll get hurt," he said. Coming to the bed, he bent over her to force their mouths together, in spite of her spitting and cursing. "I'm keeping you safe, Squirm. I don't care what it costs. I don't care if you leave me in the dust when this is all over. That's what your life means to me."

Producing a length of material from the nightstand drawer, he tied it tight around her mouth. With her trussed up, he pivoted and marched out the door. She tried to call out and kept on trying until the front door closed. Only then did she relax. All she'd produced were useless muffled shouts. He wasn't coming back for her yet.

This was a kneejerk reaction. This was what he did when he panicked. Right then, she couldn't put words to her level of upset and anger. He'd chained her up and hadn't trusted her enough to keep her word. What did that say about the trust in their relationship?

Still, there was better than the bathroom floor.

After grumbling to herself for a while, she closed her eyes and tried to sleep. Yeah, right. Her worry for Archer wouldn't let her get a wink.

THIRTEEN

NOISE CARRIED FROM the apartment; he was back. About damn time. Wriggling, battering the chain off the headboard, she'd show him anger. Though he'd probably ignore it. Selective ignorance was one of his special gifts.

Her guy, if she wanted to call him that right then, was used to keeping people captive. People who screamed and cried and just generally made a racket, hence her gag. She wasn't beyond calling his name on repeat until he was forced to address her. Not like she'd never done that before.

Just as she suspected, there was movement in the apartment, footsteps. Except, hmm, they weren't as heavy as Archer's. Thinking about it, no one slammed the door either, Archer's trademark. There was no scuffle. Whoever it was, they were alone. What were they doing? Sound didn't carry well with the doors closed.

Shit, should she be scared? Look up vulnerable in the dictionary, there would be a picture, just like her, tied down, silent, no way to defend herself. Shit.

"Archer!" A female called out from the living room. "Are you home, honey?"

Oh God, okay, so the visitor may not be there to kill them. Didn't really make her feel better though. Strapped to a bed, helpless, was not the way she wanted to meet one of his exes who'd probably rocked up looking for a good time. Under normal circumstances, she'd handle it, but her dignity was in the damn toilet. First impressions were everything when trying to scare off the competition.

Staying quiet, she hoped, whoever this woman was, that she would disappear or maybe serendipity would shine on her and Archer would come back before she was discovered.

No such luck. Hope was dashed when the footsteps closed in, and the door opened. A woman, yes, who stepped inside, tall, blonde, sleek, with a voluptuous fake chest… wasn't what she would've expected from Archer's range of exes.

"Well…" said the blonde, cocking a hip and drumming her shocking pink nails against it. "There's hope for my boy yet. This is some kinky shit."

The woman came over, scrutinizing her. She didn't want to struggle. All she could do was maintain wild eye contact and beg the woman would show mercy.

Sitting on the edge of the bed, the woman's pink dress rode up, showing the lace tops of some fancy white stockings. The visitor leaned over to untie the knot balled against Nya's cheek.

"So, sweetheart," the blonde said. "I'm his mother, Ester, who are you?"

The gag loosened and she gasped for breath, both out of necessity and shock—this was his mother?

"Girlfriend," she said, trying to control her panting. "Nya."

Ester's eyes trailed down her body, taking a measure of her son's girl. "And he just left you here? Why've you got your clothes on?"

So she thought this was a sex game, maybe some sort of power play, kinky for sure. Good guess, and she'd prefer the woman was right, rather than the reality of her position.

"He's pissed at me," she said. "Insists this is how he can keep me safe."

"Oh," Ester said, running her hand over the edge of the nightstand. "Then where the fuck is the key?"

"Dresser," she said, gesturing with her chin to the unit beside the door.

Ester got up and went to retrieve the key. Holding it up in triumph, she spun around to eye Nya again.

"Now, you're not bullshitting me, are you? He's not looking for some kind of information from you, is he? 'Cause all you've gotta do is tell him and he'll cut you loose. He's like that. He keeps his word."

"If he was, I'd be chained under the bathroom sink," she said, shaking her head to get rid of the hair from her mouth. "It's a really long story."

"I bet it is," Ester said, crossing to lean over and slip the key into the lock.

Oh, and lovely, she got an eyeful of the woman's generous breasts as they hung near her eyes.

The lock snicked free and she sat up, rubbing her wrists.

Taking a deep breath, she rolled both hands to lessen their ache. "Thank you."

"What's that?" Ester asked, snatching her hand to yank it upwards, examining her mark.

"I told you," Nya said. "I belong to him."

Ester smiled as she traced her fingers over the shape. "You're not pissed about this?"

"Pissed about it?" she asked, standing up to press her fingertips against it. "It's my favorite part of my body."

"You and me are gonna get along, I can tell already." Ester took her hand and linked their arms to draw her out of the room. "Now, let's find the liquor."

FOURTEEN

NYA COOKED AS Ester tracked down the booze. After their meal, Ester consumed the lion's share of the alcohol. The woman had some kind of immunity to its potency. In contrast, she did her best to appear that she was drinking but had always been a bit of a lightweight.

"He was an asshole," Ester said, lurching forward to snag the wine bottle from the coffee table. They sat at opposite ends of the couch, their legs stretched toward each other. "I mean I thought he was all that. I thought he was cool. And he went and fucked around on me."

"You don't deserve that," she said to the slurring woman.

No woman deserved half the things Archer's mother talked about. Ester had plenty of experience with men. Plenty of stories. Captivated, she loved listening to her talk, loved her confidence and her joie de vivre. Ester had constant optimism, even in the face of all the horrific things that happened in her life.

"He thought he got one up," Ester said, sloshing the wine onto the edge of the couch as she poured it. Archer would go crazy when he saw that stain later. Rather than rush to clean it up, she hid her smile behind her glass. She wouldn't be snitching either, he deserved everything he got. Karma worked in mysterious ways. "He told me to pack my shit, said he wanted me gone by the time he got back from having his smoke." Ester slammed the bottle onto the table with such force that liquid shot out of the top, creating a puddle on Archer's pristine coffee table. "I went in that apartment and threw my shit in a bag, took me thirty seconds. Then I went in the bathroom and used a pin to poke holes in all the rubbers I found."

Ester laughed a wild kind of cackle and ran her hand through her hair when she tipped her head back to gulp down half her wine.

Should she be shocked, horrified, or amused? Ester didn't hide her own emotion on any issue.

"Wow."

"Thinks he can leave me for some dumb little nineteen-year-old bitch, that'll show 'em," Ester said and polished off the wine after her next breath.

"I guess it will."

This woman could handle her alcohol; she'd already drunk one bottle and was on to the second. Ester could down it flat, without pausing to breathe, it was quite impressive.

"Do you use rubbers?" Ester asked, pointing her glass at her.

She shook her head. "No, we... we don't."

Ester's head went up and down, her voluminous hair bouncing in radiant waves. "You trust him, that's good," she said, sort of melting off the couch to reach for the bottle again. Except she turned it, read the label, and screwed up her face. "He must have something stronger than this."

Ester used both the couch and the coffee table to clamber onto her feet.

Nya laughed. "Are you okay?"

Ester ignored the concern. "Most women get scared by the size of his cock," she called out, her face scrunched like she'd forgotten why she was on her feet.

Nya squeaked when she inhaled. "What?"

"His girlfriends, Archer's girlfriends, they get freaked out by it. You shouldn't be freaked out," Ester said, shaking her head, picking up the wine bottle. She still stood between the couch and table, searching for the reason she was there. "His daddy was hung, seriously hung… There are tricks, you know? For dealing with guys who are well-endowed. I can show you—tell you, I can tell you. Teach you, that's what I meant."

Oh, Archer would love that. What exactly would that involve? His mother went off toward the kitchen, wine bottle in hand, slugging from it a couple of times before opening the first cabinet.

"He hides the hard liquor," Ester said.

Putting her glass on the table, she was about to respond when the front lock clicked. Archer made his usual entrance and slammed the door. First, he looked at her, next, at his mother, then back at her.

"You're not where I left you, Squirm."

Pissed as she was, she could already tell this experience would be payback enough.

"Honey," she drawled, "we have company."

Ester chastised her son. "Who the fuck do you think you are?" she said and tripped over but caught herself on the breakfast bar.

"Shut your trap, Ester," Archer said. "What the fuck are you doing here?"

"Drinking," she said, holding the wine bottle aloft.

He huffed. "When are you not?" he asked and came in to dump the paper bag from his loose hand onto the table.

"I've been getting to know your girl," Ester said, coming out of the kitchen, using the wine bottle as a pointer. "I like her, she's good."

His eyes grew a fraction. "You like her? Goddamnit," he said. "How much have you had to drink?"

He stomped into the kitchen. She got off the couch, eager to know what happened while he'd been out. His scowl wasn't optimistic, though that might be caused by what he'd come home to rather than what happened out there.

She leaned on the corner of the fridge as he made coffee, strong coffee if the number of scoops he put into the machine was anything to go by.

"No more booze," he said, marching past her to his mother somewhere near the back of the couch.

He grabbed the wine bottle and wrestled it away to take it into the kitchen.

Nya expected Ester to object, she didn't.

"She's pretty," Esther declared. "You've done well, son."

Archer tipped the wine down the sink, then put the empty bottle on the counter as he glared past her at his mother.

"Ester," he warned.

"Got a good figure too," Ester said.

Nya laughed when Ester's hands came around her body from behind to cup her breasts, giving them a squeeze and a shake.

Archer's jaw ticked. "Ester, take your hands off."

"Oh look, he doesn't like it," Ester said, taunting him. "I think he's jealous."

"Maybe I don't want my mother's hands all over my girl," he said, coming over to snatch Ester's wrists to pull her hands away.

"She's got a pretty face too." Scooping her hand around to Nya's opposite cheek, Ester used her free hand to stroke Nya's hair. "She's got those big Disney princess eyes, look, look at them!"

Archer had to grit his teeth. "She's not a fucking Disney princess."

"Sure, she is!" Ester exclaimed. "Every woman's a fucking Disney princess." Ester laughed and turned around, happy to stagger away on her own. "Now where's the music? You used to have a killer sound system, where did it go?"

"I sold it," Archer said, coming up close to lower his volume. "How long has she been here?"

"A couple of hours."

"She let you go?" Nya nodded. "And you didn't walk out on me?"

"Yeah, imagine that," she said, folding her arms. "I told you I could be trusted."

"So you stayed to prove a point. Now what?"

"Do you care?" she asked, looking up at him. "You said keeping me safe was all that mattered. You didn't care if I loved you or not when the Hexam situation was through, as long as I was alive."

There was no apology on his lips. "If I have to choose between your life and your love, I choose your life." His hand came up to curl around her chin, forcing her to crane her head back. "But if I can have both, I'll take it."

"I'm tired!" Ester exclaimed from the other room. "Tired! Tired! Tired! Time to get some sleep!"

There was only one bed in the apartment. Archer had slept with his mother before, to keep the woman in check, so that was her cue.

"I'll get going," she declared to both people in the room, but wrapped a hand around Archer's bicep. "Look after her tonight. I'll look after me."

"No! No! No! No! No! No! No!" Ester said, shaking her head and rounding the couch to join them. "You need to go to bed." She grabbed both their arms to pull them in the direction of the kitchen table. "You go in the bedroom and you screw each other senseless. Yes, yes." Putting their hands together, Ester squeezed them. "That's what you need to do. You're young, and Archer gets irritable if he doesn't get regular pussy."

"Ester!" he chastised.

His mother seemed impervious because she sauntered to her purse and raked inside for a minute before coming back.

"A present from me to you, son," she said, slapping something down on the table, then lifting her hand to reveal it.

Nya laughed at the two wrapped blue pills and covered her mouth with a hand, but it was too late to conceal her amusement.

Her love wasn't entertained. "What the fuck is that?"

Ester came right over to lower and whisper in her ear. "Sometimes he gets performance anxiety when his mom is in the next room."

Archer wouldn't appreciate the grin that twisted her

lips, but she'd never heard anyone talk like this about him, or to him.

Clearly, it riled him. "I've never had performance problems," he said. "And who the fuck carries Viagra around in their purse like it's gum?"

"I do," Ester said, holding up both hands as if it was something to be proud of. "When you get to my age, son, sometimes the talent isn't as lively as us ladies need it to be."

Now she did laugh, straight out, and had to curl into Archer to bury her face against him. Her hands just wouldn't do the job.

"Right, enough, you need to sleep," he said, pointing at his mother. And to address her, he grabbed her hair at the back of her head to pull her away from his chest. "And you're not going fucking anywhere, Squirm, you know it. Both of you, bedroom."

She was to sleep with his mother? He wouldn't want either of them in the living room alone. Her out of worry for her safety, and his mother out of fear for his liquor.

"Both of you, go to bed," he said, pushing and cajoling them down the hallway into the bedroom.

Tossing back the blankets before he took two tee shirts from the drawer, he threw one to each of the women.

"You should have sex," Ester said and tried to walk out the door. "Don't mind me."

Archer put an arm out to catch her shoulders and urge her back. "We'll have sex when you're sober and out of here. Now get in the fucking bed and go to sleep." As Ester began to get undressed, Archer turned his back, directing her in front of him as he went. "She'll be out fast, she always is. She'll chatter for a minute and then start snoring."

"What about you?"

"I'll be on the couch if you need me."

Now it made sense why he had a super long, super wide couch. She'd always thought it was a strange purchase. It must've been expensive, yet he always stood at the back of it. The only time he enjoyed it was when he was enjoying her. Now she knew it doubled as a bed when Ester was around.

"Okay," she said. "I'll look after her."

He cleared his throat. "Did she say anything? You know…?"

"Inappropriate?" she asked, grinning again. "Just about every word out of her mouth is inappropriate. She's fabulous. I love her."

He blinked, his expression went completely blank until confusion became curiosity. "You like her?"

"Why wouldn't I? She's a blast. She says exactly what she thinks." Nya got closer. "She even promised to teach me a few techniques for dealing with your monster," she said, batting his groin.

He caught her wrist and yanked it high. "You fucking dare talk about that—"

Nya laughed. "I'm kidding," she said, stroking his face with the hand he hadn't captured. "I'd never talk to her about our sex life. But I do love her and even though you're a complete bastard, and I hate you for what you did to me tonight, I do love you too."

"Aww," Ester wailed, coming close, wearing Archer's tee shirt. She wrapped an arm around both of their backs and pushed them together as she pulled herself close. "You should totally screw now."

Nya made strained eye contact with Archer when Ester backed up a step.

"We'll wait 'til you're asleep," Nya said to appease Ester.

Archer kissed both women's heads and went to the door. "I'll be out here if you need me."

"We'll be fine," she replied, ushering Ester to the bed and laying her down.

Yes, he was a bastard and there were several issues they had to address, but they weren't going to fight in front of his mother. Those issues would keep until after they'd all gotten a good night's sleep.

FIFTEEN

ON COMING OUT OF the bedroom, she paused in the hallway. Opposite, she could hear the shower on in the bathroom. To the left, when she craned to listen, some daytime chat show blared from the TV.

Nope. Not her guy's bag.

Archer had to be in the shower. There was just no way he'd be watching that, sound or no sound. Plus, she had a clear view straight to the front door. If Archer was there, he'd be standing at the back of the couch, blocking her view of the exit.

Mmm, and the bathroom door was unlocked, she closed it as quietly as she could and slipped out of the tee shirt he'd given her to wear the previous night. Creeping forward, she ignored the pipe she'd once called home and let her hand snake around the curtain.

Inching the fabric aside, she saw him washing soap from his face. As soon as her hand made contact with his ass, his snapped down to grab her wrist. Spinning around, he was growling, ready for a fight.

She smiled and pushed her shoulders back. "Don't be mad, I have tits you can play with."

His grip changed from aggressive to supportive as he

pulled her arm higher to help her over the edge of the tub into the stream of water.

"Don't fucking do that," he said, drawing the shower curtain rings right to the end of the pole.

Stroking his abdomen and up to his chest, she purred out her delight at being so close to his naked form. With her fingers spread wide, she sank her mouth onto his chest and tasted as much of him as she could.

"I realized that's the first time I've slept in that bed and not got laid," she said, giving him only a brief view of her smile before she went back to her kissing.

"So you thought you'd come in here and change that?" he asked. "My mom's in the kitchen."

"She's watching TV," she whispered. "She won't care." Maybe she would, she couldn't know for sure. The uncertainty didn't prevent her hands skimming down his ribs, over his obliques to his hips, and curling both hands around his proud cock already trying to say good morning. "Have I persuaded you?"

He fondled her breasts, tweaking her nipples, rubbing his face in her wet hair. "When do I ever need to be persuaded?" he asked, grabbing her shoulders and spinning her around to plant her back on the wall.

Dipping down, he hooked one of her knees over his elbow and raised it as high as it could go until she was perched on one set of tiptoes.

Using his shoulder for support, she gripped him tight and hopped up to hook her other leg around his hips.

"That's why I fell in love with you."

Despite the unstable surface he was standing on, he didn't hesitate or waver; he gave her all the support she needed as he slid his shaft into her.

"You didn't need much prep time either," he said. "One of the reasons I picked you… you're easy, girl."

She hadn't even kissed him good morning or needed to. Waking up surrounded by his scent was enough to get her body started. She'd woken up wriggling, squirming, her dreams must have been carnal.

Her legs spread wide in that bed, seeking him out,

hips arched. She'd turned to reach for him only to find herself alone. That was when the memory of the previous day returned. No need to be disappointed because there he was, pampering her with full-service treatment in the shower.

"Oh, God," she panted, suddenly remembering how impossible it was for her to stay quiet when he was inside her.

"Don't even think about it," he grumbled, pressing his forehead into hers, forcing her head back at an awkward angle with the weight of his. She didn't give a fuck about the pain in her neck when her pussy felt so good being massaged by his pounding.

"I can't," she yelped. "I can't… not!"

"You fucking can," he said. "Hush."

With his head still on hers, he smacked a hand over her mouth forming a damp seal, stifling her moans and shrieks, making it harder to get the air she needed.

Mumbling, grumbling, she wriggled against him as she bucked and writhed through the orgasm he ignored. He kept on going, fucking her good and hard. And maybe because they weren't supposed to be doing this, and they'd stolen the moment together, her excitement climbed to the point of madness.

Her wild eyes met his in deep concentration. She wished he would kiss her, wished she could taste his tongue, wished she could do more than run her hands over his shoulders and drag her fingernails through his hair.

On the apex of her third orgasm, she grabbed his hips, and dug her nails in deep, begging for him to stay right there, filling the hollow space in her body, designed and destined to berth him alone.

Pressing his mouth into the back of his hand still clamped over hers, it acted as a barrier to a full kiss. She tried to yelp, to ask for his lips, but he didn't give her the chance. With a brutal thrust, Archer hit her hard in her deepest, most sensitive spot, then exhaled. His eyes lifted to hers very slowly as he allowed his hand to leave her mouth.

"That's a good morning," she whispered and tipped up for his mouth.

He eased back. "I love fucking you. You came just

when I needed you."

Literally? Had her orgasm matched his or did he mean she'd appeared in the shower at the right time? Didn't matter. She draped her arms around his neck, hanging her body from his, and this time he did kiss her. As she enjoyed the sweet slide of their tongues saying their intimate good morning, the insistence of his cock prodded her belly button.

Lowering her mouth to check its girth, she confirmed her suspicion. "Didn't you come?" she asked, sure she'd read his signs right. A familiar expression had contorted his features before he'd pulled himself out of her body. Her guy put her on her feet and took half a step back. In an involuntary action, she touched her own core and looked at her fingers to see that yes, his seed was mingled with her juices. "You did."

"Yeah, I did," he agreed, erection in hand.

He'd always been virile, he worked out and recovered from their bouts quickly… but not this quickly.

"You want more?" she asked, unsure if she should be terrified, concerned, or amused.

He certainly didn't seem to understand his arousal. And then his shoulders sort of sagged and an expression of annoyed understanding crossed his features.

While she was still confused, Archer sucked in a breath. "I'll fucking kill her."

"What is it?"

He threw back the shower curtain and with the water still thrumming on her body, she watched him grab his towel from over the rail.

Opening the bathroom door an inch, he hollered into the apartment. "Ester, you fucking bitch, what was in that coffee?"

That was when she got it. Hiding a laugh behind both hands, she didn't want to upset him further by giving into her amusement.

But seriously? Damn!

"What?" Ester asked, her voice floating down the hallway.

He put the towel around his hips before his mother pushed the door. Nya grabbed the shower curtain to cover her body, so she could watch the scene unfold while maintaining some modesty.

"You fucking bitch," he said. "What was in the coffee you fed me?"

Ester gave Nya a finger wave, but she was too busy hiding her mouth behind the shower curtain to reciprocate.

"You left that girl chained to a bed," Ester said, folding her arms to drum her talons on her upper arm. "And not for fun reasons. I think she deserves an apology. A proper one. And I just made sure she'd get it."

Ester was proud of herself and, hey, she wasn't complaining. Archer was fuming and she didn't know where to look.

"You put drugs in my coffee?"

"Only to save your relationship. Nya is gold, I won't let you lose her," Ester said on a sigh, examining her manicure. "You're welcome, son." She patted his shoulders. "I have some errands to run this morning. You kids have fun. I'll be back later."

Ester turned and flounced away.

Archer couldn't exactly follow given his current state of undress. When the front door closed, he swore again, and turned to look at her. She had to keep the shower curtain over her mouth, otherwise she'd lose it for sure and he was not a man to be messed with right now.

"She's a fucking bitch."

She wouldn't go that far, although didn't endorse anyone drugging another person without their permission. Ester's prank would sure make the morning interesting.

She fought to keep a straight face. "How long will it last?" she asked, vindicated.

Ester was right, she had been left chained to that bed. He'd abandoned her there and hadn't trusted her word she'd stay put.

He'd left her like one of his captives and shown no respect. She'd vowed to have payback and cursed his name while lying there. Ester just served retribution up on a platter.

"How long does it last? That's your fucking question?" he spat. "I don't fucking know. I've never used that shit. She's a fucking bitch!"

Oh, her precious man was at the end of his rope. She left him to steam while she washed herself and climbed out wet. Still, he stood there just inside the door. Snagging the towel from his hips, she made a show of drying her body, but actually wanted to see if the drugs were still in effect.

"Well…" she said, after towel drying her hair and tossing the towel backwards. "I guess I'll have to make the most of it."

Taking his hand, she led him to the bedroom. This time it was her turn to push him down onto the bed.

"You're not actually going to—"

"Yes," she said, climbing on top of him, pushing him back down when he attempted to rise to his elbows. "Yes, I am." Tilting her head, she kissed him. "Because Ester got one thing right, you have a lot of apologizing to do, and since it's there anyway, we wouldn't want it to go to waste."

He grumbled. "You're a fucking bitch too," he said, but the lightness of the accusation betrayed it wasn't serious.

His hands roamed over her back and ass.

"That's why we're so well suited," she said, angling her head the other way to kiss him again. "Because you're the biggest prick I know." She cast her eyes south to the dick that probed her folds. "In more ways than one."

"Okay," he said, scooping his arms around her to flip her onto her back. "Like you said, since it's there anyway… but I'm fucking you under protest."

She laughed and accepted his kiss. He'd still be pissed at his mother when she came back. Maybe this was a gift in disguise. It gave them both a chance to exist in oblivion without facing the truth of what had transpired and the real danger lurking in their lives.

Instead, that morning, they were a couple in love, forced to enjoy each other. There were worse methods of torture to endure; they'd embrace this one and live with the consequences.

SIXTEEN

NYA WOULDN'T HAVE to work out for a month. Man, did she hurt in every interesting corner. After around five hours of almost non-stop fun, both of them fell asleep out of sheer exhaustion. Her jaw ached, her breasts tingled, and her pussy had never been so spoiled. She couldn't keep the smile off her face, even in spite of Archer shutting her down.

After waking up, they'd showered alone, and she came out to find Archer eating a sandwich. She tried to talk to him about what happened with Hexam the previous night. All he'd say was he'd taken care of it and that she was no longer in danger.

And what the hell did that mean? No idea.

Her guy was being shifty. He hadn't maintained eye contact, and his tone was abrupt, note: shifty. No matter what she tried, she couldn't force honesty from him. With the stiffness in her joints and the tenderness of her muscles, she couldn't be bothered starting a fight.

It turned out Archer had plans of his own and once he finished eating, he slunk off. Again, she'd tried to question where he was going and if she could go with him. No was the definitive answer. He had something to take care of, he said, on his own. She couldn't help but think it was something Hexam related.

Before Hexam's unexpected visit to the club, Archer told her he wouldn't take on Tag's cause again, that he wouldn't be bailing her friend out. Despite that assertion, there he was, his hand forced, doing what he didn't want to be doing. All because Tag's mess put her in the firing line, again. Guilt swamped her, she held on longer than normal when saying goodbye. Yes, her guy's secrets infuriated her, but whatever was going down, he was taking on a burden that should be rightfully hers.

Ester hadn't come back yet. Archer wasn't worried about his mother, so she wasn't either. The woman had her own life to live. Archer said in the past that Ester often swanned in and out of his life depending on her relationship status and need for money.

Having missed the mother-son exchange at breakfast, it was possible Archer handed over money, or promised to take care of Ester's latest ex. If the boxes were checked, maybe Ester wouldn't be back at all. Either way, she had some time to herself.

After eating alone at Archer's, she went to her apartment to change clothes, then set Tag's place in her sights. Archer said her friend was lying low but hadn't said he wasn't home. Hexam couldn't have been in town for long if Kristof just revealed his return to Archer the previous night. Maybe Hexam hadn't gotten around to knocking on Tag's door.

Wherever her friend was, checking the apartment was a good start. If Archer was fixing this problem, and she was being threatened for it, confronting Tag was inevitable. She needed to know if what she'd said was true, did he really love Farrah? Was he willing to go all the way to protect their relationship or was Archer on a fool's errand? Committing himself to helping a man he didn't even class as a friend because he loved her?

Foregoing knocking or shouting, she elected not to draw attention to herself. She also didn't want Tag to come to the door and show himself. Although no one overtly watched, that didn't mean there wasn't someone lurking or a camera planted nearby. She didn't want to be responsible for confirming Tag's location to Hexam.

Putting her key in the lock, she went inside, and dumped her purse in the entryway. The last time she'd walked into Tag's living room, she'd found Farrah wrapped in nothing but a sheet. Surely nothing could be more shocking to witness given Farrah's identity.

Turned out she was wrong.

When she went into the living room this time, Tag sat in an armchair by the fireplace with Archer in the one opposite. Both men stood up fast. If that wasn't an immediate indicator of guilt, she didn't know what would be.

She waited for one of them to exclaim this wasn't what it looked like, except, she didn't have a fucking clue what it did look like. Archer was being cagey. Tag hadn't been in touch. And they weren't the kind of men who'd get together to shoot the breeze.

"What are you doing here, Yorkie?" Tag asked her.

Her mouth opened in an exhale of disbelief. "Yeah, I'm the one out of place here," she said, frowning in time with her accusation.

The bedroom door opened.

Farrah spoke as she emerged. "Okay, I've booked us three one-way tickets to Bogota, but the flight leaves in an hour and—"

The beauty stopped talking when she lifted her head and spotted the unexpected guest.

Nya descended further into her stupor. So they were running away, but why together? Why now? Why was she out of the loop?

"A vacation?" she asked. "How nice for you all. Bring me back a keychain."

Glad to be close enough to the door that she could spin around and hurry out, she snagged her purse before slamming the door. The elevator came as soon as she pressed the call button. Glad to avert a scene, she was so grateful when the doors closed, and it began to descend.

Idiot, what a fucking idiot. No, a fool, that was a better word.

Should she be angry or upset? The burn of tears in the corner of her eyes were just as confused. Was she just embarrassed about them planning a getaway that excluded her? Was she upset about being abandoned while the two people she cared most about in the world were picking up and leaving the country without her?

Her upset came from the deception. A lie of omission was still a lie. Archer must've known this was a possibility before he left her in his apartment. Yet he hadn't hinted he was going to Tag's or out of the country.

Getting out onto the street, she hooked the first right into an alleyway and picked up her pace. Cutting straight through would get her onto a crowded city street. Perfect, she needed to lose herself for a while. Apparently for an hour because after that the trio would be on a plane.

Two streets over, the truth was obvious. Why panic? No one was coming after her. No one was worried about her feelings or her perception of what she'd seen.

If Archer was getting on a plane in an hour, he would need to get home to pack. That would take priority over soothing her. The schedule was too tight to add in an argument with his girlfriend, who wouldn't be easily appeased.

Disappointment weighed her down; at least clarity also gave her direction. She got into a cab and gave her address. No point hiding when no one was seeking. Of course, the phone rang during that cab ride. She wanted to answer but didn't want to argue in front of a stranger. She'd only end up getting angry and shrill, so she diverted it.

At least Archer made an attempt, whether to explain, or tell her to get over herself, he'd tried to get in touch. Tag hadn't. Her supposed best friend had plenty going on in his life with his new girlfriend and the woman's intimidating brother. Archer had been right about her sliding down Tag's priority list. She hadn't been naïve enough not to see that, but she hadn't expected to fall off that list completely.

She paid the cab driver and ran upstairs to her apartment. The chime of a voicemail. In her studio, she retrieved the device from her bag when she got inside and laid it on her tiny kitchen table. That was it. Just… there. Nothing else.

She made coffee, more to stay busy than because she

actually wanted to drink it. Her gaze flitted back to the phone time and again. Curious about what he might say, she didn't want to listen to any excuses or half-answers.

As much as her love for Archer was immense, some part of her feared his call would be his last, that he might utter the word, "goodbye," and maybe even, "good riddance." Filling her mug, she sipped her coffee. Okay. Inhaling vibrated her throat. After clucking her tongue, she sank into a chair and rested a hand over it.

She wasn't fooling anyone. Not herself anyway. She was going to listen to the message eventually, might as well get it over with.

Dialing into her voicemail, she put it on speaker. "You have one new message," came an automated voice who listed the date and time it was left.

The trio must be at the airport by now. May even be queuing to get on the plane.

"Squirm." The word burst from Archer through her phone speakers, scaring her. Noise behind him, probably the airport bustle, didn't encroach on his voice. "Goddamnit! You know why I'm doing this. Something happened with Hex last night. I came to see your boy today to figure it out and I was roped into a job. That's all it is, Ny, it's a job." He barked the words like he too was warring with anger and upset, though he'd never admit to the latter. "I'm fucking doing this for you. I don't give a shit about this fucker!" Anger won out in that sentence. She traced a fingertip around the edge of her phone. "I'll call tonight and you're gonna pick up the fucking phone, Squirm, or I'm leaving this bastard to rot. If you're not around, I don't need to risk my life for him."

There was a long pause. Not silence, but not Archer either. Was he doing something? Thinking?

"What?" she whispered, anticipating what he'd say next.

"I love you, Ny," he murmured. "Watching you walk away from me with that look on your face..." his voice trailed away.

"Archer, we have to go," said a female voice in the background.

Although it wasn't distinct, she'd guess it was Farrah's.

"I'll call you later," he said into the phone one more time, then the message ended.

He'd call her later, what did that mean? Her time or his? She had Sizzle that night. If nothing else, work would keep her busy. Though so much for protecting her, she didn't relish the idea of Hexam cornering her while Archer wasn't even in the country.

Still, she'd rather be there, surrounded by people with things to do, than sitting staring at the walls, waiting for Archer to call. She trusted why he was doing this, trusted that his intentions were good and motivated by love for her.

Guilt and worry swirled in their conflict for dominance. He shouldn't be doing this. Her love shouldn't be anywhere near this mess, yet he was traveling to one of the most dangerous countries in the world, for her.

The only reason he was part of this mess? Her. Wherever he was going, for whatever reason, this mission had to be dangerous, he'd said he was risking his life. She didn't want that, especially when she couldn't trust Tag to have her man's back.

Unsettled, she did her best to fill the rest of the day with mindless jobs like household chores. Where was Archer? What was he doing? And was he thinking of her? Probably that answer was yes, he'd be cursing her for getting him into this.

Tag had drawn them in to another dangerous scenario. This time she'd been left behind. Not being at Archer's side meant she couldn't support him. All she could do was hope he'd come back to her in one piece… and that their relationship would survive this trial.

SEVENTEEN

COMING TO WORK IN Sizzle was supposed to distract her enough that she wouldn't sit staring at the phone like a lovesick teenager, waiting all night for it to ring.

Yeah, that plan worked for all of three minutes.

Sitting in the office, legs crossed, one foot tapping against the leg of her desk, she'd done nothing but fixate on the device.

Chin propped on the heel of her hand, she nibbled on her pinkie nail, wiggling her pen between her first two fingers. Archer said he would call. Work it out. Okay. The flight would be like nine or ten hours. From there, God only knew how long it would take him to get from the airport to his final destination. And who knew what cellphone reception was like in Columbia? Maybe he had to wait for a landline; did they have those down there? Maybe it wasn't easy to make calls out of the country. How would she know? She'd never been.

Getting the call would only be a first step. How long would he be down there? When would he come back? What if he never got to a phone? She could be waiting for days or weeks, never hearing from him, jumping every time the door opened, straining to hear every whisper, desperate to pick out his voice.

Tag was gone too. Her support network had up and left the country, left the continent, and she didn't have the first clue why. Sizzle was no consolation. Keeping the place going was her job. It was Tag's club, Archer had put in time there, so she had to keep it together. But still, listening to the pulse of her pen and the thud of her foot, she had to admit, if she had more confidence in their destination, she'd probably be on a plane by now.

What would be the point in chasing after them? It would be tough enough to find them if they stayed in Bogota. If they traveled, which was likely, given Hexam and Tag's trade, they could be anywhere on the continent, dealing with the worst kind of people.

The only hope was Farrah's presence. Hexam wouldn't have sent his sister somewhere dangerous. So long as Farrah stayed with the two men, Archer and Tag should be safe. Hexam did business with men in that country. Farrah could be secreted away to some fancy house somewhere. This could be Hexam's opportunity to separate her from Tag. Maybe the whole thing was a ruse.

Archer would know what was going on. He knew everything; he'd have ferreted out information without Hexam's knowledge. Wouldn't he? Still, she stared at the phone, praying for it to ring.

Ridiculous as it was, when the door opened, she pounced to her feet. For a split second, she expected Archer to walk in. If he'd gotten on a plane, he would still be in the air. If he hadn't boarded the flight, he'd have been back with her by now. Damn, still an idiot.

Jada came in. "There's some guys here to see you," she said. "They're causing a problem out front with security."

Men. Plural. The club was open, in full swing, she couldn't handle a brawl. And this wasn't a random attack if people were asking for her. Curiosity was satisfied when a familiar man walked through the door.

Shoving Jada aside, Hexam focused on her. "Nya," he said. Shit, she hated being right and didn't trust the smile on his face for a second. "You have pretty employees."

He looked Jada up and down.

"Get out of here," she demanded of Jada, this was not going to be Jamie two point oh. "Tell security to leave them be."

"That's right," Hexam said. "Take your fine ass out there and get my men a drink."

He used the door to push Jada out. To her credit, the youngster made eye contact like she was worried. Nya had lost one employee to this man, in the most horrific way, she couldn't lose another. The door closed.

"Your men can have anything they want," Nya said. "You don't have to scare the staff."

"I'm not here to scare them," he said, folding his arms.

"Just me?"

An odd moment passed between them. A sort of charged tension sizzled. They both knew, to an extent at least, what cards the other held. But they stood facing off waiting for the other to break.

Alone, Nya had no safety net. Hexam could take anything he wanted. Archer wouldn't walk in. Tag wouldn't stumble on the scene. Some insecure part of her subconscious was transported back to her father's kitchen when she was fourteen years old, when Tag's brother first put his hands on her.

The impact of dread was the same; it hit her so hard she couldn't inhale. Back then, she was a scared kid. Now she was all grown up. She pushed that fear down, dampening it with every ounce of strength. Archer told her the nightmare would never come true, and there she was, living it. If only she'd known then, the true nightmare was nothing to do with the horror of how her night might end.

"I'm here to make friends," he said.

Yeah, like she'd trust that.

No longer smiling, Hexam examined her expression, her body language, probably trying to assess her nature.

"If you wanted to make friends with me, why did you bring a posse?"

"I brought three guys," he said. "I don't travel alone

in shitty neighborhoods like this."

She'd spent too much time with Archer. When her mouth opened, sass almost leaked out. She got away with her sarcasm with her guy because he loved her. Not every strong guy, bigger than her, would accept it, especially when she had no intention of softening the verbal blow with a kiss or caress.

"I could've come alone," he said. "There's not a guy out there who doesn't owe me something or that I couldn't bribe. Besides, your security isn't as strong as you think. I walked right in here the other day, didn't I?"

"I have enough friends," she said and sat down to pick up her pen.

He swaggered closer. "That's not the way I see it. I think you need a friend. A friend who can do you a favor."

Intrigued, she stopped fake reading the order sheet on the desk to look at him. "What kind of favor?"

"When a guy goes out of town, it takes him a few days to catch up. It didn't hit me until I was sitting looking at you that you have a right to be pissed at me."

"Thanks for the permission," she said and pretended to make a note on the paper.

Well, she did make a note, just had no idea what it said. It was a distraction from looking at the bulk of his muscles, or the colored tattoos of curse words and weapons on his biceps. A tattoo of fire from his wrist to his elbow implied he'd been borne by hell. Just what she needed. A guy with no morals and everything to win.

"My guys fucked up when they came in here. They dropped your bouncers in the street outside. I don't know what shit went on in here, but I know your girl didn't make it out."

Clenching her fist around the pen, she wouldn't let her anger show. Archer's voice in her head told her to "Calm it." To "Hush." To hold it together.

"No, she didn't." Nya fixated on the figures on the paper. "What's your point?"

"Those guys pissed me off and I think you're pissed at them too. Means we've got something in common."

She glared. "Good for us... Do you think I'm stupid?

Do you think I'm going to believe you actually came here to make friends?"

"I've known Archer a long time," he said, sitting down and lifting an ankle to his opposite knee. "A lot of years. We've worked together, close together, and sometimes we're on opposite sides. It's the way the game's played."

Which was basically the same thing Archer said.

"I know," she said. "I know men like you. I've known men like you since I was a kid. Men like you lived on my block when I was in diapers looking out the window. I watched women on street corners being pushed and heckled into cars, by men like you, crying and screaming women. Some weren't even women, they were girls, who didn't want to do what they were told. But they were beaten there on the street like dogs if they didn't. I've seen good people sucked into your world. They owe you some money. They owe some more. They do you a favor. You do them one back, and then you own their ass."

"Good." While she'd meant to take the wind from his sails, she'd somehow managed to bolster him. "Then you'll know what I'm about to do for you isn't free."

"What are you about to do for me?"

He wouldn't sign his baby sister over to her best friend just to make everyone's lives easier.

"I'm on my way somewhere and I want you to come with me."

She laughed. "Yeah, right, why would I do that? Besides, weren't you told to stay the fuck away from me unless Archer was around?"

"Archer's my buddy," he said. "I'm not here to hurt you. I'm here to bail you out. I'm doing it because you're Archer's girl, that's the reason. And I know where he is right now, so do you."

Bristling, she didn't know whether to admit the truth. Except Archer would never have gone south and claimed he was saving Tag's ass, if it wasn't a job he was doing for Hexam.

"I don't know where he is," she said without intending to play dumb. "But I know where he's not."

"Here," Hexam said. "Arch plays everything close to

his chest, even with his whores, don't take it personal. 'Scuse me." He held up a hand. "His *lady*, that's what he calls you, isn't it?"

In front of others he did, not in private. If he was there, he'd take exception to her being called a whore. She appreciated Hexam taking the time to correct himself, even if it was mocking.

"Maybe."

"Archer's a stand-up guy. He's told me he'll do a job, it'll get done. You know why he's on the hook?" he asked, pulling his chair closer to the desk to lean over it. "Because I don't trust your boy, Taggert. One guy could do what I sent them down there to do, but I know your weasel of a friend will find a way to wriggle out of it. You might think Arch is putting his ass on the line for me. He's not. He's putting it on the line for you. Do you know how fucking tough it is to get Arch to work when he doesn't wanna? 'Cause if it was anyone else and I called Arch and said, 'Hey, man, you wanna go babysit for me?' He'd laugh in my fucking face. You know it, I know it. That guy got on a plane to go to the world's asshole, because I can't trust Taggert to do any fucking thing right."

Much as she'd love to jump on Tag's defense, she couldn't. Her friend had a way of looking out for himself and could be bullheaded. If someone told him to do something he didn't want to do, he would dig his heels in and wouldn't do it. She'd always been the exception, but even her influence had limits.

Maybe Farrah was different and maybe that was why she was there. That didn't matter. If Tag was sent to Bogota to do a job, to prove to Hexam he loved Farrah, he would have to do it. If he didn't, he'd lose her. Whatever this job, it was important enough that Hexam needed it done either way.

So whether Tag tried to back out or not, Archer was the safety net who'd stand behind him and make sure it got done. Hexam stood to lose nothing. The thing he needed done would get done, Archer would make sure of it. Tag may lose Farrah if he didn't do it. God only knew what Archer would lose. Again, the only reason he was there? Her.

Guilt gnawed every day, this one would weigh on her

for a long time.

"Why would you come here to do me a favor?" she asked. "If I'm just the bitch that got your bro, Archer, messed up in this shit, why would you do me a favor?"

Hexam opened his hands, then brought them together in a clap. "Because you're his lady. You ask any guy in town who they'd want on their side and they'll tell you Archer." Archer didn't have property. He didn't have a patch. He didn't deal drugs or weapons or anything like that. "'Cept that sonofabitch won't give his loyalty to no one. He stays neutral all the fucking time and won't give his allegiance or withhold it. Sometimes I think he works against folks just so they don't get the wrong idea he might be soft or on their side."

Archer worked best when he was neutral.

"It's worked for him."

"Archer knows everything and everyone. I know guys he's screwed over who'd still suck his dick if he put them on their knees. Because if you control Archer, you control half the board. I don't know anyone who doesn't owe him something from some time even way back. And anyone else? He has dirt on so deep, they're scared to take a piss without his permission."

Fear, gratitude, blackmail, Archer had so many plates spinning, and he did it without breaking a sweat.

"What do I care?"

"Are you kidding? The gal who sucks the cock makes the man dance."

Hexam wasn't subtle.

"And you want me to make Archer dance for you?"

"Not right now," he said, "but there might come a time…"

He wanted her in his back pocket. "Thanks, but no thanks."

"You don't even know the favor I'm offering. It could be big."

"There's nothing I want from you," she said. "Except…"

The last word slipped out and it was too late to take

it back.

"Except what?" he asked, peering at her. "What do you want?"

"I want Archer home safe. I don't want you sending him away on planes anymore."

"That's sweet," he said, mocking her with his smile. "Unfortunately, not even I can make a plane turn around and they must be landing soon, right?" He looked at his watch, though not for long enough to actually read it. "They'd need to land to refuel, so while they're there, they might as well do the job."

She wasn't going to beg for information about when they'd be back. Would she even believe what he said? Hexam might imply they'd be on the tarmac for minutes only to turn around and come home; she didn't believe that.

"Why don't you come with me?" he asked. "You can leave any time you want. All you've got to do is get in a car with me. I'll send my boys away. Just you and me, boo. We'll take a ride."

She wasn't a soft touch. "I get in a car with you, and you could drive me anywhere. There could be a thousand guys waiting for us wherever we go."

"Maybe this will change your mind." Lifting his hips, he reached behind him and produced the biggest handgun she'd ever seen in her life. He opened the clip, showed her the bullets, slammed it back inside and loaded it before putting the piece down in the middle of the desk not far from her phone. "Does that make you feel safer?"

Guns. Nya didn't know what to do with guns. She'd seen them at Tag's place in the past, had boyfriends who used them, even her father had a shotgun. But she'd become accustomed to Archer's knives and wasn't sure how she felt about holding a gun.

As if in her thoughts, Hexam reached behind him for something else. "Or maybe you'd prefer this," he said and slapped a sheathed knife about five inches long beside it. "You can keep hold of them both. I swear to you, no one will hurt you. Archer must've told you something about me. What did he tell you?"

That he didn't order quick hits. The people Hexam wanted hurt weren't hurt quickly, they were hurt slow. Whatever he was planning, even if it was sinister, she wouldn't end up dead, not tonight.

Not to be shared, those hints would stay between her and Archer.

Weapons weren't supposed to be allowed in Sizzle. Hexam wouldn't have let himself be searched. Bringing a group to distract security would've let this guy sail through without a confrontation.

"No," she said. "I won't do it."

"Listen, boo, I could've come in here and dragged you out kicking and screaming. There wouldn't have been a fucking thing any of your men could do about it. Archer isn't even in the country. The chances of anyone getting word to him in the next forty-eight hours are nil. Not close to nil, Nya. Nil. And even if by some sheer miracle, someone managed to talk to him, do you have any idea how long it would take him to get back here? At least a day, not a short, daylight-hours day, I'm talking twenty-four hours, and that's without delays… Just so we're clear, we'd make sure there were delays. Do you know what kind of fucked up shit could happen to you in twenty-four hours?"

"Our friendship was short."

"Far as I'm concerned, you delivered. I came in here and told you I wanted Tag on my doorstep, now a day later, he's my bitch. That was you and Arch made that happen. You're a helluva team."

She didn't want praise from this guy. "So you want both of us on the books now?"

"You've got something, boo. Some way of convincing guys to do what the fuck you want. And that's interesting to a guy like me."

Interesting Hexam was exactly what she didn't want. The idea he might have his eye on her, now or in the future, in a professional way or otherwise, was insanely unnerving.

"I think you should leave now," she said.

"I could." He didn't move, just watched her rise to her feet. "These clubbers of yours, they'll be fucking off soon, then it will be you and me back here. And all those young, sexy servers we'll line up for me and my boys."

This guy didn't know the meaning of friendship. What to do? She needed Archer and he was half the world away.

"I get in the car with you and then what?"

"I told you. I'm not gonna hurt you. I wanna do you a favor, show you we can be allies. I can be useful to you. I can give you what you want."

This guy thought he knew her so well, she wasn't falling for it.

"What do you know about what I want?" she sneered.

"Plenty."

The conspicuous weapons were unsettling, she tidied her desk around them. Hexam couldn't honestly think they would make her feel better. He was stronger and quicker. If he got hold of one of them, she wouldn't be quick enough with the other to even the odds.

"Tulio." The name stopped her straightening papers. "That's right, boo. See, like I said, it takes a guy a few days to get back in the loop, but now I am. And I know what you want." Hexam clasped his hands. "I know every fucking thing, boo, and I can give you it. I can give you the revenge you want. You don't have to do it bit by bit, I can help you rain down hellfire because the same guys who wronged you, wronged me. We have something in common."

Back to that. And he was right. He knew everything. All the problems she and Archer discussed were becoming reality. Hexam knew about Tag and Farrah, and he knew about her plan for revenge. Archer said Hexam wouldn't care what happened to these guys as long as they weren't in his inner circle. This offer had to be evidence they weren't.

"How did you…? What did you do to Tulio?"

"You marked him," Hexam said. "It wasn't Archer's trademark, but the work was pristine. There's only one guy with the skills to do that."

"And Tulio… he told you what…"

Hexam smirked. "Made us promise to protect his women."

She'd seen how Tulio cared for his women. "And that's when he told you…"

Hexam shook his head. "But after putting two bullets in his whore's head, he got chatty."

Tatiana. That was the name of his mistress, she remembered Archer saying it. Pain clenched her heart.

"Why would you hurt your own men?"

"He wasn't a serious player. He's expendable. Just like the fuckers who hit Sizzle and fucked up your friend. They did sloppy work under my name. Whether you come to watch or not, I'm taking them out tonight."

"You have them?" she asked, dropping into her seat. Her hands folded over the gun.

Proud of himself, he stretched out in the chair. "I do. Four of 'em lined up and ready to go."

"Does that include Tulio?"

He shook his head again. "We let him live, 'cause he gave us useful info."

So four, plus Tulio, plus Jonno, that left only one unknown. "Who are they?"

"Come and see for yourself. I've got them all for you, boo. Not even Archer did that for you. I've got the little guy who shot your bouncers, and the three who screwed… what was her name?"

Dazed, she was slipping out of reality. "Jamie. If you have them, why didn't you tell Archer?"

"He knows. I guess you guys never got time to talk about it."

No, they hadn't, and she glanced at her phone that still hadn't rung. Maybe that was what he was going to tell her. That he was doing this job in exchange for time alone with the men who'd killed Jamie.

Hexam smiled again. "You've got the bloodlust, I can see it. You want to see them suffer and you've got nothing to lose. You can come and watch with your own eyes, then I'll take you home and leave you alone."

This wasn't the time to be shocked. She had to keep it together.

"How do I know you'll let me go?"

"What would happen if I held you? I can't force Archer to stay away forever. It took me a whole fucking hour today to convince the guy to go. One of his conditions was that he wouldn't stay down there for a breath longer than he had to. You must do mad things to his cock, 'cause there's ample pussy down there, and he doesn't give a fuck about it. Told me to keep it the fuck away from him."

She did. But that wasn't why he was so eager to come home. If she was in Archer's position, she'd be eager to come home to him too.

"I can't trust you," she said. "I'll have to pass."

Regardless of her desperation to see these men taken down a peg, Archer would go postal if she went. He'd told her she should never put herself in danger for him because if she did, they'd be through. The same rules probably applied if she did something to endanger herself by choice.

"Come on, Nya, you know I wanna be your friend and do you a favor—"

"And then I owe you."

He didn't deny it but wasn't offended. "Way I see it, you owe me either way," he said, with his elbows on the edge of the desk.

"How do you figure that?"

"Because you can come with me now and get exactly what you want, watching these men go down. Or you don't come with me now and you miss your only chance to see it."

"Then I pick door number two."

"Fine," he said, standing up to brush his hands down his jeans. "But you're making a mistake. Don't forget, Columbia's a dangerous place. There's lots of gangs down there who see Americans as a payday, grab one and they get a helluva ransom. Lots of stray bullets and machetes swinging too, accidents happen all the time. You wouldn't believe how easy it is to fuck people up down there, no one gives a shit."

Hexam had a way of doing this thing with his eyes where he could cool them and intensify them at the same time, conveying his threats while keeping his words implicit.

"You're telling me something might happen to Archer or Tag?"

"I'm saying if I get upset, like I will if you don't come with me, I might forget to give the guys down there orders to protect the Americans' asses. Might forget to tell them to put the safety on their guns. You might've heard I can be unreasonable. When I'm in a bad mood, I make bad choices. You don't want me to be in a bad mood... Do you, boo?"

She stood, angry, confused, offended. There was no reasoning with this guy; he put her in an impossible position. Choice was an illusion. He wasn't asking. He was giving her an order.

"You said Archer was your friend."

"And if he picks a girl who hates my guts, that friendship will sour fast. So what do you say, Nya, spend a couple of hours with me, or your boyfriend comes home in a box? What's your pleasure?"

Like she had any option.

Archer would be hurt if she refused. Tag would never make it alive either. On top of that, she would make an enemy out of a gangster just to complete the fucked-up trifecta.

"Okay." Bowing to grab her purse from under the desk, she slung it across her body and picked up both weapons. Putting the gun in her purse, she strapped the knife to her hip and hid it under her shirt. "But just you. Get rid of your understudies."

"This is the beginning of a beautiful friendship," he said, holding out his arm.

Though it went against instinct, she went to step under it. Just as they were about to walk out, her phone buzzed; she glanced back to see it light up. His hold on her shoulders strengthened.

"Leave it, Nya. You can tell him all about it in the morning."

If Hexam held to his word, as Archer said he did, she would see bad men being punished, then taken back to her apartment and left alone. But if Hexam didn't keep his word, she might still be with him when Archer came back. *If* Archer came back.

EIGHTEEN

JADA WAS WARY, as were the security guys. Nya gave them quick instructions she was leaving for the night and wouldn't be back.

Hexam sent his men away, though they wouldn't go far and were probably just traveling in another vehicle. Whether it was those men or others, she didn't know where they were going. How many people would be there? Hexam didn't travel alone, he'd already confessed that.

The last thing she expected was to be driven to an office block in a decent part of town. Hexam went to an underground parking garage open for them. He'd tried to make small talk in the car, she didn't understand why, their "friendship" was a myth. Maybe his goal was to confuse her and keep her on edge.

Two guys flanked the elevator. She hadn't really seen the guys in Sizzle, could be the same ones or newbies. Didn't really matter. Sending away the original three men meant nothing, because he had plenty of backups.

They got into the elevator alone and traveled to the fourth floor of ten. Stepping out, the environment was weird, almost eerie. An empty bullpen filled with desks and chairs and low partitions between them. Clearly this was an office in use, in daylight anyway, there were knickknacks on desks, pictures stuck to computer monitors. On the walls were highlighted schedules and colored writing on whiteboards. Not a single soul awaited them. The lights were off, the shadows around them managed to transform the benign space to sinister.

Hexam took them in a U-turn down a corridor. That was when she heard music, loud enough to muffle the sounds of whatever was happening in the room ahead, but not loud enough to carry to the street below. Basking in privacy, no one would hear anything concerning or annoying. It got louder. It was some kind of heavy metal, nothing she recognized.

Hexam opened a door. She expected a secret knock or a lock, there was neither. He went in like it was any other room and—she came to a stop. Plastic drop cloths covered the floor, and most of the walls, some sort of metal sheeting beneath it, making the floor hard and unyielding.

Two guys, one in each of the back corners, said nothing, just watched the four men facing forward, kneeling in a line in the middle of the floor.

All of them were crying, bloody, naked. How long had they been at Hexam's mercy? Hands bound in front of them, they also each had a different colored ball gag in their mouths.

"And here's tonight's entertainment," Hexam said. Drawing her into the room with his arm around her shoulders, he closed the door at her back. "You might not know these guys, boo, 'cause they were all wearing masks, right? They'll tell you. You recognize who this is, don't you, boys?"

Hexam stood behind her, squeezing her shoulders. The shortest one at the end was so battered she didn't see tears. His eyes were so purple and swollen, he wouldn't see anything. When Hexam didn't get the answer he wanted, he clapped his hands once.

"I didn't hear you!" he called out. The trouble was, all they could do was nod and give muffled responses. "You two, out. Stay on the door."

The two men from the corners went out, leaving her and Hexam alone with these four men.

"Archer's probably given you a crash course but let me help your education. We've been dragging these guys around for weeks. I was sort of impressed when I heard you and Arch were going for them too," he said, sauntering away to wander around to the back of the men.

He clapped twice in close succession and all four rose higher on their knees like they'd been trained to react to the noise.

Hexam said more, "See, I don't hurt guys quick, I hurt guys slow. Any way you can think of to hurt these guys, me and my men have done it." He kept circling the men. "They've been on their knees for weeks." Bloody bruises and welts on the kneecaps of each man in the row proved that. The wounds radiated up their thighs where they'd been cut. "We drag them from place to place, let them dig their own graves a couple of times. Tossed them in the lake and watched them fight not to drown. It's fun, especially when you tie them together, you see the primal instincts come out. The little one's struggled."

Hexam grabbed a handful of his hair and gave him a shake. Piss spurted from his dick, reflex took her a step back.

Hexam called out in disgust. "Oh, man, not in front of the lady," he said. "You see, boys, this is why we don't feed you or let you drink, 'cause you just embarrass me. See they've lost all shame; they know they're close to the end."

He came back around and laid his arm across her shoulders. "This is a gift to you," he said. "You can do anything you want to them. Anything, Nya. What is it you wanna do?"

It was funny, when Archer was at her side, she felt confident and empowered, now she felt weak and incapable.

"I… I don't know."

"That's okay," he said. "You're new to this. We'll start small. You wanna humiliate them? We can do that. You want to give them back what your friend got? We can do that too. We got guys on staff who'll fuck anything, and we've turned them on each other a few times. Believe me, these guys have felt it. Each one of them's taken it up the ass ten different times, twenty maybe."

The biggest one sobbed, Hexam went over to slap

him. "I'm surprised you didn't like it," Hexam said. "Since you enjoyed bashing in that little girl's skull so bad. I say we give my boo here a shot." Hexam turned to her. "You want to cut him? You want to force your blade down his throat the way he forced her to take his cock? You can do it. No one judges here. You want something to shove up his ass yourself, we can do that too. How hands-on you wanna get? We'll have the boys dig you up a strap-on and you can take them all."

She shook her head. "No."

"Okay. Well what about their junk?" Hexam kicked the second in the line in the groin. He doubled and Hexam kneed him in the face. "I didn't tell you to crouch." He spat in the guy's face. "They're all disgusting. Weak. None of them deserve to work under me and they sure don't deserve pussy. Where's your knife? Cut off their balls, they'll eat each other's dicks, anything you want, boo. It's yours."

Nya was speechless.

"Maybe you'd prefer to get it over with," he said and went to open the door a couple of inches.

As he spoke to the men outside, she was still fixated on the four kneeling in a line, just five feet away.

The biggest one blinked and tried to talk, no dice with that gag. They were pathetic, tortured, their bodies a mess. Their bloodshed and bruises were deserved. The shoulder of the third in the line was bent at the wrong angle, obviously broken, his collarbone pressed on his flesh from the inside.

Maybe they'd been drugged, maybe pain was the least of their problems.

A silenced shot startled her. She jumped to the corner as the smallest one fell, blood oozing from his skull. Her eyes jumped to Hexam just inside the door, holding a gun, bearing a silencer, in an outstretched hand.

The middle two shook and cried again. The biggest one tried to shout and object. The little guy lay on the floor on his side in a puddle of his own urine and blood. It was the end for him and she wasn't sorry.

"That's the guy who killed your bouncers," Hexam said. "Now, how do you want the next one to die?"

Hexam was enlivened, aroused, by playing with life

and death. It could be intoxicating, she'd felt that rush when standing with Archer.

This didn't feel the same.

"Where's your gun?" Hexam asked her. "The weapon I gave you, where is it?" It was in her bag. Sliding her hand inside, she curled her fingers around the butt and pulled it out. "Good." Hexam wore a smile as he waved his gun around. "We're like Bonnie and Clyde, you and me. Natural Born Killers."

The comparison wasn't appreciated. Not that she'd argue while he brandished a weapon, one he'd proved he would use.

"Now, they know how their night's gonna end," Hexam said. "Do you want to hear them beg? Does that get you off, boo?" She shook her head. "Then what do you want?"

She wanted Archer. The minute his name popped into her head, tears stung her eyes. She wanted her man. It wasn't that she felt compassion for these scum suckers, she didn't. They were in a sorry state, stripped, skinned, and scarred, exactly as they deserved to be. Each one of them had to pay for what Jamie went through.

If the positions had been switched and she'd died, witnessing this from the great beyond would vindicate her. Jamie would be cheering her on. Telling her to beat the shit out of each of them and force them to swallow each other's cocks, as Hexam suggested.

With mistrust, she couldn't get over the niggling truth there was nothing stopping Hexam from putting a bullet in her when he was through with the guys.

Begging and crying for Archer wouldn't help.

"I want them punished," she said because she had to say something.

His curious sneer might wonder at her discomfort, could he feel it? He'd been so pleased to put bruises on her arm in the Sizzle office. This guy got off on pain, causing it for sure, maybe not receiving it. He swaggered over and slid the edge of the silencer barrel up her arm, to her neck, and crowded her in close to the covered filing cabinet she'd been cowering against.

"Some women get off on this," he said again. "If you're one of those girls and want to let them watch what a real man can do with a woman, I'll make that happen, Archer never has to know."

Was he propositioning her himself or offering to set her up with a stranger? Sex wasn't an option. She wouldn't have sex with Archer, the man she loved, in front of these lowlifes. For sure she wasn't going to do it with anyone else.

Her doubt was confirmed when he leaned in. Gun still in her hand, she pushed him back.

"Archer's your friend," she whispered.

He almost laughed. "I'm curious about the girl who's got him by the balls," he said. "Guess I want a taste of that magic you use to keep him on a leash."

"I don't."

"You don't?" With his gun in hand, he reached past her to lean on the filing cabinet, penning her in. "Tulio would never have walked away alive unless you called Archer off."

Her guy hadn't been insistent about killing Tulio. He'd given her the decision.

"Archer doesn't…"

She didn't want to use explicit terms in front of these men, even if this truly was their last night alive.

"Doesn't he? Maybe not as a rule, but when his girl gets involved, he has no boundaries. One of my boys grabbed Archer's girl's ass once. She slapped it away and got offended. Know what Archer did? Strung the guy up by his ankles for four days," he said, then laughed. "It was fucking hilarious. He let everyone take a shot at the guy. He didn't just get spanked. He got whipped, spat on, pissed on, shit on, there were no rules. Every guy Archer knew got a call to come and take a shot at this guy. All because he touched her ass. Know how he died? Archer cut off his hands and let him bleed out, took a long fucking time."

Archer was possessive. Hearing what he was capable of was disturbing. Conflicting feelings warred with each other. On hearing something like that, she should be appalled, angry, scared, but she wasn't any of those things.

"And that was your guy?" she asked. "Didn't that piss you off?"

Hexam tilted his head and lifted a shoulder. "I don't give a fuck. He shouldn't have had his hands on another man's girl." This from the guy who'd just tried to kiss her. As if he read her mind, he explained. "Archer wouldn't come after me. We've shared women before. It's no big deal when you see some of the shit him and me have seen together."

"But you threatened his life in my office."

"Did I?" Hexam asked. "Is that what I did?"

Although his back was to them, Hexam somehow noticed one of the guys sagging. He turned, lifted his gun, and fired off a shot with such precision, she dropped her gun and both hands leaped to her mouth.

"Don't panic, sweetheart," he said and picked up the gun. "Maybe this isn't for you." He dropped the gun into her purse. "Try the knife." Insinuating his hand beneath her shirt, he pulled it from its sheath and put it in her palm to curl her fingers around it. "Has Archer taught you how to use a blade?"

Archer wouldn't teach her how to use a weapon even if she begged. She'd spent more time at the sharp end of his knives than the hilt. The scars on her fingers proved it.

"Come over here," he said.

Guiding her forward, he maneuvered them until he stood behind her and captured her knife-wielding hand. Holding it out in front of her, he moved her toward the two remaining men.

Hexam pushed her blade to the center of the biggest one's throat. "This is the guy you want," he said. "He's the one who taunted her. The one who fucked her pussy and fucked her skull. The one who beat her to shut her up. The one who goaded the others on and thought he was all that."

As he spoke, the blade pushed farther into their victim's skin. Blood budded at the tip, when he tried to scream, and his Adam's apple moved, a streak of red formed against it.

"You hold him there, see how that feels, take your time."

Hexam let her go. What did she want to do? She kept looking at the point of her knife pressed against this man's throat. Archer had spoken before about what it was to see the shine of sharp metal pushing into flesh and how rich and exotic blood looked as it seeped from a human body.

There were no lights, only windows at the back of the room, behind the men. Stretching from the ceiling, down a couple of feet, she could see nothing beyond, but ambient light from them allowed her to witness what she was doing. Twisting the blade, left and right, she studied the glint against the metal and understood.

She must have pushed deeper than intended because her victim cried out behind his gag. The quick succession of a silenced bang, bang, startled her away. The two men who were already dead just received a shot each to the chest.

Hexam turned around, wearing a grin. "Just to be sure."

He enjoyed putting more bullets in the already deceased men, she could read his glee.

The one beside her victim pissed, so she retreated further. He was crying and blubbering, tears ran from his distraught eyes. Hexam whipped him hard with the butt of his gun.

"You fucking pig, she'll get to you! Wait your fucking turn!" he yelled, snatching her blade to bend over the trembling man.

Everything faded out. She heard nothing, saw nothing, until her awareness zeroed in on the steely gaze of the guy on his knees before her. The one she'd been holding a weapon on. When she looked into his eyes, she saw it, the evil anger radiating from the bastard who'd stolen Jamie's life. This was the man, the evil bastard who took what wasn't his. The need for revenge burned bright.

The cry from the man beside broke their stare. More blood on the floor, a lot of blood, spurting from somewhere she couldn't see. Hexam stood up and backed off. It didn't take long to see the pisser was kneeling in a puddle of his own blood, his severed penis lying between his knees.

"Solves that problem," Hexam said, pleased with

himself as he wiped the blood on the big one's shoulder before giving the knife back to her. "Sorry, boo, you were in the middle of something. I didn't mean to interrupt."

Blood pooled from the screaming man, more than there was from the two corpses. His fuss prompted Hexam to turn up the music blaring from the stereo by the door.

The noise crowded her mind, her ears rang, her head hurt.

She didn't want to look at the man who'd been under her blade.

"You should try it," Hexam said. "It's a lot of fun."

She couldn't let the big guy at the end see her distress. It wasn't that she feared for her safety, no, she felt superior to the piece of shit.

"Oh, wa, wa," Hexam called out to the guy still crying behind his gag. "Stop making a fucking racket! What do you want? It's done! You'll be fucking dead in a minute anyway."

He had no sympathy.

"You're going to kill them all?"

Hexam whipped around. "I've done my two. The next two are yours."

Murder. She wasn't ready for that. Archer started with Tulio because he was a nobody they didn't need to kill. Her guy was helping to build up her immunity against what might have to be done. He had never once suggested she should take a life herself, he'd only ever offered to do it for her.

"I don't know if I can," she admitted.

Much as she hated showing weakness, she couldn't stand there all night making excuses while he expected her to take action. He'd told her when he was in a bad mood, he made bad decisions. If she took all night, he'd be pissed off and might take his impatience out on her.

Hexam still had his gun in hand, he raised it and shot guy number three right between the eyes. Immediately, the victim dropped.

"That one's a gift," he said. "Because the noise was giving me a headache." That was rich. The music was loud enough to throb through her skull. "But this guy…" Hexam walked between her and the kneeling victim to grab the back of his neck. "This one's all yours, boo. This is the guy who killed your friend. This is the guy you want."

Lunging around, he seized her wrist and pulled her forward to push the knife into the guy between them. This time, slightly off-center, the edge of her blade met the underside of his jaw at his carotid.

"All that hatred, Nya. All those times you probably lay awake thinking about what a bastard he was, thinking about that poor girl and what she went through. Did you think about the blood spurting from her as he pounded her skull into the floor? Did you think about that? He smashed it in, she had no chance, none. Three guys on one little girl. How many of them were raping her then? How many dicks did she have inside her? They fucked every hole, did you know that? Fucked her 'til she bled inside. You know you want to punish him. You know he deserves it. The things they did to that girl, they cut her tits, her belly, sliced her to pieces, and through all of it, she was still alive."

Archer said she'd been alive in the ambulance. These monsters raped Jamie and the only reason she got out was Archer. She didn't know what happened to Jamie when he was taking her out of there, or what they'd done after.

"They cut her face, cut her hands, one of them had some idea of hiding her identity, stupid fuck, her blood was everywhere. That only turned them on more, didn't it, Nya? You saw it. You tell me what you saw."

"I saw bullies," she said, gazing into the eyes of Jamie's murderer. "I saw men use an innocent woman like she was an object they could destroy. I watched them strip her and touch her. I listened to her cry, listened to her scream as they took her apart."

Her teeth gritted together until she could hear them grind. Tears streamed from her eyes, not like normal, they felt thick like blood. Anger swelled her sinuses until they burned. Curling her fingers tight around the handle of the blade, adrenaline surged.

"And that pissed you off? That made you angry!"

"Yes," Nya said. "I heard her say no and beg for her life…" She lost the words in a whisper as her lips cracked and her tongue dried. "How could you do that to her? How could you do that to anyone?"

Did she want an answer? Hexam loosened the gag and tossed it aside.

The guy gasped. "She was a fucking whore," the rapist croaked, his voice hoarse and weak. "And you'd have fucking got it too, bitch."

Her breathing became a pant. "You don't deserve to live."

"Then kill me," he growled.

Maybe it was what he wanted. After what Hexam put him through, he probably did want death. Jamie would've wanted to die too. Nya would've taken that over what they did to the young woman. She hated this man more than she'd hated any other. She hated like she hated Tag's brother and her father, and Damien, like every other man who'd thought they were better than the women they hurt.

"You tortured her. All so you could get yourself a quick lay. Was it worth it? Was it worth it to be under my blade now?"

He leaned forward just a fraction of an inch, but Hexam grabbed his hair to pull him back. The rapist winced and a spurt of satisfaction curled her lips into a sinister smile.

"Oh yeah."

"You're a piece of shit," she said.

"You're a dirty fucking whore standing here now pissed off her friend got to go first. My dick's right here, sweetheart, why don't you do the only thing you're good for, get down there and suck me off."

Rage growled from her, she didn't think and pulled the blade up in both hands above her head and drove it down into his chest until horror spread on his face. Yanking it out with a grunt, she stumbled backwards.

Seconds passed. Seconds of nothing. The rapist spat blood. It dribbled down his chin, and his gaze fell to the wound. Hexam jumped out of the way to let the guy fall and land on the floor with a thud.

Nya couldn't breathe. She couldn't think. She couldn't lick her lips or blink or do anything.

"Wow," Hexam said and clapped his hands once before he came over to put an arm around her. "We make quite a team, boo." He squashed a kiss to her temple that she didn't have the wherewithal to avoid. He whistled. The sharp sound startled her backwards. Hexam held up his hands. "Don't worry. I've got guys for clean-up. We take away the plastic and the sheeting. There are no slugs. Inside twenty minutes, this office will look exactly like it did before we got here."

Someone tossed him a rag. Hexam rubbed his hands and then cleaned the blood from the blade she still clutched tight, ridding it of the stains left by the blood of the man she'd killed.

She'd killed. She was a murderer. She'd taken a life.

Her desperate eyes landed on Hexam changing his boots and his shirt. "Just like I promised you, boo. I'm gonna take you home."

Nya was still dazed as he led her out and put her in the car. Someone offered her a chance to change, but she didn't feel like getting naked in front of these guys.

Hexam was hyper, his chatter was faster and more animated. Either murder got him high or he'd had a little chemical lift at some point.

It didn't even occur to her to think twice about how he knew where she lived when he stopped outside her apartment.

"Want me to come up?" he asked.

That was really the first thing she heard since they'd left the office.

"Not a chance," she said on autopilot, her thoughts still adrift.

"Go up, take a shower, get some sleep," he said. "You'll feel better in the morning. You'll feel pumped. I'm betting that's the first time you've done that."

Nya only looked at him for a second before her gaze fell to her lap and the knife she still held in both hands.

"Want me to take that?" he asked.

She shook her head furiously because it was almost like her hands were glued to the thing. The reminder would be unwelcome. If she was thinking, she should want the weapon as far away from her as possible. Yet it was her only tangible evidence the night happened.

"The boys can get you a souvenir from your victim."

A trophy, she'd heard about those, but wasn't interested. That led her to face the next truth.

"What is it you want from me?" she asked. "You told me tonight wasn't free."

He leaned over and stroked his fingers through her hair. "Just enjoy this," he said. "And don't be scared. Friends do each other favors all the time. It's just that now you owe me… I told you we'd be friends. Feels good, right?"

She owed him one, for what? For lining up the men, for murdering them in front of her, or for setting her up to take a life?

This is what she'd wanted. The worst part was, she didn't feel bad about the lost lives. If she distanced herself enough from the shock of taking a life, she could be pleased the disgusting men responsible for Jamie's death were gone.

Hexam's methods might be unorthodox. But together, they'd done a good thing and made the world safer.

"I'll see you around, Nya." He leaned over to kiss her cheek. "My boo."

This wasn't Archer's car. Took her a minute. She didn't have to wait for someone to open the door. Letting herself out, she crossed the sidewalk, but didn't remember much about getting up the stairs or into her apartment.

She lifted her purse over her head and dumped it on the floor with a thud, all the while, staring at the weapon.

God, she wanted Archer, she needed him to tell her he'd take care of it, to tell her what she should do now, that he would help her. He would make her feel better… after he calmed himself down.

But he wasn't there and couldn't help. She'd just done something final in front of a man she didn't trust.

Dropping to her knees, the tears came again. Her fingers opened and the blade clattered onto the wooden floor. Falling to her side, she curled into a ball, and wept. Tears of guilt were washed away by tears of satisfaction; she'd got her revenge.

All at once she was devastated and elated, terrified and free.

What she'd done, she couldn't take back. Even if she could, she wouldn't. But until Archer looked her in the eye and told her she'd done the right thing, she wouldn't be secure. He would know if it was the right thing and he wasn't even there to support her.

NINETEEN

"YOU FUCKED UP."

These were the first words she heard the next day. They came from the most unexpected of visitors. Nya had been drying her hair when the pounding on the door started, and it didn't stop until she opened it. She was still blinking in surprise at Kristof standing on her threshold.

"Are you just gonna stand there and gawp at me?" he asked. "I said you fucked up."

At some point in the night, she'd crawled into bed. Which she only knew because she'd woken up there a half hour ago. In an attempt to find some normality in her topsy-turvy life, she'd showered like it was any other day. Seemed unlikely when she had virtual strangers standing at her door scowling.

He pushed her aside and marched in.

"Uh, excuse me?"

Still glaring, he spun around without any apology. "Do you know how many times Archer's called me to check on a girl? In his whole life, do you know how many times?" he asked but didn't wait for an answer. "Zero." He held up his thumb and finger in an O. "Zero. Even you can count that high."

"Archer," she said, ignoring Kristof's condescension to slam the door and rush over. "You've spoken to him?"

"Yeah, and you were supposed to. Where the hell have you been? He's been trying to get hold of you for hours. If I don't call him back…" he lifted his watch to her face, "in the next eighteen minutes, know what happens? He gets his ass to the airport and leaves your buddy to deal with his own crap."

"I'm fine," she said, holding up her hands to calm him. "I'm fine. Look, see, I'm fine."

It was funny 'cause she'd thought the same thing when looking in the mirror. The woman staring back at her that day was the same one she'd seen the previous day. Yet, she was different on the inside, in a way she couldn't articulate.

He eyed her brand; she ran her fingers over it.

"So why didn't you pick up your phone?" he asked. "You still busting his balls?"

He made it sound juvenile, and damn it, now it felt like that. She should never have turned on her heels and stormed out of Tag's. She'd been so surprised, and embarrassed, about being the only clueless one in the room. Running had been easier than causing a scene.

Except she had a valid reason for not answering the phone and it wasn't impudence.

"I left my phone in the club," she said. "I was just gonna go over there and get it."

"How long?"

His sneer got her hackles up. "I didn't even know if Archer would call," she said, feeling the need to explain herself.

"He told me he said he would," Kristof said, backing away from his haughty position for a blink.

"He did. But who the fuck knows what reception is like in Columbia, or even if he'd be allowed to keep his phone? I don't know where he is or what he's doing. He could be in a fucking jungle for all I know. So I'm supposed to sit by the phone, stare at the thing all night, waiting and hoping it would ring?"

That's exactly what she'd been doing until Hexam

walked into her office. She should never have ignored the call, except if she hadn't, Hexam might have left without her. Confused though she was by her metamorphosis, she still wasn't sorry those scum suckers were dead.

"His mistake, I guess he thought you might give a fuck," Kristof said. "Being that he went down there—"

"I know, to save Tag's ass," she said and folded her arms. "Nobody asked him to do that, you know?"

"You're pissy? Wow, no wonder you get along with Ester."

Doing some quick familial math in her head, Nya hadn't quite put the pieces together, but it made sense. Derren was Kristof's father and Ester was Derren's ex. Their odd misfit family must still somehow be in contact.

"You've spoken to her?" Nya asked. "Is she okay?"

Ester was supposed to go back to Archer's, and she hadn't bothered to check if the woman made it.

"Yeah, she called all pissed off that you and Arch weren't home. Least she started off pissed, by the end of the call she figured you'd snuck off to screw somewhere."

At least she could be reassured Ester was safe. "So she was happy?"

Kristof bobbed his head in confirmation. "She was drunk, she's always happy drunk."

"Did you tell her where Archer really was?"

"No, that'd just give her more of an excuse to act crazy and she's got that routine down."

Kristof was new to her, she hadn't even known he existed until meeting him at Archer's place. Now she could see he was more integral in Archer's life than her guy let on.

Archer kept so many secrets. It was his default not to trust or offer any more information than necessary. Mental note, she should start prodding him for more personal information on a regular basis.

When she'd asked about his history with Derren, he'd told her, but she knew nothing of their present relationship. Which would be why Kristof never came up in conversation.

"Do you know how long Archer will be gone?" she asked. "What did he tell you about—"

"Listen, I'm here to make sure you're alive," Kristof said. "Get to the club and get your phone. I'll tell Archer to call in an hour. He's rolling out today, so he'll be pushing it for time. And I warn you…" He went to open the door. "If you don't pick up this time, your buddy's on his own."

Kristof exited and slammed the door. It didn't startle her, it made her smile. Although he and Archer weren't blood, they were alike, and there was comfort in that.

TWENTY

AN HOUR FELT LIKE an age. It didn't take that long to finish getting ready and over to the club. There wasn't enough time to get home again, and she didn't want to be in a cab when the phone rang, so she busied herself with bullshit tasks in the Sizzle office. She couldn't stand staring at the phone any longer.

She'd missed eighteen calls over the course of the night. Zero voicemails. Was he that pissed off or did he not want to leave evidence? Whatever the case, she'd just locked the safe when the phone rang at its highest volume.

She leaped into her chair to snatch it up. "Fella?" she asked, pleading and desperate.

Every emotion she'd experienced since last seeing him came together to infuse her with fresh adrenaline.

The caller said nothing. She took the phone from her ear to check the line was still connected. It was, to a number simply listed as, "Unknown."

"Archer?" she asked when he still didn't say anything.

Was he angry with her? Did he know what happened? So many questions and she couldn't get started until he acknowledged her and confirmed it was him.

"When you put a guy in the doghouse, you do it

right."

Relief curled her lips. She exhaled a long breath and closed her eyes. Just the cadence of his voice was enough to restore some of her equilibrium.

"Oh, God, I missed you."

He didn't sound as happy to hear her voice. "You wouldn't have fucking had to if you'd answered your fucking phone. Where the fuck have you been?"

He swore a lot at the best of times. When he was emotional, angry, upset, his cursing increased tenfold.

"I left it at the club."

It might take some time to calm him down. "I told you I'd fucking call. You're lucky I'm not on a fucking plane right now."

It couldn't be easy to be so far away and out of touch, especially for Archer, who was used to being in the know.

"I know," she said. "I'm sorry."

Still snappy, his words were quick. "And what the fuck do you mean you left it at the club? The club was still open when I called."

Back to reality. "I left before closing," she admitted, staring at the now empty chair Hexam had sat in.

"Yeah, I heard there was trouble."

She laughed; the first time she'd had the urge since he left. "Of course you fucking did," she said. "Only you could be halfway across the planet and still know what happened in Sizzle last night."

"That's funny?"

Bringing her bare feet up onto the seat, she wrapped one arm around them. "Yes, it's funny, and it's comforting, and it's terrifying, and it makes me love you so fucking much."

Again, there was silence. Such an elongated one that she didn't have to be near him to know his mind was working. When he spoke again, his voice was low, as was his volume, his concern suspicious.

"What did you do, Ny?"

There was a limit to even his knowledge. He'd have known there was trouble. If anyone told him about the random men showing up, Archer would want to know everything. Kristof probably would've found out if he came looking for her after she missed Archer's calls.

Sizzle had a landline, people rarely got through unless the person in the office picked up. But it was possible someone heard it and answered, only to tell him that she'd left with a well-built stranger.

Nya couldn't even say "nothing" because she would have to tell him the truth. If she didn't, Hexam would, with his own flair. She wouldn't let him put any kind of wedge between her and her man.

Except, as far as she was concerned, explaining over the phone wasn't an option.

"When are you coming home?"

Archer was focused. "I don't like that answer. Try again."

And he shouldn't like it. He probably took it as an avoidance of his question. It wasn't. She just didn't want to tell him the whole truth over the phone. For one thing, the line might not be secure. For another, wherever he was, if he reacted badly, he could get himself into trouble or hurt.

She could give him some answers; this wasn't withholding or game-playing.

"Hexam came here last night. I left with him," she said to more silence. "I can't tell you what happened over the phone, that's why I asked when you'll be home. I know you need to know everything and I will tell you." She sighed. "As soon as you hang up this phone, you're going to call Hexam. I don't know how he's going to tell the story, but whatever extras he slides in, I need you to know… the basics of the story…" She took another breath. "Are true."

"What the fuck does that mean?"

"Fella, whatever he tells you I did… is true. I did it."

Being this far away from him had nothing but disadvantages. It seemed every minute that passed brought another one. While he was silent, all she could do was wait. She couldn't poke at him or play with him to influence his mood. Nor could she read his expressions for hints about his emotions and assumptions, as she did during their conversations in bed.

All she could do was wait for him to be explicit.

With a fingertip she drew a shape on the desk, the outline of the gun that sat there the previous night and the blade lined up beside it.

"Did anyone touch you?"

"No," she said.

Because he knew better than she did what Hexam's men were capable of and would have his own fears about what they could do to a female.

Her guy didn't believe her. "Squirm, I swear to God, if one of them laid their hands on you—"

"They didn't. I'm not just saying that because you're far away. Nobody touched me against my will, I promise."

More silence. "You didn't..." he trailed off, quiet again. Nya opened her fingers on the desk as her brow came down. What was in his head? "Consent, did you?"

So if she hadn't been raped, he worried she'd screwed around on him?

"There was no sex involved," she said. "Not directly. I really can't talk about it on the phone."

"Why not?"

"I don't know where you are or what line you're on. I don't even know anything about my phone," she said, glancing at it again.

There was so much talk of law enforcement agencies listening in on phone lines. She might just be a regular Joe, but what did she know about technology and its capabilities to monitor and record conversations? She'd committed murder; she couldn't shout that out willy-nilly, she had to be cautious.

"Go to my place and shut the door," he said. "I can be home in twelve hours."

Stern commands were his way of masking concern. He had to feel like he was doing something. Right then, that meant getting to her. Except he was in South America doing a job that had to be done to solve their other problem. To come back now would make the trip pointless.

"No, you don't have to come rushing home, nothing bad happened."

His angry impatience forced his words out faster.

"Something bad is happening now, you're withholding."

She wasn't. "Trust me, Arch, Fella, nothing bad happened… to me, anyway."

"Nothing you're saying's making me feel better, Squirm," he said, with a sort of urgency to his severity.

Keeping herself calm, she didn't want him to read anything into her tone, so kept her voice as level as possible.

"Brett told me it would take you twenty-four hours to get back from wherever you are."

Turned out her tone was less important than her words.

"Brett?" he asked, spitting a laugh. "What the fuck, Squirm?"

She hadn't used his first name before and hadn't made the choice to now, it just came out. Stupid.

"Hexam."

His contempt was so thick she could hear the sneer in his breathing. "Yeah, I know who he is," Archer said, his irritation growing. "Why the fuck were you talking about me?"

Unable to react to his mood, the last thing she wanted was a fight. "Because we had a long conversation before I left with him," she said. "I didn't come to the decision to do what I did lightly. But when you hear what happened. You'll understand why I did it. And I hope you'll support me."

She'd been preoccupied by her own need for Archer and how he would make her feel better. At no point did she stop to think whether or not he'd agree with what she'd done.

Archer was supposed to have been a part of taking down those men. Except Hexam made it clear he was going to do it whether she was part of it or not. So she couldn't have waited for Archer, those men wouldn't exist when he got back. Hexam wouldn't have waited.

It seemed she'd done something right because he sounded more reasonable when he next spoke.

"Two things we have to get straight," he said. "You didn't have sex with anyone last night?"

"No."

"You didn't get naked or dance or suck cock or play with anyone's balls, did you?"

Narrowing her eyes, she sought clarification. Was he really accusing her of cheating on him? He might sound rational, but if he was going to toss accusations at her, she would put him in his place.

"Is this part of the same point or a new one?"

"Ny," he warned.

The reminder of the torture sat her straighter. Hexam had when he'd cut off that guy's dick, but she didn't think that counted. She herself hadn't touched anyone's tackle.

"No."

He inhaled. "Then I support you," he said, satisfied.

Amazing, he didn't even need details to be sure he was on her side.

Okay, good, they were back to themselves, she could, should, share one secret.

"There's one thing I should tell you that Hexam probably won't."

"Tell me."

Being paranoid, she kept it vague and prayed he'd follow. "Our friend, you know the one we marked together?"

"Yeah."

"He's a rat," she said.

Archer was quick to respond. "No fucking way."

She nodded at no one. Her surprised reaction had been the same, though she hadn't been able to express it.

"Hexam saw the mark. He got it out of our friend after he disposed of the mistress."

Interesting as she believed it to be, Archer took the news in stride.

"Hex wouldn't have told me that. Our friend still around?" Archer asked.

She guessed he was asking if Tulio was alive.

"Yes."

"Not a problem. As long as Hex lays off you 'til I get back, I swear our friend won't talk again."

Did Archer intend to kill him? She couldn't get her head around what she wanted for Tulio or Jonno or the last mystery man who'd pressed her into the wall. That guy had touched her, she had his number.

"I miss you so much."

His concern crept back in, his tone softened. "You need to fucking talk to me, Ny."

"I will when you come home. Is Tag with you?"

"No, and you're not fucking talking to him anyway. The slimeball piece of shit's been doing nothing but pissing me off this whole fucking trip."

"Keep your cool," she soothed.

It was ironic to be calming him down when she'd lost her shit last night.

"You're not gonna ask why we're down here or what we're doing?"

Specifics were irrelevant. For one thing, she wouldn't say anything on the line that could incriminate any of them.

"I know what you're doing."

He was down there to do a job for Hexam. She'd grill him for details when they were alone again. But as everyone kept reminding her, Archer was down there protecting her friend because he loved her. She didn't need any more details than that, not when her head was full of everything else.

Taking the conversation away from criminality, she diverted it to family. "Ester is worried. You should call her."

"Do you know how fucking difficult it is to make a phone call?" he asked, not taking her hint about the subject change. "And now I've got to waste my time calling Hexam too. He's gonna tell me a story, is it gonna make me want to rip him apart? Tell me now, did you start another war for me?"

Was he pissed off? Probably. If Tag was annoying him that much, he was probably struggling to keep it together and missing his knives. They had to still be in the closet at his apartment, he wouldn't have been able to take them on the flight.

She sighed. "I don't know what you'll be. I think you'll be pissed. But I didn't start a war. If anything, I think it will be easier now we're all on the same page."

"Okay, I've got to go phone this guy 'cause I want to rip him apart already, don't know if I'll let him get through the story."

His anger wasn't helpful, she needed him calm

because he had to keep his head focused to be safe.

"Arch," she murmured. "Please, baby."

"Don't leave your fucking phone anywhere else. I'll probably be calling you straight back."

"Don't. You're gonna be so pissed that you're gonna want to shout at me and you're gonna want to ask a zillion questions." That she wouldn't be comfortable answering over the phone. She smiled. "I'm holding that information to ransom until we're together again."

"You don't think I already want to come home to you? I don't need incentive. This shouldn't take us more than a week."

Stunned, she yelped. "A week!" Her heart broke. That was too long, she wanted him home now. "I can't wait a week, Fella!"

"Great, I'll grab a cab and meet you at my place later. Time me, bet my estimate is better than Hex's."

Scowling at his sarcasm, she put her own selfish needs aside. She had no control.

"I guess I have to wait a week if a week is what it will take," she said. "Do you need a ride from the airport?"

"I have never seen you drive," he said. "The picture on your license is cute though."

She laughed again. "How have you seen my driver's license?"

"Don't ask stupid questions," he said. It was gratifying to hear his smile too. "I thought you'd be pissed at me, Squirm. I thought you'd be making me grovel for weeks."

Inhaling, she reflected on how much had happened since she'd last seen her lover.

"If you called last night, I would've been. I was so embarrassed when I walked into that room and found the three of you together like you were having some sordid affair."

That seemed ridiculous. "Yeah, a three-way with your best bud and my friend, slash, enemy's sister. That's not a recipe for disaster. After all that action you gave me in the morning, I think we're good on the sex front for a couple of weeks."

"Don't count on it," she said, sultry and seductive. "I

wanted to crawl inside you last night. I've never needed someone so much in all my life. Hexam brought me home and I… I needed you, Arch. I needed you so bad."

Suspicious, he hummed before he spoke. "Because Hex turned you on so much?"

She didn't blame him for being unimpressed.

That wasn't what she'd meant. "Not in a sex way," she said. "And I know how you feel about emotional women. You'd have been in hell. I just needed to be in your arms."

"You will be soon. Once I come back, I won't be going anywhere without you again."

"I don't have a valid passport. You probably already know that."

"I meant I'll be sticking with you at home."

Seeing the opportunity for a tease, she knew it would calm him down if she played with him. "Are you rethinking us living together?"

"No, but I got you a new place."

Okay, that did surprise her, but in a wonderful way. Impressed and in awe, she licked her lips as she absorbed his fast work.

"Who flies all the way to Columbia to complete some dangerous mission, spends all night worrying that his girlfriend's been carted off to a gruesome death, and manages to rent a new apartment all while blazing through his long-distance minutes?"

"A guy of many talents."

"You just gave my landlord rent."

"In your shithole that didn't add up to much," he said. "And don't worry, I've already given him your thirty days' notice and booked your movers."

Incredible didn't begin to describe his dedication and thoroughness. Even with his flaws, she was amazed she'd lucked out with him.

"Chase," she said, her feet sliding to the floor. "Why do you love me so much?"

This silence wasn't like the others. It wasn't charged with judgment or suspicion. She wished he had her same depth of need to have his arms around her.

"You're a fucking mess and the most together person I know," he said. "You've never had anyone look after you. I know you think Tag does, but he's a bare minimum kinda guy." While Archer was an all-in sort. "I'm gonna show you it can be different. You need someone watching your tail. I plan for that person to be me for a long time."

It wasn't a sonnet, but it touched her heart. Except he wasn't the soppy sort, he had his moments, but didn't like to focus on mushy for too long.

"Okay, so where is this great new place you got me?" she asked. "Do I get to see it?"

"You don't need to."

Uh, okay, but she had to know its location. "I'd like to know what the neighborhood is like and how it's laid out. What if the neighbors are a nightmare?"

He exhaled a laugh. "The neighbors would kill for you, and you know the other two things already."

"How do I?"

"Because I rented you the apartment under mine."

Her smile was slow, but she'd never worn one wider. "You did not!"

"I did. I knew the guy was thinking about moving out, so I leaned on him 'til he made a decision on a schedule I liked. He called me after I left the apartment yesterday and told me he was moving out right then. The landlord knew I wanted it. Gave him a call, dropped off the deposit, and the first year's rent. The place is yours to move into this week. Your name's on the lease."

A bona fide one-bedroom apartment. Nya hadn't had one of them since living with her last boyfriend. She wasn't going to ask how Archer got her signature onto a legal document. It didn't matter when he'd done it for love.

"When were you going to tell me about this?" she asked.

"I just did. Your landlord is jumping for joy, he gets to double dip for a few months. I told him the movers will be coming to get your shit on Thursday. They'll pack up the place for you and move everything to your new joint. You don't have to lift a finger."

Because with the timing, Archer wouldn't be around to do any heavy lifting. It must have meant something to him to make sure she wasn't stranded with the job on her own.

"What made you pick there? Most guys don't want their girl breathing down their neck if they're not living together."

"Easy," he said. "I know how much you like being under me and now you get to live your life there."

The cocky bastard was right. She did love to be there. Being in such proximity would mean he'd never have to worry about walking her home after a date. They'd be going to the same place anyway. He'd never have to be apart from her when he had a captive either because he'd be able to monitor the guy from a floor away. He might even be able to spend the night. It would be like living together without actually living together.

"What if I was mad?" she asked, kind of messing with him. "I mean you ran away with my friend and another woman. What if I told you to go to hell?"

"Hell is anywhere without you," he said, ignoring her teasing. "I'm already here. And, you know, you fell in love with me while you were chained to my wall. If I have to go through that again to make you want me bad, I'll do it. I've got plenty of chains and plenty of time."

Nya wanted to kiss him, leap into his arms and thank him. It wasn't that she was unhappy in her current apartment, it was that he cared so much he wanted her to have a better place. He wanted her to be near enough to him, always be under his watchful eye.

"You're in luck. It just so happens, I love the idea. You can keep your chains in the closet."

"Good, 'cause the rent's non-refundable, so you're stuck there for a year at least. Now I know we're good, I've got to go."

And her mood dropped through the floor. "Already?" she asked, sinking back into her chair.

"I've got to call Hexam, don't I?"

Yes, he did, and he would be angry when he heard the story. Archer couldn't blame Hexam for what happened.

"Just remember to stay cool," she said. "No one forced me into anything. I know I can't ask you not to call him because you'll go insane if you don't know. So do it, listen to him, and then do what you're down there to do. Stay focused. Don't worry about me. I'm fine."

"Kristof didn't believe you when you said that either and the guy's only met you once. What do you think those words say to me?"

She didn't need him thinking too hard about her. "I'm fine enough that I can last a week until you get home, Fella. If you don't keep your head in the game there, you'll get hurt. Then you'll never be able to come home and yell at me, will you?"

"You got that manipulation thing down perfect, Squirm. Just promise me you won't go off with some other guy again. Your place, my place, Sizzle, no place else, understand?"

Casting her eyes up, she let him issue his commands. If they had said goodbye properly, he'd have said the same thing then. After Hexam told him what happened, Archer would probably want to tighten her leash.

"I understand. You just promise me you'll stay cool."

"Always."

"I love you," she said because she didn't care who was listening to that truth.

"I love you too, Squirm." The response made her grin. Either he was alone or didn't care who was listening. "Do me a favor. Stay at my place tonight."

"Your mom might—"

"Just stay there. Don't argue with me."

If it was going to make him feel better, it was pointless to fight. "Okay."

"Be good."

Those were his final words before the line died. Nya didn't know why he wanted her at his place or what purpose her location could serve. Maybe it was because Ester was there and there was strength in numbers. And she'd keep an eye on the place too. Archer wouldn't want it turned into his mom's party palace when he was about to have a new neighbor.

Whatever the reason, she didn't mind spending a night in his bed or even on his couch. It would make her feel closer to him. While he was so far away, she needed something to remind her he still held her close.

TWENTY-ONE

"YOU'RE ABOUT AS ORGANIZED as I am when I move," Ester said, picking up her wine glass.

The move was the previous day. She was pretty sure Archer paid over the odds for the movers, or maybe he'd threatened their lives, they were damn efficient. There was no company name on the van, could be they weren't even official and just owed her guy a favor.

It didn't take long to pack, she didn't own that many things. They got everything out of her place in less than an hour. Locking the door for the last time was always bittersweet; she had experience. When she returned the key to the landlord, he was grinning ear to ear, happy that he could let the place again and keep the money Archer already paid him.

Ester had arrived in Archer's car as the tail end of work was being done. With the burly guys doing the hauling, Ester was in her element, flirting it up, and voicing her upset at not showing up sooner. The woman may not have been all the way sober, but Nya appreciated having a ride to her new place.

The guys put her boxes in the space between the kitchen and the front door and took the time to position her furniture where she wanted it. They even went so far as to re-build what had been dismantled for the move. On their final walkthrough, the movers were eager to be told they'd done good work. Yep, that was confirmation Archer had put the fear of God into them.

Electing to put the couch in the same position as Archer's in the apartment above, she didn't kid herself she'd had a choice in that decision. Archer always grumbled about her crappy nineteen-inch screen, which could be why a monster of a flat-screen was already wall-mounted beside her living room window, just where Archer's was upstairs. A Post-it stuck to the top read, "This stays here."

It wasn't Archer's handwriting, didn't mean the message wasn't from him. Being on his secret Hexam mission didn't slow her guy down, he'd already put his stamp on her place. Her lover was a creature of habit. If having this screen would make him feel better, she'd let him keep it, made no difference to her. Ester, on the other hand, turned it on to explore the channels only to then declare with excitement that she had full cable.

Archer would have some explaining to do.

Between the move and racking up all the hours she could at Sizzle, fighting her urge to pine for him was a full-time job. As the days went by, it got tougher to ignore his absence as the days went by.

Ester spent most of the week with her and slept most nights at Archer's. The matriarch had taken to hanging out at Sizzle, probably because she got free drinks. Even Kristof popped into the club twice to check on her, although when he discovered Ester was there, he didn't hang around.

That Friday night she'd blocked off from Sizzle to get to work on unpacking her boxes. She'd got through most of the kitchen things. Not that she'd packed by room, everything was mixed together, so it was a lucky dip on each box she opened.

The apartment was laid out exactly the same as Archer's, and, to her surprise, it was as pristine clean. She'd never moved into a clean apartment, didn't know they existed. Before praising the previous tenant, she'd ask Archer if he'd had a cleaning crew in there before she arrived.

The carpets were plush, Ester was sure they were new, but couldn't say whether Archer bought them or if maybe the landlord put them in to impress his latest tenant. Archer had wooden floors and rugs, but she liked the comfort of carpet.

Sitting on the floor under the TV, she sifted through clothes, and drank wine with Ester. Though, as usual, they were drinking at a 1:4 ratio. With a box open beside her, she folded the apparel into piles on the coffee table, sorting them into what would need to be put in drawers and what had to be hung in the closet.

Her previous apartment didn't have a closet with a rail, so she'd stolen some of Archer's hangers to hang up her outfits. Some of which never made it out of boxes and bags in her last apartment.

The stack of boxes behind the door needed her attention. It didn't matter how many she emptied, there was always another waiting. Most of the important stuff was out, she thought, all that was left were the books, knickknacks, and pictures that she would have to find places for. Her bathroom closet looked kind of empty, though there were still stacks of linen and towels to find. It would all fill out eventually.

Ester loved getting involved in helping out, she'd been a godsend. Like they'd been conditioned, the television was on mute with the subtitles, neither of them was actually watching it. Ester had put it on earlier, suggesting she might miss her son, or be worried about him. Although she hadn't said anything out loud, maybe to spare her feelings.

"The guy next door is cute," Ester said, picking up the wine bottle to fill up both glasses.

She herself had only taken a mouthful from hers, but Ester still took the time to top off the difference.

"Which guy?"

Just like Archer's apartment upstairs, Nya was at the end of the corridor and there were another three apartments on this floor.

"Next door," Ester said, waving the bottle toward the kitchen before she put the bottle back on the coffee table.

"Georgie-Boy."

She smiled and folded a top. "For you or for me?"

George was nice, probably in his forties, he took care of his physique and had been nice enough to come out and ask the women if they needed help when they were carrying bags up from the car. That must have been when Ester got talking to him. Thinking about it, she had been alone in the apartment for a while before her pseudo-mother-in-law returned wearing a grin.

"For me!" Ester exclaimed and as outraged as she sounded, she followed it with a wink. "All the single men are mine, you're off the market. Sorry, daughter!"

Ester had taken to calling Nya "daughter" at every opportunity. What was a surprise at first had actually become a comfort. Having never known her own mother, it was nice someone wanted to claim her, even if she was just on the right side of thirty and really beyond needing a mother's nurturing.

"If you make a move on him, it might make things awkward for Arch when he has to kick his ass."

Ester picked up her glass to take a gulp. "No, he can do for me what he did for you. If Georgie-Boy stops doing it for me, we'll get him kicked out, and I'll move into his place."

Nya laughed. "You think Archer would like to have his momma next door to his girlfriend?"

"Maybe."

"It would make paying our bills easier," Nya said.

Every utility company she called stated her accounts were already in credit. The bastard had got to looking after her already and he wasn't even in the country.

"We'll make this the girl-only floor," Ester said, sitting back to stretch her legs up onto the couch.

There was a girl in the apartment opposite Nya's, about the same age as her, Ella. She'd already seen her twice. Once yesterday, when she was trying to tip the movers, who, of course, refused her money. And again that night, when she'd taken out the trash.

"We haven't seen who's next door to Ella yet," Nya said. "There could be a big, scary tattooed biker dude with a beard and a vicious dog or something."

Ester purred and narrowed her sultry eyes. "Oh, don't tease me, daughter. Maybe I should double-check that before I make my move on Georgie-Boy. Wouldn't want to start on seconds."

She wiggled her brows and winked again. "You're incorrigible!" She laughed. "You haven't been on the market for long, give yourself some time. Has Pierre knocked up his girlfriend yet?"

Ester glowered. "Who knows? I'm keeping my ear to the ground. Haven't heard anything yet."

Pierre was the last guy Ester had been with. The one who'd dumped her for the nineteen-year-old before Ester poked holes in all his condoms.

"Archer will hear if he does."

"I'm hoping there will be the patter of tiny feet closer to home soon," Ester said, then returned to her scowl. "Though I don't know how I feel about being Grannie Ester."

Nya was still laughing. "Archer doesn't want to get me pregnant yet."

Ester sat up, folding her arms on her knees, the wine glass hanging in her fingertips in front of her.

"You've talked about kids?"

Nya lifted a shoulder and a pile of clothes as she stood. "In a kind of indirect way, yeah." With one hand on the top of her clothes and the other on the bottom, she turned them over. "He'd said he'd knock me up if I asked."

Riling Ester was easy and could be a lot of fun. After delivering that bombshell, she slunk to the bedroom to put the clothes in her drawer. When she came back, Ester was on her knees, arms stacked on the back of the couch, wine still in hand.

"Then ask him," Ester said, shimmering with excitement. "Tell him it's what you want, and he'll do it."

"I don't know if it's what I want."

"Sure it is!" Ester exclaimed. "Sure, sure it is!" Ester leaped onto her feet and drained her glass. "This is too exciting, daughter!" She rushed over to hug Nya and kept an arm around her as she rubbed her belly. "Oh, a little baby, a hundred of them! How incredible would that be?"

Ester screeched with enthusiasm and ran away to the bathroom. She put Ester's frequent bathroom trips down to the volume of alcohol she consumed.

She went into the kitchen to make coffee, better that than drink more booze. Archer should be home the next day. When he showed, she wouldn't be hung over. No, he wished. She'd be ready and desperate to make up for lost time. Bastard would think twice before leaving her again.

Crouched at the lower cabinet in the unit connecting the breakfast bar, she searched for filters. She'd just picked a stack from the box when the front door slammed.

"Daddy's home!" Archer declared and something heavy hit the floor. Pouncing to her feet, she was struck dumb as his eyes slid around to her. "And, Momma, you've got some explaining to do."

Oh, she didn't care if he was pissed off. Be pissed off. Tossing the filters to the floor, she would've vaulted the counter if she was able. Instead, she darted around the breakfast bar, and sprinted across the room to leap into his arms.

"Oh, Fella!" She squashed her mouth onto his, wrapping both arms and legs around him. "Oh, you're home. You're home. You're home."

She punctuated the words with a kiss, each one longer than the last. His splayed fingers ran up her back, one to her ass, one into her hair, then they slid back the other way to switch places.

She didn't know whose tongue made contact with the other first, all that mattered was the thump of her heart, echoing in his chest, making their bodies pound in time together. When the generous length of his cock grew hard against her, she moaned, a long, languorous sound of pleasure. Rubbing against him, she used her arms around his neck to build a rhythm up and down. Dry humping him through his jeans, she gained momentum toward the release she'd been deprived of all week.

"Happy to see me?" he asked when he gathered her hair in both hands to pull her face from his.

"I'm not done with the kissing," she said, trying to

consume his mouth again.

He gave her hair a yank and pulled his head away. "I am pissed. We've got some talking to do."

"Whatever," she said. Her parted lips begged for his; she couldn't take her focus from his mouth. "One more, baby, please?"

"Don't wanna show me round your new place? Have a chat? Catch up?"

She shook her head. "Sex first."

"I guess we can take the edge off, horny one," he said, like he was doing her a favor, but she read the arousal in his smile.

He only got two paces when a scream stopped him dead.

"Oh! My baby boy is home!" Ester shrieked.

Honestly? She'd completely forgotten the woman was there.

She exhaled and Archer's forehead fell onto her. "A heads up, next time, maybe," he grumbled.

Ester came over, put a hand around his head and dragged him down to smack a kiss on his cheek. Nya didn't let go, she tightened her limpet hold and rested her head against her arm on his shoulder.

"You need to treat this girl right, Chase," Ester said, slapping the back of his shoulder. "You don't fuck off for some stupid job and leave her dealing with shit herself. The girl would've been lost without me."

"She has been a help," Nya said.

Ester went to grab her jacket from the breakfast bar. "Now you two have got a job to do," the woman said, winking. So the baby thoughts hadn't gone far. "I'm gonna get me a piece of Georgie-Boy, you two be naughty!"

Ester sailed out of the apartment and closed the door.

"Who the fuck is Georgie-Boy?"

"The guy next door," Nya said. "Ester plans to move in with him."

"When did they hook up?"

She nuzzled his neck. "For the first time? In about twenty minutes if Ester gets her way." That was as much of an explanation as he was getting. "You came home," she said, kissing the corner of his mouth. "I thought you were coming in tomorrow."

All week she'd been terrified he'd call to say there was a hitch and he'd be delayed. He'd left on Friday, and they'd spoken on Saturday, so when he'd said a week, she wasn't sure which day he'd be back. Anticipating the Saturday meant she wouldn't be disappointed, and she wasn't.

With her limbs coiled around him, her eyes closed, basking in his heat was all she needed to sustain her. Nya didn't care about details. Dropping down, she took his hand and led him across the room.

"The TV looks new," he said, following her. "Nice."

They both knew he'd provided it. "I don't need cable," she said, pulling him down the hallway. "It costs a fortune and I never watch TV."

"The cable's for me, not you, and neither of us are paying for it. I know a guy." He gave her a shove into the bedroom. She was happy to go, but he stopped to frown at the layout. "You've gotta move the bed."

Oh her love didn't like anything out of place. His headboard was against the left wall, while she'd put hers against the far wall, beside the window.

"I like it there."

He shook his head. She only had one nightstand; Archer went over and picked it up to take it to where his was in his bedroom. It took him less than three minutes to pull the bed away from the wall, turn it, and reposition it in the same place as his on the floor above.

"Better."

"Why did you do that?" she asked, hands on her hips.

"Because…" He jumped up to land on the bed before he kicked his boots off and sat up to discard his tee shirt. "When I'm lying here, I'm between you and the door," he said, stroking her side of the bed.

"And you think I might run away if you're not in the way?"

"I think if you piss someone off, they're gonna meet me before they even see you."

Even in his sleep, he was protecting her. Thrilled just at the sight of him, she let excitement drive her forward. There would be time for talk later and she'd missed their conversations in the wee hours, that would come after their physical reunion.

She wasn't wearing shoes, or even a bra, so she slipped off the straps of her dress, pulled off her panties, and threw herself on top of him to unite their mouths again.

He rolled over, putting her on her side of the bed, taking his place on top of her. "I think I'm gonna deprive you a lot more often."

Curling her nails into his hair, she pulled him down for another kiss. "You better fucking not."

"You get excited and happy when you haven't had any in a while."

Tilting his hips, he thrust his concealed erection against her center and the mass of it was enough to make her moan.

"Oh, I've missed you so bad," she whispered, licking his lips, savoring his taste.

Her hands wandered from his cheeks to his hair, to his shoulders, and his chest. The texture of his skin, the warmth of his heavy form as it pressed her down into the mattress, she wanted to remember it all.

She wished his jeans were gone because if they were, he'd be fucking her already.

"How much prep do you need?" he asked, shifting onto his side, suckling her as his fingers moved between her thighs that opened eagerly to accept his digits.

He squeezed the breast he'd been teasing and switched to kiss the one closer to him.

"None," she said, wriggling against his fingers that drummed against her clit. One then the other, they sped up and slowed down, teasing her. How did he have the willpower to hold back? "Fella, please."

Lifting her hips, she tried to force his fingers closer to her passage.

"You were naughty," he said. "So naughty, I nearly got on a plane and said screw your friend."

Archer licked her breast, kissed her cleavage, and traced his tongue up her sternum to her throat where he placed short, soft kisses to her tingling skin, distracting her mind. Two fingers plunged into her, jarring her back to reality.

She gasped and grabbed for his hair. "Archer!"

"I'm not sure you deserve to be fucked," he murmured near her ear.

Panic opened her eyes to meet his. "I'm sorry for the way it went down," she said, rubbing his torso, kissing him and curling in to treat his chest, his neck, his arms, everywhere her mouth could reach.

Rolling to his back, he scared her this might become a fight. Turned out all he was doing was getting rid of his jeans. When he was naked, she breathed in, and sat up; he grabbed a fistful of her hair and jerked her back to toss her head onto the pillow. Then she was beneath him, her excitement soared to fever pitch.

"You're in luck. I'm horny as fuck. So I'll take what I want from you, Squirm. And then you're gonna give me an explanation."

She hissed in a breath when he pushed his cock into her. It had been a week and she'd behaved. Although tempted to play with herself a couple of times, she hadn't. He scowled at the resistance he met.

"Relax, Ny. I'm playing, you know I want you, what's wrong?"

She shook her head and snatched his hips when he pulled away. "No, no, I want this. Please!"

"You're tight as a vice, I won't fit."

Forcing the tension from her body with an exhale, this was a clue how tight she'd been wound.

"Again," she said. He pushed forward, taking his time. "Just do it, Arch!"

But he withdrew. "I won't hurt you." How could she be so desperate for this and be putting up a wall? She hit the bed with both fists. "Easy, baby. I've missed my Cheerios, that's all it is."

Sinking lower, he kissed her most sensitive spot. Playing with her, he licked and sucked her clit. Stretching his arms over his head, he stimulated her breasts with his hands. Curling her feet to his back, she stroked them up and down, arching into the pleasure of his mouth.

Her worries lightened, her body loosened, and she relaxed long enough for him to push her into the spasm of orgasm. Before she'd even recovered, she sat up straight and urged him onto his back.

Climbing over his body, she snatched his cock to guide him into her. This time, he went all the way.

Sucking in his groan, he tensed. "Oh, your pussy's fucking stubborn," he said, grounding out the words as she moved on top of him. "The bitch wouldn't let me in 'til she got hers."

She grinned and bowed to taste herself on his lips. Sucking his tongue, the evidence of what he'd done sped her intent. Building a sweat, her hands went into her hair to lift it from her sticky neck.

Squeezing and groping her breasts, he sat up to bite one nipple and lap the other. "Oh, keep going."

The angle let her undulate her clit against his groin. After a few seconds, he scooped his arms around her, and dropped them to their sides, giving them both control of the rhythm. It slowed, drawing out the pleasure promised at the end of their exertion.

With their eyes on each other, she felt more love coming from him than ever before. Combing her fingers through his hair, she welcomed the lazy pace of the next kiss. It lasted a score of seconds, until his pelvis began to pound faster. She was forced onto her back while he linked his arms under her thighs. Pulling them higher, he forced his way deeper, and slanted her hips so his shaft could stimulate the cushion of desire inside her.

Her volume grew. Good thing her upstairs neighbor would never complain about the way she screamed when her lover sent her into the spiral of climax.

"Oh, you scream, baby. Scream louder."

Her throat was almost hoarse. She loved that he was happy for her to let go. Damn anyone and everyone who might hear her. Making a fool of herself, she screamed out the ecstasy he gave her.

Pulling her hips up, he slammed into her, and she curled her nails, scratching them across his shoulders, over his collarbone, to his chest. He swore and bit her lip at the same time he fucked his load into her.

When his seed was seeping into her every crevice, he pulled out and lay down at her side, saying her name again.

"Did that take the edge off?" she asked, stroking his chest with one hand because she couldn't move off her own back.

"Think it made it worse," he said, still panting. "This is gonna be a long night for you."

"Good. I missed you so fucking much."

He turned his head to make eye contact. "Now it's time to pay up," he said. "I've paid the ransom, now gimme the goods. I want every fucking detail."

TWENTY-TWO

NYA TOLD HIM EVERYTHING. Everything between her getting into Hexam's car and getting out of it again. She told him what happened, how it made her feel, her impressions of Hexam. More spilled out than just the facts. She covered what it was like to look into the eyes of Jamie's killer and know she'd done the right thing by taking his life.

Archer didn't interrupt much. He asked the odd question and wore a set expression of scowling concern throughout. Without slowing, she was clear about what had gone down. It hadn't been her intention to ever lie to him, she just wanted to tell him the story in person.

"What did Hexam say?" she asked. "After our call when you got in touch with him?"

Archer called her just one other time after that. The conversation had been short and clipped. No, he wasn't happy, but they'd ended with an "I love you," leaving her confident their relationship was secure.

"He told me you killed him… He enjoyed telling me he'd goaded you into it. He was proud of himself."

While thinking about it this week, she'd concluded Hexam had manipulated her. Yes, she was uncomfortable knowing she'd taken a life. Yet she couldn't feel guilty about exterminating such a monster.

"Are you mad?" she asked.

Lying on top of him, her body nestled between his thighs, her abdomen was resting against his cock. It had been requesting attention for a while, but he'd ignored it. With her breasts pressed into him, she had both hands on his chest. One of his was at the back of his head, while the other played in the ends of her hair.

"I'm mad at him," Archer said to the ceiling. "He shouldn't have put you in that room without me. And I'm mad at you."

He lowered his eyes to hers.

"Because I killed someone?"

For a split second, he was amused, though quickly switched back to pissed. "No. Because you did it in front of Hex. That was incredibly stupid, Ny."

"What choice did I have? He said he was going to kill them either way."

"So he didn't need you to do it for him," Archer said. "He wanted you to kill while he was standing there, after that you owed him."

Exhaling, she didn't like it, but knew it was true. "I know that," she said. "I'm not naïve. He told me it wasn't free. I know he'll want something from me."

Rolling over, he put her on her back. "Not anymore."

A confusing statement. "What do you mean?"

"The point wasn't to get to you, Squirm. It never was. The point was to get to me."

Hexam had said he wanted Archer on side, and how frustrating it was that her guy insisted on staying neutral. At worst, she'd thought that meant Hexam asking her to use her influence to persuade Archer into doing something.

Now it didn't seem like that was the case.

"What did you do?" she asked.

Having spent all this time talking about herself, she hadn't asked what he'd gone through that week.

"I cleared your debt," Archer said.

Dread chilled her. Sitting up to cross her legs, her knees rested on his torso.

"How did you do that?"

It wasn't his place to take on her burden. Archer had been in Columbia, saving Tag, because of her. Apparently, while down there, he was talking to Hexam and cleaning up more of her messes.

"Forget it."

"How did you clear my debt?" she asked. He didn't respond, just stared up at the ceiling. She poked his ribs. "Archer, don't ask me to be honest with you then ignore me." He still didn't answer, frustrating her further. "I didn't want you to clean up after me. I was willing to do whatever he asked because he did help me."

"That's what he wants you to think," Archer said, linking his fingers behind his head. "Is that how he got you to go with him? He told you he was doing you some big favor and you went along with it, convinced he was being a good guy?"

Being so desperate to get the story out, some earlier details may have been missed. "I told him I didn't trust him, and I refused to go. I must have said no five times."

"Still, you went," he said in a way that betrayed her decision displeased him.

His muttered words dismissed her. "Hey, I did what I did to protect you," she said, amped. "I wasn't going anywhere. I was willing to give it up. He told me everything and I said I didn't care. I said I was willing to walk away from Jamie's killers and never know what happened to them until he threatened you. It was his last play. He said if I didn't go with him that something might happen to you in Columbia. That there could be an accident, and you could be hurt. Killed, Archer. He threatened to kill you if I didn't go."

Why couldn't she get through? If violence came more naturally, she'd be inclined to punch him in the gut or grab him by the balls—he wouldn't ignore her then. Just as she was about to growl at him, his head moved.

His eyes descended until they landed on hers. "You did what?" he asked, his voice low, threatening.

"I…"

Frustration left in light of him growing so cold.

Archer sat up, scooped his hand under her chin and forced his mouth to hers. He didn't kiss her for long and didn't slip his tongue between her lips. He just drove their mouths together. Then he let her go, stroked her jaw, and picked up her arm to kiss her brand.

Puzzled by the power of his harsh kiss followed by such a tender one on her wrist, she didn't know what to say, what to think. Then he turned around to put his feet on the floor. Touching his shoulder, she was shocked when he bent down, away from her caress, to pick up his jeans from the floor.

"What are you doing?" she asked.

It was the middle of the night, and he lived right upstairs. Not like he had a long journey home to think about or an early day. They never had early days, both preferred the night, which they spent together whenever they could. They didn't have captives or nightclubs to worry about either. Why would he be collecting his clothes now?

He stood up to pull on his jeans and righted his boots to shove his feet into them. Stretching farther, he snagged his tee shirt from the floor, and pulled the laces on his boots without tying them. Stuffing his tee shirt into his back pocket, he fastened his belt.

"Archer?" she asked, rising on her knees.

Reaching for him, she didn't manage to touch him because he took a step back.

"We're through," he said.

The words were so blunt and detached that they were like icicles jagging into her. "Very funny."

But when she tried to reach for him again, he retreated farther, though she hadn't got close to touching him.

"I told you if you ever did anything to put yourself in danger to protect me, we would be done, Nya."

She couldn't ignore his seriousness, her pulse raced. "Archer, you don't mean that," she said with a disbelieving laugh. "You're not gonna leave me."

He scrutinized her body, the body he'd pleasured himself in not so long ago. A body he'd come back from Columbia to seek out. A body he hadn't been able to resist even when he had a thousand questions and was desperate for information. He'd put that curiosity aside to slide himself inside of her and satisfy them both.

Without another word, he turned around and left the bedroom. In astonished silence, she stayed still for a second before adrenaline drove her to leap up and run through her new apartment.

"Archer, no! I won't let you go." Already he was picking up the bag he'd dumped at the door. "Archer, hear me out! It wasn't like that."

He stopped, dropping his hand from the door to turn to her with his bag in his other fist at the back of his shoulder. "Be very careful before you think about lying to me."

Opening her mouth, her inhale stuttered. "I… I wouldn't."

"Did Hex threaten me?" he asked. "Did he threaten that something would happen to me if you didn't go with him?"

This was her chance. All she had to do was say no. All she had to do was backpedal and explain it hadn't been meant like that. She could even point at Tag and say Hexam only threatened him. But her guy knew her too well. Knew her integrity. Beyond that, no matter how she'd tried in the past, since they'd got together, she could never bring herself to lie to him.

"I love you," she said, skirting her puny kitchen table, pathetic in the space it was supposed to dominate. "What was I supposed to do?"

He grabbed the back of her hand when she tried to touch his jaw and lowered to growl in her face.

"You were supposed to tell him to go fuck himself, Nya. I'd have been so fucking proud of you."

"I couldn't take the risk," she said. "I couldn't take the risk he would hurt you."

Archer thrust her hand away. "And that's why we're through."

She leaped out of the way of the door as he flung it open. The slam that followed was so final, she jumped. Why? His loud entrances and exits were a part of her life… weren't they?

Naked, open-mouthed, and stupefied, she didn't know what to…? Her boxes by the door, half unpacked, drew her focus. Her apartment wasn't even set up and she'd already outstayed her welcome. The man she loved just dumped her.

A crash from above made her jump again. Archer was home. He'd just slammed into his own apartment. His heavy footsteps stomped across the floor. There were raised voices, feminine and masculine, the exchange was brief, then the footsteps carried on and another door slammed deeper in the apartment.

If he'd gone to his room, he wasn't worried about Ester's drinking. Maybe he'd told his mother to beat it. Frozen where he'd left her, it was…how? How had they gone from enamored lovers to strangers in a heartbeat?

No, shit, pull it together. She smiled. He didn't mean it. He couldn't. He was teaching her a lesson. Okay, she'd let him sulk for a night. She'd let him sulk and apologize the next day, in all his favorite ways. She'd pout, suck him off once or twice, cook him something nice to eat, then they'd talk about what happened on his mission.

After that, they'd forget this horrible night ever happened. Although her skin prickled and anxiety lingered, she checked the door was locked and went back to bed. Wasn't quite the same as the real thing, but at least she had the scent of him to keep her company.

Staring at the ceiling, he was right there above her, probably pissed as hell. They'd figure this out. They couldn't be over. She wouldn't let him walk away.

TWENTY-THREE

NYA WAS WRONG. Of all the things she'd been wrong about in her life, this was the one that counted.

Tag was crazy in love with Farrah, things were going great for them. She'd had dinner with the happy couple the previous night. It was weird to see her friend pandering to Farrah's canoodling. They weren't charged in their attraction to each other. From her point of view, there was little mature or intense about what they shared. Apparently, Tag liked Farrah's giggling and the way she stared at him with gooey eyes.

In other circumstances, she might have made fun of her friend for being so enamored. As it stood, all she'd been able to focus on was keeping her food down. They were so sickeningly in love and that was the last thing she could face.

Nine days. That's how long it had been since Archer told her they were over. He wasn't budging.

From the day following his departure, he wouldn't even let her into his apartment. Of the four times she tried, he glared at her like she was an unwelcome stranger before slamming the door in her face.

Yeah, she got the message.

Sizzle was the only thing keeping her going. When

she got tired of analyzing every noise in the apartment above hers, she forced herself to go out and spent most of her hours in Sizzle. The place had never been so efficient.

All jobs on the to-do list, that had piled up for years, were done. All the maintenance was up to date, as was the paperwork. She worked every minute of every shift, and that night was no exception.

Ester disappeared within a couple of days of their break-up. She'd come down looking for scraps of information. Apparently, whenever she mentioned Nya, Archer shut his mother down. She couldn't tell Ester the whole truth, his mother hadn't known about Columbia and Tag and Hexam.

Protecting his mother was important to Archer; she wouldn't beg the woman to make a case for her. Ester didn't stick around in the tough times. When things got tough, Ester found herself a new town, or a new man, or a new job. She was a party girl, interested in fun; she didn't want to deal with her son stomping around the apartment or any negative vibes.

Spending time with Tag wasn't an option. Her friend was too caught up in Farrah and his work with Hexam. Whatever had gone down in Columbia, it must have been successful. Still out of the loop, her friend refused to share details. He hadn't asked about her mood. Did he need to? After all these years, wouldn't he recognize the signs of her heartbreak?

No break-up in the past met the level of this one.

The music in Sizzle pissed her off. It grated on her every night. Maybe managing a nightclub wasn't a good career choice for her. Yeah, 'cause this was the time to quit her job. She'd just given up an apartment that was hers in deference to a place that wasn't. And she'd lost her man. She couldn't handle another change.

She wanted this night to be over.

"Your boyfriend's here," Jada said, popping up at the side of the register.

"My what?" Nya asked, her thoughts too busy to concentrate on what the girl was saying. "What time is it? Isn't it nearly—" Just at that moment the music went off, and she exhaled in relief. "Oh, thank God."

This was the point of the night when she could start urging her customers to the exits. But it would be another half an hour to forty minutes before everyone was out.

"I said, your boyfriend's here," Jada said.

Turning to Jada, she intended to correct her and tell her Tag wasn't her boyfriend. Then it hit her. Jada had never met Tag. Whipping around, she saw that yes, there by the entryway, on the other side of the room, was Archer.

Seeking her out? No, he had a group of her security men around him. They were engaged in intense discussion. Except she needed her security guys doing their jobs, not shooting the breeze.

So she closed the register, left the bar, and marched over to see what was going on. Eight of them huddled around Archer. All were twice her size, that didn't stop her pulling their arms to yank them out of her way.

"Can I help you with something?" she asked, fixated on Archer, irritated he'd bypassed her in her own place.

"No," he said. "Toddle off and count your money."

Oh, his condescension, she wasn't surprised.

"This is my job. I'm the manager. If you have a problem, I'm the person you need to talk to. These men have a job to do too. In case you hadn't noticed, the music is off, that means it's the end of the night, which is when these guys have to get everybody out."

Archer's jaw ticked.

"She's got a point," Robbo said.

Archer leaned back against the doorframe and folded his arms. "I'll wait," he said, glaring at her like he wouldn't be beaten.

Glancing at her employees, she smiled. "Let's see if we can break our personal best and get these people out in twenty minutes. I want to be home early tonight." She didn't care about getting home early. The security guys took her at her word and scrambled to get the patrons out. "If you're gonna conduct business, you should show up earlier," she said to Archer when they were alone. "Our opening hours are on the door. Don't tie up my employees; bring your own if you need shit done."

"I follow orders," he said. It was insulting he could show up and lounge around the place, using that damn cool, lazy voice, like she was just another obstacle in his day that meant nothing to him. "That's all I do these days."

Except Archer didn't follow orders, he was his own boss.

Her expression scrunched. "Whose orders?"

After pushing away from the doorframe, he walked away from her. The rabble was getting too much; this was the bottleneck that forced the large crowd to squash into the tight corridor to get out the front doors.

Archer didn't have the patience to listen to the din, but he could've answered her instead of being outright rude. She was sick of him ignoring her. The pity she'd lived with since they split began to change hue.

Spinning around, she spotted him heading for the office. Before he went in, he looked across the floor and made eye contact. Did he want her to follow him? Whether he wanted it or not, she was going.

Hurrying across to the office, she didn't know what to expect when she went inside. That room held memories for them, and they were about to make another one, positive or otherwise. This was the most he'd spoken to her since he'd left her standing naked in her apartment, so she'd hear him out.

Closing the door, she rested her weight on it and wasn't surprised to see him sitting in her chair at the manager's side of the desk. There was a blue file on the surface that didn't match Sizzle records.

"Hexam," he said and probably because she didn't understand, he explained. "I follow Hexam's orders now." Linking his fingers, he laid his forearms on the desk over the blue folder. "And so do you, Sweets."

That was the pet name he used in front of other people when they were doing something wrong, he had never used it in private before.

"Me?" Leaving the door, she went to sit in the guest chair. "Is this about—"

"No," he said and picked up the blue file to hold it out to her. She didn't know what would be inside but took it and opened it to read. He gave her just enough time to figure it out before he spoke again. "Your boyfriend signed over ownership. I guess that's what happens when you're in love."

She couldn't believe it. But he was telling the truth. This was a document transferring ownership of Sizzle from Tag to Hex.

"I can't… I can't believe it," she stuttered. "When did this happen?"

"They've been talking about it for a few days. He didn't tell you?"

She shook her head, numbed by the words in front of her eyes. "I had dinner with him before my shift. The bastard never said a word."

"I guess he thinks it doesn't matter. You get to stay on."

Whoop-de-do for her, instead of working for her best friend, who gave her free rein, she would be working for the only man who'd ever seen her kill.

"He's changing things. That's why you were talking to my guys." When she looked up, he was nodding. "And you're here to oversee the transition?"

"I don't know his plans. I didn't fucking ask," Archer said. That he didn't seem to care about being in the dark was a stark contrast to the man she knew. "I was told to come here and make sure those guys knew what was what."

Security was the first to know, probably because Hexam would want his friends to get priority and his enemies barred.

"Why would Tag do this?" she asked.

"His price for Farrah."

"Why would Hexam want a nightclub? Why would he want *this* nightclub?"

His eyes didn't warm. Her Archer wasn't the man in the room with her. This wasn't the man calm and patient with her questions, the guy who'd take time to explain whatever she didn't understand. He was switched off. Professional. Detached.

"Just keep doing what you're doing. When Hex wants to shake things up, you'll know."

"How?" she asked when he rose.

"He'll send someone."

"Will it be you?"

"I go where he points. Tonight he pointed here. Who knows where he'll point tomorrow."

Archer came out from behind the desk.

She couldn't let it end like this. "You're doing this because of me," she said, and he stopped halfway to the door. "You're running Hexam's errands like a bitch because of what I did."

He'd said he cleared her debt and now she got it. This was the price. Archer had agreed to put himself in her place, to put himself under Hexam's boot, freeing her from the position.

"I don't want you to do this, Fella," she said, leaving her chair, tossing the file to the desk. "I don't want you to compromise yourself. This isn't who you are. If I fucked up, I fucked up, that's my mess. Let me pay the price. You shouldn't."

He spun around with his fist raised, finger pointed. Anger crackled behind his gritted teeth, but he didn't say anything. The words were in his eyes, there was something he wanted to say, she almost felt them lodge in his throat. He'd never shied from giving her a piece of his mind before. Maybe he was different with women when they became his exes, maybe he'd shut them down and shut them out.

Good luck to him. She wouldn't give up without a fight.

"What?" she asked, getting into his personal space. "Tell me, Arch, what is it? What is it you're desperate to say to me?"

And he was. He had to be. There was no way he didn't have an opinion on what had gone down. When she poked a finger into his arm, he grabbed it. Physical contact. The first they'd had for nine days. It was ironic he held the same hand he'd tossed away before slamming out of her apartment.

Still, he didn't speak.

"You know we're only over 'cause you're an idiot," she said, taking a risk. Already she could see it paying off because his anger intensified. He'd only be able to take so much before he exploded. "You might be able to turn it off, Arch, but I can't. I don't feel any different. I love you. If you can so easily switch it off, like you've been doing these last nine days, then do yourself a favor. Go to Hex, tell him I'm a dumb slut from your past that you don't give a fuck about anymore. Let him charge me whatever he thinks I owe."

It made sense. Archer had done everything in his power to prove they were through. He hadn't called or tried to get in touch with her. He'd severed all ties. Even conversation with her when she showed up on his doorstep pissed him off, and he cut it off as fast as he could.

"You don't owe him jack shit," she said. "Anything he thinks *you* owe was cleared by whatever the fuck went down in Columbia. You're free and clear. You tell him to go fuck himself and make me proud of you. I got myself into this. I'll pay the price for it."

"No," he growled.

"Why not?" While he still had one of her hands in his vice grip, she rested the other on his hip. "It's no big deal if you don't love me anymore. If you don't love me, you don't care what happens to me."

She wanted him to admit he cared, but he never would.

"I gave him my word," Archer said. "I won't go back on that."

"Before you broke up with me. You gave him your word before you ended our relationship when you still gave a fuck about me. Hexam has the club and Tag is mixed up with Farrah. I'm in it all the way, Fella, there's no getting out for me. But you're not bound by any of that. You're not bound to Tag, Farrah, or this club. The only link you had to any of it was me. Getting rid of me might be the smartest thing you could've done."

Clarity changed her thought process and she put selfish desire aside. Lowering her hand, she was still in his grip.

After a second, he released her. She backed away until they stood four feet apart like strangers.

"Shit, Archer," she whispered. "It makes sense." The truth might hurt, didn't stop it being the truth. "Getting rid of me was exactly what you needed to do."

The tension in his shoulders eased until he said, "You don't know what he'd ask you to do."

"I don't care. I got to watch that bastard die. It was worth it. That lowlife, pervert, piece of shit—"

"Hex could put you on a street corner," Archer said. "He could send you to one of his downtown dens; you'd never see daylight again."

As far as she knew, Hexam was a drug dealer, his involvement in the sex trade was a mystery. Although, being as widely known and highly feared as he was, she'd guess he was involved in many different enterprises.

"I'd be a useless sex slave and we both know it," she said. "Guys would pay as much for my skills in the sack as they would for a day on the beach during a hurricane."

He narrowed an eye. "Are you fishing for compliments, Squirm?"

She smiled. "You were easy to please. I think any client who pays to be locked up with a girl would expect some serious bang for their buck."

He didn't understand her confidence, it was written all over his face. Confusing him was something she enjoyed. Nice to know she was still capable of intriguing him.

"It doesn't scare you that Hex could hurt you any second?"

"It terrifies me, almost as much as the idea of being tied to any bed but yours. But I have a choice, Archer."

"He won't give you one. If you're thinking about running—"

"I'd suck at that too," she said. "I've thought about this, you know, I've had a lot of time and you're right. Hexam put me in that position because he wanted something to hold over me and he probably did it to manipulate you too. But Hexam can't make me do anything against my will."

"Yes, he fucking can."

"No, because if he tries either of the things you just said, I'll turn myself in."

His expression blanched, it wasn't confusion, it was shock. "You'll what?"

"If it's a choice between working in one of Hexam's brothels, or twenty-five years in a cell, I'll take the second."

"You would hand yourself over to the cops?" he asked like the suggestion was unfathomable.

To her, it just made good sense. It was practical to accept that one day it might have to happen. "What would you prefer, Archer? To be raped every day until you died or three square meals and a roof over your head? I don't want to go to jail, but I'm not sorry for what I did, and if that means I have to do the time, I will."

He sealed his lips and took a breath. "You're a fucking mess and the most together person I know."

Going back to him, she laid her palm on his cheek. Those were the words he'd used when she asked why he loved her so much.

"Tell Hexam you're out. Fella, please. If you keep doing his work, he's gonna get you too, he'll own you forever."

"I won't turn my back on you."

She'd wanted to know he still cared, but the words didn't change their relationship status. Being without him broke her heart. The ache in her chest wouldn't ease until he healed it by claiming her again.

"I slept alone last night and the night before that, Archer… you already have. The worst thing I could ever have done to you was dump you, and you got to doing it before I could. I have no chips to play." She couldn't influence or manipulate him. If he'd done what he did for her because he was worried about losing her, that fear was gone, they weren't together anymore. "Your need to protect me is the same need that drove me to go with Hexam."

He shook his head once. "I don't accept that," he said, retreating from her touch. "I can't accept that, Nya. I told you straight not to do it. I told you if you did, I'd take that as a betrayal."

"How would I have lived with myself? Hexam made promises that nothing bad was going to happen, that I would get payback with the men I was desperate to see punished. He was offering something I wanted anyway. He promised me he'd let me go. He promised me he'd take me home and let me leave alone. And you were the one who told me he was true to his word when he gave it. I trusted you, not him."

Anger hardened his features. "So why did you keep saying no? If you were so goddamn sure you were going to be safe. You told me you kept saying no, why?"

What was the point of the conversation? Was there any chance of reconciliation? As stupid as it sounded, she would rather spend the rest of time arguing with him in that room than another minute anywhere else without him.

"Because I didn't want to upset you. I thought if I went you'd be mad that I'd taken the risk."

"I would've been. I was. I am. You did it anyway."

"I did it after he threatened your life and Tag's. And I never made you any promises, Archer. Every time you told me to give you up if I was asked, I told you I wouldn't be able to do it. Why are you surprised?"

His brows rose. "That you disobeyed me? I'm not. I'm pissed I let myself fall for you when I know exactly what you're like."

Offense made her exhale. "And what the fuck does that mean?"

Folding her arms, she cocked a hip in expectation of his explanation.

"You're emotional," he said. "Maybe it was too much to ask you not to betray me, you were always going to. Everything you do is driven by emotion. You couldn't give Tag up because of your guilt. Because you were stubborn. Because you knew you'd never be able to live with yourself if you just gave a simple address."

"You or your buddies would've killed him."

"And you," he said, peering at her. "You never look out for yourself. You're always looking out for someone else. If it's not Tag, it's Jamie, or my mom, and now me. Maybe I need to be with someone only occupied by their own interests like I am."

On a bark of a laugh, she gaped at him. "You think you look out for number one? My God, Archer, you went to Columbia to bail out my friend—a friend you can't stand—because you knew it would upset me if anything happened to him. You, right now, are standing here in front of me running errands for a man, resenting the shit out of it, and you're doing it because you gave him your word. Which you only did to get my ass out of the fire.

"Your mom embarrasses you. She pisses you off and frustrates you. She's everything you're not. She's loud and fun-loving, and careless and irresponsible. She's nuts, promiscuous, and messy! But you never turn her away. You never judge her. You mutter about her and act as if she's an inconvenience, but you pay every one of her bills, and let her stay with you whenever she needs to. And you punish every boyfriend that pisses her off, even if they don't really deserve it!"

"This is who you think I am?" he asked. "Because I pay my mom's bills and look after the pussy I'm fucking, you think I'm some kind of saint?"

The rising emotion got her blood pumping. "I know you're not. I know you've hurt people. I've seen you do it. I've seen your anger, heard about your jealousy. But I won't let you pretend to be some kind of demon. If that's what you need to believe to get through the day, and help you do the job, then do that. But that's not the man who shot me full of antibiotics to make sure my wound never got infected," she said, holding up her wrist to show him her brand. "That's not the man who pinned Bryant to a wall and scarred him for life for touching me when I said no."

One of them moved, maybe both of them, they were in each other's personal space, somehow. Her brand was close to his lips, got closer when he turned his head.

"You can get that removed," he said, curling his fingers around the back of her wrist to trace his thumb over the mark. "They use lasers to reduce the scarring. It's effective."

Did he think explaining that would make her feel

better?

"Never," she said, so protective of her scar that she was offended by the suggestion. "You marked me as yours and nothing changes that."

His ire landed on her. "Hexam isn't the only one who keeps his word. I said we were through and I meant it."

Because he was stubborn, or because he figured she was trouble and he was better off without her?

"I don't care if you hate me or if you never lay a hand on me again. That brand tells the world where my heart is. Nothing will change that."

He was so cool, but she couldn't calm down. "That brand tells the world you're mine and you're not."

"I am," she said. "Yours and waiting."

He wanted to be mad and was doing a good job of it. She could believe he wanted her to disappear, but hope sent her to her tiptoes praying he'd let go of his resolve. If he kissed her, the desk would be their next stop. A tryst would be all he'd need to remember they belonged together.

The door opened and Jada burst in, shattering the intimacy of the moment. The girl's glee dropped.

"Oh, shit, sorry," Jada said. "I guess I should've knocked. You guys could've been going at it in here."

A few weeks ago maybe, not anymore.

"That's okay, what is it?" Nya asked

Wasn't like she could curse the girl out.

"We just didn't know if you were gonna cash out 'cause the place is almost empty."

Hmm, word had got out they were trying to close up in record time. The other employees wouldn't complain about that. Her intention was to ask for another minute, right up until Archer walked away and slipped out behind Jada.

She sighed. "I guess I'll come and do it now."

The whole time she was emptying the register, she was aware of Archer around talking to different employees, most of them security. The others might be asking questions, now news they were under new management was getting around.

She didn't like the idea of working under Hexam and

had worked under people like him before. Usually when they took over any establishment, they wanted to make it their own. They could be looking at something as simple as a name change, or something as complex as a complete function overhaul. Hexam could turn the place into a restaurant. Although that would require getting new licenses and this probably wasn't a neighborhood people would come to if they wanted to eat out.

He could turn the place into a strip joint or a tittie bar, or even an S&M club. Whatever Hexam decided to do, she was apparently staying put. Though she'd have to find out if that was voluntary or not. If she could get out, this might be a good time to hand in her notice. Let them do whatever they wanted with the club.

The staff began to ask if they could leave and when she looked around for Archer, she didn't find him. He was gone. Her heart broke all over again. When they were together, he'd never let her walk out of there on her own. At the end of the night, he'd always wait for her, no matter how long she took. They were going back to the same apartment building and he probably had his car.

Instead of doing the decent thing and waiting to give her a ride, he'd fucked off. And that was the confirmation, they really were over. Archer was the adamant sort. The guy insisted on walking every date back to their doorstep and putting them into their home. He'd done it with her, but not anymore. Obviously, he didn't care whether she made it back alive.

It also meant she had to keep staff back while finishing up as fast as she could. By the time she walked out and locked up, the numbers she'd written down were already gone from her head. She'd recheck everything the next day.

Talking to Archer hadn't resolved anything. She felt worse than before, not better. The life she'd built was falling apart. She'd lost her man, might be losing her job, and her best friend was distracted by the latest pretty face in his life.

Enough. No more feeling sorry for herself. She had to start taking responsibility. Finding a purpose was the only way to get through this. How the hell was she supposed to do that?

TWENTY-FOUR

KNOCKING ON HIS DOOR gave her butterflies. The good kind or the terrified kind? She wasn't sure.

Two weeks had passed since their conversation about Hexam taking over the club. Archer had been back to Sizzle more than once, without uttering a single word to her. Security was fine, he could chat it up with them. And the other guys he brought with him? They got conversation too. And got to buddy with him any time he entered the office. Archer stayed as short a time as he could and left without giving her a chance to get him alone.

His apartment door opened. Just like old times, he was chewing on whatever was filling his mouth. Nothing in his hands to suggest what it was.

"Not today, Ny," he said around his mouthful of food and tried to close the door.

Slapping a palm onto it, she couldn't let him shut her down. "Business," she said. "I have business."

Pulling the wad of bills from her back pocket, she held them up at his face.

He frowned. "What's that for?"

"Rent," she said. "I figure since you're the guy who paid the landlord, I should pay you."

He swallowed and crooked a brow. "This is your excuse to see me?" he asked. Swiping the bundle of bills, he dug his thumb into the crease to count it. "I didn't ask for rent."

Nya lifted her shoulders as she slid her hands into her back pockets. "I know, but it feels right. I can't live in an apartment you paid for, using utilities you've covered, and not give you anything. I'm still watching your cable too."

"I told you, no one's paying for that," he said, stuffing the money into his jeans. "Cool, see you around."

He tried to close the door again

She pounced forward, putting herself into the narrow gap between door and frame. "I need a favor."

That got his interest. His brows went up and his mouth opened, though that may have been more to do with whatever morsel his tongue was trying to dig out of his teeth.

"This is gonna be good," he said, bringing his forearm to the frame again.

A female voice chirped from inside. "Okay, I'm going!"

Her butterflies became lead. Archer kept a hand high on the door when he opened it to let the speaker bounce out beneath his arm. She glared at the smiling woman, not just any woman, Ella, who lived opposite her.

"Hi, Nya," Ella said. "Archer, you're amazing, thank you."

The beauty frolicked away down the corridor. Archer leaned out the door to watch her go, completely ignoring Nya standing with her arms folded, making no secret of her judgment.

Only when Ella was gone did she slap both hands onto his chest to shove him.

"Are you fucking her?" she demanded.

"Maybe," he said, his casual attitude infuriating her. He rested his upper arm on the doorframe. "What's the favor?"

She was too mad to discuss her reason for knocking on his door. "I want an answer. I want to know if you're fucking her. I want to know if you're fucking my neighbor."

"I figured I'd work my way round the building. Ester and I are having a race to see who can screw the most tenants."

She squawked when her chin fell, and she shoved him again. "You better be messing with me, Fella! I didn't give you permission to screw around."

"Permission?" he asked. "We haven't been together for a month."

"Twenty-three days," she said, correcting him. "And you might have cut me loose, but I didn't give your cock permission to sniff around."

"So that's how it is? You get to do what you want, and I'm supposed to sit here celibate?"

Smug, she liked his concise question. "Sounds good to me," she said and wouldn't apologize for being territorial.

He grabbed her hand to hold her wrist between them. "So why you wearing this again?" he asked about the cuff she'd only ever worn to conceal her brand. "Finally realize you don't want to be owned by me anymore?"

Ah, good that he'd noticed. Her satisfied smile bridged the time it took her to unbuckle the cuff.

"You told me to have it removed if I didn't want to belong to you anymore."

Shedding the cuff, she held up her wrist, and he got a shot at being shocked. Leaving the doorframe, he straightened back to full height and took hold of her wrist, elevating it enough for him to examine.

"So you went and did the fucking opposite," he murmured, tracing his fingers around the lines on her arm.

She shivered at the contact and closed her eyes, relishing the sensation of his skin on hers. Instead of removing the brand as he demanded, she'd gone to a tattoo parlor and had it outlined in black ink.

The original brand was still as it always had been, but now it was unmistakable. It couldn't be fobbed off as any kind of accident. Archer's initials were emboldened by careful work. With a clear idea, she insisted the artist use deliberate thick lines around the outer edges and the insignia inside. The design accentuated the art of the mark she was proud to wear.

"Nya, what the fuck did you do?" he exhaled.

"I put the cuff on because it's still healing," she said, snatching her arm away from his judgmental grimace. "I got it done a week ago, it's getting better."

Attaching her cuff, she didn't have to see him glare to know his expression was tight. "You don't let go, do you? If I told you to suck my cock right now, you'd do it."

"Yes," she said, finishing with the buckle. "I probably would." She landed her fists on her hips. "If you hadn't just been balls-deep in Ella's pussy."

"If you'd come round an hour earlier, I could've had you both…" He pondered for a second. "That's an interesting factoid to record for later."

She couldn't tell if he was playing with her or not. While mad, it was easy to focus on that powerful emotion. Then she got an unwelcome flash of Archer's body entwined with Ella's.

Nausea brought her hand to her mouth.

"You look sick," he said. "Pale." He put the back of his hand to her forehead. "Did you take your pills? Did you fill your script? You better look after yourself, Ny. If I have to come down there every day and force the goddamn pills down your throat, you know I'll do it."

His anger betrayed a sensitivity she hadn't seen since they were together.

"I might stop taking them just to see if you back that up," she said. Archer coming down to her apartment every night would be a dream come true. "Except if I collapse in the middle of my apartment, it would take weeks for anyone to notice. Sizzle would have to run out of beer first. I'd definitely be dead by then."

The scowl he wore was a continuation of his worry. "Where the fuck is Tag?"

She shrugged. "With Farrah. He's not really checked in for a while. I'm happy he's so in love. I can't argue with that. I know what it's like," she said, making herself smile because she meant it, though she did miss her friend too. "I know what it's like to be caught up in a person like that and I can't argue he hasn't gone to hell and back for her."

"I don't get it."

That wasn't surprising, the men never saw eye-to-eye. "Tag didn't get how I fell in love with you," she said. "He'll come back to me. Once him and Farrah settle into a groove and they get over the excited sex part at the start." Nya grinned. "This is how it is with Tag and me. Sometimes we don't talk much for a few weeks or a few months. If I needed him, I could call."

"But he might not be there," Archer said, still not happy. His tension was flattering. "The guy's selective with when he gives a fuck about you, Ny. Your friendship isn't equal. When he needs you, he wants you a hundred percent. But when you need him—"

"I don't need him," she said. "I mean, yeah, it's been tough. I won't deny that. I could never lie to you. But Tag can't do anything to make it better. He can't force you to love me. He could try, but we both know how that would work out."

This time when he said nothing, she couldn't guess what he was feeling, if he was feeling anything at all. Taking the wins when they cropped up, she liked he was moving beyond his cold attitude toward her. Although if what he'd said about Ella was true, he'd moved onto cruel. She didn't like that any better.

There wasn't much he could say to that, so it became awkward.

"What's the favor?" he asked, returning to her original reason for knocking on his door.

"It's not a big one, not like before when I was the one sucking your cock. I need a meet."

"With who?" he asked, so dubious that he tilted his head away from her.

"Hex."

When Archer stood up straight to dig his hands into his pockets, he wasn't enthusiastic. "It's not safe."

"What do you care?" she asked, stating what was obvious now.

If he was half as heartsick as she'd been, staying away from her would've been impossible. Especially given their proximity. Much as it ripped her apart to know his love hadn't endured, losing her hadn't made him blink. After twenty-three days, she was getting to a place of facing the facts. Archer, her Fella, wasn't coming back to her.

"Tomorrow night. At the club. I have to talk to Robbo and the guys anyway, so I'll be around."

"What are you gonna do? Jump in between us if he gets too close?" she asked, trying not to laugh. She'd love it if he was still that protective, but his leaving her at the club without a care showed how little he valued her safety these days. "If he wanted to kill me, he'd have done it when he was holding a gun, and we were alone with four corpses. And he has no interest in raping me, he can have any girl he wants."

"He can't have you," Archer said, adjusting himself in the space between his door and its frame.

Everyone else got invited in for a conversation like this. That courtesy wasn't afforded her anymore. Archer didn't like conducting business in public, but he kept her out, separate from his personal life.

If he'd been having sex with Ella before she arrived, maybe he didn't want her walking in and witnessing whatever carnage they'd created.

"I'll set it up," he said.

"Thank you."

Maybe they could be friends, maybe that's what this was a sign of, that he was willing to give a little. Maybe they could still be a part of each other's lives. Or maybe she was just being filtered into Archer's long list of contacts and that was why he wanted them on good terms.

She side-stepped, reluctant to leave, but there was no reason to stay. Not until his next word reminded her of something she hadn't considered.

"Payment."

"Right," she said, nodding. A self-conscious quiver shook her windpipe. It hadn't occurred to her, Archer always got paid for everything he did. Except she'd just handed over all the money she'd managed to scrape together. "Sex on demand works for me."

Her joke just came off as awkward. She folded her

arms over her abdomen.

He smiled. "Been there, done that."

Ouch. She didn't say the word aloud but wanted to. So he'd had her and didn't want her again? Nice.

"I'd do no make-up for a week, but you wouldn't be around to know if I followed through. I don't have a lot of cash, but if you let me make payments… You know where I live, and where I work, I can't run out on you."

"I don't want your money."

The certainty in his voice betrayed he had something in mind.

"Then what do you want?"

He looked down the corridor toward the stairway at the end, but there was no one there. Then he licked his lips and came out of his apartment. His choosing to get close, to crowd her, was a thrill.

Although he was looking at her, and she'd embarrass herself, she closed her eyes, drugged by his scent. No scent of Ella or any other woman. This was just Archer. Just her man.

He scooped a hand under her chin and dropped a straight arm onto her shoulder to shake her out of her daze. "The murder weapon," he said. "I want the murder weapon."

Why would he want that? Surprised by the request, she stumbled away from his touch, backing up to the hallway wall.

"Why?"

He was intent. "Do you still have it?" She nodded. "I need you to give it to me."

Shocked and offended, she was confused. "Is this about your thing for knives?" she asked. "Because you have a thing for collecting them? You think—"

"Knives?" he asked, surprise and curiosity hit his expression at the same time. "Hexam gave you a gun."

That was part of the truth. "He gave me both."

Again, his intrigue was perplexing.

He stood tall to peer down at her. "Nya, what did you use to kill him?"

Horrified he'd said those words so loud in this public space, she rushed forward and pressed herself to his chest, urging him backward into his doorway.

"We can't talk about this out here," she hissed in a whisper, searching for eavesdroppers. "Why do you want the weapon? Does Hexam want it? Is he going to use it against me?"

Archer grabbed the back of her neck, reversed through his apartment door and gave it a kick to close it behind her. When they were inside, he planted her against it.

"Answer my fucking question, Nya. How did you kill him?"

"I… I stabbed him," she said, replaying their bedroom conversation.

Didn't they already cover this? What had she said? What had she missed?

"Where?" he asked, picking up her hand and pressing it flat on his chest. "Where did it go in?"

With two fingers, she fumbled his shoulder and let them slip down. Closing her eyes, she tried to recall the image of the man before he fell. She pressed them to the top of Archer's left pec.

"Right here," she said. "I had to hit him hard."

Her voice broke. She hadn't grieved or thought about that night for a while. Losing Archer had taken priority. Her eyes would be glistening, Archer hated emotional women. Why the fuck couldn't she keep it together?

She swiped at her tears, but he grabbed her hand. Covering it with his own, he pressed the tips of those two fingers back to the same point.

"You're sure, Nya? Focus."

"I think, I… I don't know."

This was important. Archer was hyper-alert. On the spot, she wasn't confident her answers were all the way accurate.

"Was he bigger than me? Shorter?"

"He was kneeling," she said. "I told you the room was dark and…"

Her inhales turned into sharp, short pants. She didn't want to lose it. It was too much to be talking about this in an apartment she hadn't seen since she was happy, with the man who'd broken her heart.

Archer dropped to his knees, keeping her hand right there on his chest. "Like this?" he asked. "Show me what you did."

Desperate, she wanted to forget, not relive the horror of that night.

"Why are you doing this, Archer? Please don't make me talk about this."

"I want to see the blade. How long was it? Like this?" he asked, holding up his forefingers about twelve inches away from each other.

"No."

"Bigger or smaller?" he asked. She guided his hands closer until they showed the distance between the tip of the blade and the butt of the handle. "This was the blade or the whole thing?"

"The whole thing," she murmured in a small voice.

"Did you aim straight or did it go in at an angle?"

God, Archer seemed to think about everything. It came back to her now, the only thing she hadn't done was describe the kill, she'd just said she'd killed him. Hexam was talking, he cut off the gag, the rapist angered her and then, "I killed him." Those were her three words to Archer while they were lying together downstairs in her apartment before he ended their relationship.

He stayed on his knees but cupped her moist face in his hands. "It's important, Squirm. I need you to think for me. Can you do that, baby? For me?" he asked, brushing his thumbs over the tracks of tears on her face.

"He told me to suck his cock," she said, her words only just loud enough to be heard.

"And that's when you did it?"

Raising her fist, she held an imaginary weapon toward Archer's chest, as she had in that room. "I had it like this. He told me to do all I was good for and then I…"

She lifted both hands together above her head then plunged them down, letting them come to rest against him, although her own blade had never gone that deep.

"Did it go all the way to the hilt?" he asked, clasping

her balled hands in his.

She shook her head. "I don't think I was strong enough."

His disbelieving exhale was nearly a laugh; she cast off the haze of the memory.

"Oh, Squirm. We're fucking idiots," he said, scooping both hands under her chin, he rose and captured her mouth in the same breath.

Unexpected? Yes. But there was no chance she'd reject it. Clinging to him, she wrapped both arms around his neck and angled her head to let his tongue delve deeper into her mouth. He tasted so good, like the essence of life she'd missed for twenty-three days. This was the medicine she needed to sustain her, and it came only from him.

The fervor in his kiss forced her hard against the door that blocked her entry on so many recent days. When she curled her fingers into his tee shirt to hold on with tight fists, he broke away.

His stunned expression was quickly covered by the fist he pushed to his mouth. "Fuck," he said. "Sorry, forget that happened."

Feeling as bewildered as he looked, she struggled to get herself together.

One thing she was certain of? "No," she said. "No forgetting."

She tried to pull his fist away from his mouth, but he uncoiled her fingers from his shirt and ran a hand through his hair as he paced away and turned his back on her. She stayed against the door, panting, trying to remember what day of the week it was and what reality she'd stumbled into. It wasn't one she wanted to leave.

"Fella?"

Shutting down emotion was easy for him. "Bring me both, the gun and the knife, and I'll set up your meet with Hexam."

"But I—"

"That's it, Nya," he said. "I shouldn't have kissed you. It didn't mean anything." Just when she thought she was making headway, he shut her out again, returning to his discrete self. "Get out of here. We're done."

It didn't matter that she didn't want to leave. She searched behind her for the handle and released herself back into the hallway. Even closing the door was too much to master. Her mind was too messed up to think about courtesies.

"Ny."

Turning to the sound of her name, she saw Archer in the hallway just outside his apartment.

Torn as he looked, she hoped to God that wasn't pity she read on his face. "What is it?"

He took a breath and his lips moved, but no words came out. Maybe he'd thought better of saying whatever he was thinking.

On his second try, he did form a sentence. "I didn't fuck her. I'm not fucking her." He wouldn't want her to be so thrilled by that news, but relief and excitement surged up inside her. Maybe if she went back to him, now, another kiss, another—she waited too long, and he cut her again. "There will be someone someday. Soon. Not yet. But someday."

So he was making it clear there was no hope for them? He didn't want to hurt her, and he did pity her enough to toss her scraps. Not much consolation.

She needed to see Hexam to find out what lay ahead for her club. Kissing Archer gave hope. Except every time she thought there was a chance for them, he put up a wall. Was she making a fool of herself for no reason, or would persistence ever pay off?

TWENTY-FIVE

SIZZLE WAS NOWHERE near capacity. It was flat-out quiet and she couldn't figure out why. Business had been booming recently. Word could be getting out that Hexam had taken over. At first, she'd figured that news would be good for business. From what she was seeing that night? Not so much.

There were maybe only twenty people on the dance floor and ten at the bar. They could take three hundred at capacity and other than the ten or fifteen milling around at the tables, there was no one else around. The lines weren't looped around the block either.

By this time of night, there were usually groups of guys and girls coming in, at least ten to fifteen strong, looking to hook up. Men should outnumber the women five to one. The place should be alive and buzzing. So far, people seemed to be coming in pairs or threes, four at most.

There was one group of rowdy guys who'd just moved from a table toward the bar. Four of them, drunk before they even arrived. She didn't mind guys like them on nights she needed a distraction. Not until… She was collecting glasses when the guys closed in around Jada. Taking the glasses to the bar, she slid them onto the surface, and went straight over to extricate her employee.

Pasting on a smile, she wouldn't make a scene if she could avoid it. "Evening, guys, are you having a good time?"

"Great time!" one of them announced, punching his buddy in the arm.

"We want a private waitress—this private waitress," one of them said, crowding in behind Jada as another sidled up in front.

"Well, you pay for the VIP level and we'll talk," she said, insinuating herself between Jada and the guy in front of her. Pulling Jada out, she gave her a shove to put some distance between the youngster and the thug. Nya nodded to the collection of glasses she'd put at the other end of the bar. "Go wash up those glasses."

Jada hesitated but scurried off. Nya was capable if nothing else, and she'd been dealing with rowdy, handsy customers in her various jobs for years.

"Right, guys, you've got to treat a girl with respect," she said, the four closing in around her.

"Guess you want us to respect you," one guy said. Some of the innocent glee was gone from his expression. "You stole our other fun."

One thing she'd noticed since Hexam took over was the men who frequented the club were harder, coarser. She tried not to let experience cloud her decision-making. These thugs would bully her unless she stood up to them. As manager, she couldn't afford to get a reputation for being weak.

"You don't get that kinda fun here," she said. "You can go a couple of blocks over and find yourself company if you're willing to pay for it."

She tried to walk away, but one of them snagged her shoulder from behind and drew her into the circle again.

"I think you should keep us company."

A hand snaked around, beneath her arm, and cupped the underside of her breast. The guy to her right, who sneered, groped the other.

"You don't want security kicking your ass out," she said.

The tallest one moved in front. She swallowed,

keeping bravado high while her heart embraced the anxiety. Security had been stripped back since Hexam took over. Most of the systems she'd put in place were dormant. Tag had been hesitant to implement cameras and Hexam didn't like the idea either.

"You dress all slutty to get our attention and you've got it," the tall one said, snatching her to spin her around.

The one who'd grabbed her breast from behind shifted aside to let his friend thrust her down over the bar, then there was a hand on her ass under her skirt. She kicked back, and whoever she hit, swore. Good. Pain worked for her. Inflicting it on lowlifes was no problem.

"You crazy, fucking, whore!" he called out.

Something flew past them and lodged in the bar by her head, a knife… one she recognized. Pulling the blade from the wood, she rebounded, ready to fight. Except she didn't have to do a thing.

One of the bastards was already on the floor.

"Archer," she said, unable to believe he'd come to her aid when she hadn't even known he was there.

He smacked the second in the jaw, elbowed the third who came at him from behind and knocked the fourth out with a head-butt. Security came rushing over.

"Get these fuckers out of here," Archer said, snatching his knife to re-sheath it on his belt before grabbing her arm to drag her along the bar.

She needed two or three steps to keep up with his strides. Didn't matter to him, he was intent on getting to the office. As soon as they did, he threw her forward and slammed the door.

"How come wherever there's trouble you're always right in the middle of it?" he demanded, touching his upper lip.

His nose was bleeding.

"Archer," she cried out, grabbing hold of him to haul him into the manager's chair. "Oh, God, they hurt you."

Touching the blood under his nose, she pulled a tissue from the box behind her and pressed it against the stain. He snatched it away.

"Leave me the fuck alone, woman, stop fussing," he said, batting her hands away when she searched his hairline and jaw for other wounds. "Who let those fuckers in?"

She propped herself on the edge of the desk. "We're not choosy when the club is this quiet."

Taking the tissue back, she folded it and wiped the remaining smears of blood to check if the flow had stopped, looked like it had.

"Hex didn't want a lot of people in tonight," Archer said.

Ah, so the order to limit entry had come from the top, at least it wasn't a sign of Sizzle's prospects.

"You shouldn't be hitting people," she said, balling the tissue in her hand. "You don't work here. There are guys paid to do that... insured to do that."

He scoffed. "Oh? You do know that?" he asked, unamused. "Those are the guys you should've called when you saw Jada was in trouble."

Trust him to be snide and condescending.

"There wasn't trouble. I just didn't like how close they were to her."

"She told me," Archer said. "I wasn't in the fucking door three seconds and your latest project comes running up telling me some guy has his hands all over my girlfriend's tits."

"Your girlfriend?"

"Her words, not mine," he said as if he knew she might get ideas. "Consensual or not, you're lucky I didn't cut him open. Don't do that shit when I'm around, you knew I'd be in tonight. Don't play games with me."

Why was he so keyed up?

"What shit?" she asked. "I didn't do anything except my job. I've been dealing with drunk perverts all my life, since long before I ever met you. I told them to pay a hooker if they wanted action tonight."

"But they chose to take it from you instead," he said, standing up. "You can't sass drunk fuckers, Nya. Not Hex's men."

Oh, really? "I can sass whoever the fuck I want."

He loomed above her. "So you wanted those fucks to

get hold of you, did you? You wanted their hands on your cans and up your skirt. Maybe you wanted him to fuck you over the bar, did I interrupt? Strip off, sweetheart, I'll call 'em back here for you. Have a private party."

"Now who's sassy?"

Leaning over her, he forced her to angle back as he set two heavy fists in the middle of the table behind her. "I can sass you any goddamn time I want, you'll shut those fucking sweet lips of yours and take it."

Parting her legs, she raised her knees to his hips. She wasn't intimidated, she was aroused, her body awakened to his.

"I'll take whatever you give," she said. "Those dirty little fucks couldn't handle a woman like me. It took four of them to try to measure up to what I need. They'd never make the cut. They're nothing. Not worth my attention."

"What guy is worth your attention?"

Because he was so close to her, she breathed in his exhale and arched. "I like neat freaks with OCD about sharpening their blades. I need a man who's handy with a knife and will completely take over my life. And my man better have a nice big cock for me to ride when I'm wet. One that'll fuck me any time he wants, without asking permission."

"Is that what you want, Ny?" he asked. When his fingertips brushed her inner thigh, her breath hitched in her throat. "My cock?"

"I want all of you." Shifting her hips, she forced his fingers against her underwear. "But your cock's a good start."

She liked that his breathing sped up, liked that the temperature in the room was rising. She wanted to feel like this, like her skin was too tight for her body. Like the meaning of her life was to take his cock any way he chose to give it.

Archer had never hesitated to screw her in the past, but they'd never been broken up before.

Unzipping his fly, she maintained eye contact and loosened his belt. "Come closer," she whispered.

When she inched her hips to the edge of the table, he rubbed the cotton between her thighs. Maybe it was just his instinct to pleasure her or any pussy at the end of his fingertips, or maybe he wanted this too. Rocking in time with his rhythm, her own hand slid into his jeans where she found him just as immense and solid as she remembered.

"Oh, Arch, you're hard for me," she exhaled.

Relief came with knowing she could still excite him.

While she pumped her fist up and down around him, he grumbled something she didn't understand and shoved her skirt up. Hooking one forearm around her hips, he yanked her off the edge until just her spine was pressed into the sharp angle of the tabletop.

In time with that abrupt move, she tugged his erection to her core.

"Nya," he warned.

Overwhelming want radiated from him; she wasn't the only one who needed this union.

"We're so close," she said, pleading bled into her tone.

She wasn't sure if the desperation was for herself or him.

Hooking her underwear aside, his actions weren't backing up his reservations. When one of his fingers slid into her, she came all over it, yelping out his name. Waiting over three weeks for release, she'd started to think it would never happen.

Recovering, she laughed and lay down to unbutton her shirt. After undoing the third button, his hand left her core and landed on hers to stop her going any further.

"What's wrong?" she asked, sitting up again. "I'm yours. We need each other. It's been too long."

"We're not doing this."

As he was buckling his jeans, his resolve returned.

She was just plain confused. "Archer, I don't get it. You want me or you don't."

"It's not as simple as that."

"It is," she said, hopping off the desk to crowd him. "You have to tell me, do you love me?"

He probably hadn't expected such a curt question. Filling the silence might ease the mood, but she wouldn't do it. She'd wait and make him answer. Except the office door opened and while she was trying to see who'd come in, he buttoned her shirt.

"Arch," came the bass of Hexam's voice. "Leave us alone."

Archer passed her and went out of the room. Seeing him leave her alone with a dangerous person without looking back was unsettling. Hexam came over and hugged her, he actually hugged her. She was so thrown by the gesture that she put a hand to his chest and stumbled away.

"What are you doing?"

"Those who kill together have a special bond," he said, brushing a knuckle on her jaw. "What did you want to see me about?"

"I want to know what you're going to do with this place," she said, sitting down in the manager's chair, though it was probably his rightful place.

Hexam examined the office. Now that it was his, she guessed, he was more interested than before.

"For now it stays as it is. You'll have seen we've had some staff issues, we're fixing that. You're gonna have the same customers, but there is a 'no-fly list' for people we don't want near. Archer has a face-book for you. Lets you know who to look out for and who to have tossed out on their ass if they slip through."

"Everything stays the same?"

He'd sauntered around enough of the office that he was happy to drop into the guest chair and slapped his hands on the arms of it.

"We'll have a revamp probably in a month or two. Shut the place down, do some structural stuff. Spruce the place up."

"You're not gonna change what we do?"

"Are you worried I'll turn the place into a strip joint?" He shook his head. "Not in the cards yet, but with me you never know what I'll think when I wake up in the morning."

That wasn't reassuring. He took a card from the pocket of his jeans and slid it across the desk.

"You don't need to go through Archer if you want to speak to me, boo. You're one of the few with direct access."

"Why?" she asked, picking up the card.

He shrugged. "Because your best friend's dating my sister," he said. "You're the manager of my club, and 'cause, like I said, we've killed together."

No mention of Archer at all. Did Hexam know they were no longer an item? Probably didn't care either way.

"I have a couple other clubs downtown," he said. "Gimme a call and we'll check them out together. You'll see what our brand is all about."

She had no intention of dating this man. If it was a professional meeting, she would love to see what his other clubs were like. To see behind the scenes, something she wouldn't get if she went alone. Archer would probably be able to get in anywhere and see any part of the building. Too bad she'd already asked him for one favor this week and wasn't sure what quota people got. And, of course, there was the sore point, she had nothing to offer in payment.

"I can't believe you're okay with Tag and Farrah's relationship."

Could he have sinister motives for letting them see each other? She didn't expect honesty.

"I'm not okay with it," Hexam said. "But your buddy Tag has tied himself in knots, it's funny to watch what I can make him do."

Her friend was a source of amusement, but Tag was happy to go along with it. She'd tie herself in knots for Archer and he could be accused of doing the same too. It was difficult to stop herself comparing all love to what she felt for Archer. What did it matter when she couldn't figure him out? He'd been cold and cruel, except sometimes he was himself and she couldn't forget he'd kissed her.

Tonight. She didn't know what happened and would have to confront him to find out what was going on. Was he playing with her? Was it just a sexual attraction he wasn't finished slaking or did he actually still care about her? Did he want her back?

"Don't panic, Nya. We're part of the same team now. I'm not going to turn the place into a drugs den or a sex pit. I like live music. We could have more of that. If you have ideas, let's hear 'em."

For an hour, she spoke to Hexam about the history of Sizzle and the kind of people who partied there. To his credit, he listened to her vision of what Sizzle could be. Not that he wrote anything down, so he could just be paying lip service to her ideas. Why would he waste his time with her?

After he left with his men, business didn't pick up for the rest of the night. Archer had gone before she and Hexam even came out of the office, so she packed everything away and went home.

TWENTY-SIX

NO SOONER HAD NYA closed her apartment door and taken off her shoes than there was a knock at the door. Unbuttoning the cuffs of her shirt, she sloped across to peek through the hole, assuming one of her neighbors heard her arrive home.

Georgie-Boy was desperate for conversation and Ella didn't have any friends coming or going.

Yet neither of them waited on the other side of her door. Curious, she opened it wearing a frown.

"Archer, it's four o'clock in the morning," she said. "Is this a booty call?"

Heavy score if that's what it was. Yeah, she was exhausted and might not be at her best, but she'd give it a good shot. She went back into the apartment and left the door open. If he wanted to come in, he could. If he wanted to fuck off, that was fine too. Unbuttoning, she pulled her shirt out of her waistband and tossed it onto her bistro table.

As she unzipped her skirt and shimmied out of that to add it to the pile, the door closed.

Guess he was staying… the night? Oh, she wanted to fall asleep in his arms again.

"I'm here for my payment," he said. For a second, all

she could recall was offering him sex on demand. He waved once. "Can you stop taking your clothes off?"

Her thumbs were hooked beneath the clasp of her bra at her back. "Why?"

He arched a brow. He knew her game and wasn't playing. "Do you strip off when the pizza guy comes?"

"I don't eat pizza."

"Yes, you fucking do. You just don't order it yourself. Do you strip in front of other visitors?"

Shrugging, she feigned innocence. "Nobody visits me. Except Georgie-Boy next door, he comes over a lot. He seems to want to borrow things," she said, having not figured out yet whether he really didn't own anything or if his requests were excuses to see her. She smiled. "Ester won't be happy if he's making a play for me. She's got her sights on that big boy."

Deadpan, Archer didn't react. "Do you expect me to laugh?"

She sighed. "Why are you here?" she asked and then remembered what he'd said. "Payment, yes, come here."

Going into the bedroom, she opened the closet and crouched to search in the bag she'd put the weapons in. Except she'd buried them in clothes and couldn't find them. Groaning, she tried to lift the load.

"What are you doing?"

"Struggling."

Leaning over her crouched form, Archer grabbed the bag to haul it over her head and dumped it on the end of the bed.

"What's that?" he asked.

The room was dark, her eyes were still adjusting. But he nodded toward the picture propped against the wall by the window.

"It's a picture," she said. "I know you don't like clutter, but some people like to make their homes look pretty."

"Yeah, makes the place look gorgeous on the floor over there, hiding behind the bed."

Pulling open the bag, she rummaged around in the

clothes. Most of the items on top were negligees she hadn't wanted crushed, but he didn't notice.

Sitting on the bed, she crossed her legs and kept looking. "I can't put it up."

"Why not?"

Archer must have seen the gun first because he reached in and pulled it out before she could touch it. He checked the clip then stuck it in the back of his jeans.

"I don't have a hammer."

He stopped. "You don't have a hammer?" She shook her head. "Who the fuck doesn't have a hammer?"

Taking a big breath, she explained. "I used to have a hammer," she said. "I kept it next to my bed for about nine months after Damien and I broke up. I got rid of it as a kind of exorcism when I stopped waking up in fear of him every day." She yawned and sank down onto her back. "I never replaced it."

"If you need fucking tools, come see me."

She grinned although her eyes had closed. "You accuse me of making excuses to see you like I'm a lovesick stalker. If I start showing up every time I need a screwdriver—"

"You don't have a screwdriver either? Fuck, Ny, you're not prepared for the world."

She laughed. "I don't know what happened to the tools I used to have. I guess when I stopped worrying about repairs in my last shithole apartment, it didn't really matter where they went. They're probably kicking around somewhere. It's funny, I was just thinking tonight that I couldn't ask you for another favor 'cause I'd probably filled my quota, now you're saying I can come borrow things..." Peeking at him, she played. "How much will it cost me to lease your tool for an hour?"

He was wise to her innuendo. "That one you can't borrow."

"Even when you're not using it?"

"As soon as you show up, I'll be using it. My dick's always occupied when you're around."

That was a compliment, but this banter reminded her

of what she didn't have. "It doesn't matter." She stretched. "I don't have anything else to pay you with. I'll have to start saving up the green to pay for my Archer favors."

"Or you could raid Tag's safe."

That was funny. "Are you kidding? His girlfriend likes diamonds; I think he's flat broke."

"You've got plenty to barter with," he said, then his voice softened a fraction. "And you don't have a quota, Ny. My door is always open for you."

"Except when it's not," she said, thinking of all the times he hadn't let her into his place.

Even though he was standing up, just having him in the room made it easier to relax. "You didn't move the bed back," Archer said.

She opened her eyes enough to see him scrutinizing the room. "No, I didn't. Like you said, I like being under you." All his attention zeroed in on the girl on the bed in her underwear. He was doing the strong, silent thing and refused to respond to her flirting. "You never told me why you needed the weapons."

Going back to his search, he adopted his cold demeanor again. He bowed over the bag. A second later he produced the knife. When he unsheathed it, she turned her head away.

"Is this it?" he asked and she nodded.

She heard him scoop everything into the bag and dump it in the closet, which he then slid shut.

"I guess now you'll slip out and leave me," she said, then muttered, "Talk about déjà vu."

"You didn't kill him, Ny."

She sat up. "What?"

"All four bodies were found. Hexam set it up to look like some sort of drug-fueled, God-knows-what gone wrong. He used them as a warning to those in the know; he likes to put victims in humiliating setups. Doesn't matter. Point is, all four died from gunshot wounds to the head."

What was he saying? She didn't understand, couldn't follow.

"But I... I stabbed him."

"Yeah," he said, pressing his fingers into his chest. "In a completely non-vital area. The guy would've survived. Well, I guess he would've bled out eventually if Hexam left him lying there a few days. I read the ME report, Hex doesn't know I did, he wouldn't bank on me doing that. But the wound was more likely to kill him through infection than blood loss. How much blood did you get on your clothes?"

She couldn't remember, but she'd fallen asleep on her apartment floor, and it hadn't been stained in the morning.

"Not much."

"There you go. Hex wants you to think you killed him 'cause then he owns you and he owns me. But you didn't. Hex, or one of his boys, shot that guy after you left. You didn't kill him."

How should she feel about that? She wanted the bastard dead. Did it matter who ended his life? Hexam had lied to her, made her believe she'd done something she hadn't. No more Nya the Murderess.

While it was her urge to leap up and mount the man who'd given her the news. She restrained herself to ask, "Why?"

"Because Hexam thinks you'll be useful and he knows I have contacts that—"

"No," she said, shaking her head. "Why did you tell me that? Why do you even care? Why do you want the weapons?"

"Because it's a rookie mistake to keep murder weapons where you sleep."

Exhausted, she blamed lethargy for struggling to catch up. "But you just said they're not murder weapons."

"Oh, baby, you bet your sugar-sweet ass these weapons have been used to kill, just not by you. I'll get rid of them. You'll never know where. No one will ever know where."

It was incredible. "You're protecting me," she said. "That's why you were so excited when you found out I stabbed him. You already knew they'd been shot—you'd already investigated. Why would you do that if you don't love me? You wouldn't even let me in your apartment. You were so cold. You wouldn't look at me. You didn't want to talk to me. I thought I disgusted you... So why...? Why would you bother with the ME report and your own investigation if you don't love me?"

Tossing the knife to the ottoman at the end of the bed, he swore at her. "Who the fuck ever said that, Nya?"

Blinking, the shock winded her. "You told me we were over. You wouldn't talk to me or let me into your place. You told me you were fucking Ella."

"I didn't tell you that. I let you believe that for five minutes. I told you in the hallway I wasn't. I didn't have to do that. I thought if I was a cold, cruel bastard you'd stop coming by, but you didn't. I can't get fucking rid of you."

Emotion fueled her argument. "You're the one who moved me into your building, buster. It's not my fault you regret it."

"I don't," he said, finally relenting a laugh. "The sad fucking part is, every night I lie upstairs so fucking grateful I did it while I was gone. I'd thought about waiting 'til I got back. If I had, you'd still be in your old place way across town."

What the hell was he saying? "I'm confused. You want me here. But you don't want me. You love me. But you won't be with me. Now who's messed up?"

"I've always been messed up about you."

His restraint seemed to have a time limit. He couldn't stay away forever. That had to be why he was there in her bedroom protecting her.

Unhooking her bra, she slid it from her arms. "Let's finish what we started," she said. It had been in this bed he'd told her they were through. "Come back to bed, Fella. We can pretend these last few weeks never happened."

He came to sit on the edge of the bed. She shuffled forward on her knees; this was the moment everything would fall back into place. Everything would be okay again. It would be better now. Except he didn't kiss her or lie down with her, he cupped a breast and rubbed his thumb over the apex as he gave her a squeeze.

"Resisting this every night, knowing you're here and

willing… it's been tough, Ny."

"You don't have to resist," she said, stroking his face. "I'm here and I'm yours and that never changed."

"That's what makes it so difficult to say no to you. And not being honest with you… fuck, I… I can lie to anyone, I've never had a problem doing it." He'd told her that much before. He'd learned how to con people from a young age. "But with you… God, you make it so tough. Sometimes I need you so bad. I don't know how long I can keep saying no to you."

Bowing, she touched his mouth with hers. "Then don't. Don't say no, Arch. Stay with me."

But he wasn't giving in. "I can't reward bad behavior."

Matching his determination, she didn't want to spook him. "Then punish me." She brushed her mouth across his, trying to tempt his lips to part. "I'll do whatever it takes to make it up to you. If you want to chain me to your bathroom or your bed, do it. Strip me naked and flog me, Fella, I don't care."

"I don't want you in pain," Archer said, shifting to hold her face. "But I get it now. The guilt you live with. I'd never lived with that before. I get it now."

"Is that why you took my place with Hexam?"

"I took your place with him because I love you."

Those words, he said them so easily, he couldn't know what they meant to her. "I told you to walk away from him. Was it guilt that made you stay?"

"Hexam let you go, but it could've gone the other way, Squirm. He could've hurt you and I wouldn't have known until it was too late. Now that I know the only reason you were in that room was to protect me… I can't let that happen again. I can't let anyone use me against you. I don't know how to process guilt. Why is it I can rip out a guy's fingernails with pliers, listen to him scream, and then go out for burgers without giving it a second thought? But the idea of you in pain because of me… I can't handle that."

She'd lived with guilt too.

One thing he hadn't considered…

"We're not together now, right?" she asked. "We haven't been for weeks. More than three."

"Yeah."

"If Hexam walked through that door right now with twenty of his men, put a gun to your head, and told me the only way he'd let you live is if I sucked and fucked every one of them, do you know what I would do?"

Archer sneered and recoiled, filled with disgust. "I don't want to know. I don't want to think like that."

Catching his face, she couldn't let him go too far. "I love you and I'm always going to try to protect you. I could lie to you and tell you I'd never do it again. I could beg you to take me back on the promise I would always put myself before you. But I can't lie to you, Archer. I can't make you that promise."

"That's what churns me up, babe."

She sank back to sit on her feet, retreating from his caress as she accepted the truth. "I've done nothing but hurt you since the day we met. When you took me from Jonno, I caused a problem in that relationship. I've done nothing but cause problems for you since. That's why I needed to know if you loved me. Because if you can walk away, you should. I'll pack my shit and find a new apartment. I'll leave Sizzle. I'll leave the city, the state. I'll do whatever you need to get a clean break."

Getting stern, he gave orders. "I don't want you going anywhere. I look out for you. Without me around…"

If he hadn't been around, she would never have learned Hexam fooled her into believing she'd committed murder. No one else would've jumped in to save her from the chancers in Sizzle that night either.

He stood up. "I'm gonna make Hex pay for what he did to you."

"I told you not to start another war," she said. "As long as you walk away from him clean, I don't care what he does to me."

Her phone rang in the other room. It was so late, there had to be a problem. Leaping up, she ran past him to get to her purse, lying beside the front door next to her shoes.

Grabbing out the device, she answered. "Tag?" she asked because he never called at this time in the morning, not since he started his relationship with Farrah.

"She dumped me," he said. "It's over."

Unbelievable. She spun around to pin her surprise on Archer and found him turning her dirty clothes inside out, ready for the washer, in the kitchen closet by the fridge.

"What happened?" she asked Tag.

"I don't know. She told me it wasn't working out."

Having just gone through her own breakup, she understood his pain. "You guys were in love… right?"

His voice was weak, but angry and confused. "I just need you to come over. Gio's fucked off. I don't know where that fucker's at. I haven't seen him for weeks and can't find him. I'm here by myself."

"Okay," she said. "Give me a minute, I'll need to get changed."

"Okay, just be as quick as you can," he said and hung up the phone.

In the kitchen now, Archer would've heard her side of the call. "What's wrong with your boy?" he asked, cleaning up the dishes she hadn't done earlier.

"Farrah dumped him." Archer stopped what he was doing, his shock as evident as hers. "She said it wasn't working out."

"That's it? That's all she said?"

She shrugged, scant on details. God, exhaustion was heavy, she wanted to fall into bed. For weeks she'd been desperate to distract herself. Now Archer's attention might be swinging her way again, Tag needed her.

Archer must've been thinking the same thing. "Tell me, does that guy have some kind of radar that lets him know when we're in the middle of something?"

Going over to flop her arms onto the breakfast bar, she leaned across. The cool tile stimulated her naked breasts.

"He's heartbroken and I have recent experience with that… I can't believe she dumped him."

"That's twenty-three-year-olds for you," he said, returning to his dishes. "He couldn't have thought it was going to be forever. She dropped that last guy fast when she got a sniff from Tag. I told you she's a flirt."

"Does she still flirt with you?" she asked, drawing a finger around the small mosaic tiles of the counter surface.

"When I'm at Hex's, sure. I try to avoid her. It creeps me out."

Putting her phone on the counter, she tightened her arms around her breasts and leaned farther. "How could it creep you out? She's beautiful… that was your word."

His sneer was sort of grossed out. "Yeah, but…"

"But what?"

Moving around the breakfast bar, she rested back on the kitchen side.

"She's played with your buddy's junk. I gotta wonder what sort of woman would do that."

Nya laughed. "Okay, I get your point. You don't want to go where Tag has been."

"Why do you think I checked and double-checked where you'd been before I touched you?"

"Ha!" she exclaimed, going over to stand behind him. "If you background checked all my exes and found out the truth about Damien…" She wrapped her arms around him and buried her face against his spine. "You'd never have touched me if you'd learned what kind of man he was."

"Tell me."

And, unable to deny him anything, she would, soon as she didn't have somewhere to be.

"Another time." She kissed his arm beneath the edge of his tee shirt sleeve. "Okay." Taking a deep breath, she stretched again. "I have to go to Tag's."

Dragging her feet all the way into the bedroom, she couldn't make her brain work. What was she doing again?

"What did Tag do when he found out we broke up?" Archer asked.

She turned around, startled, because she hadn't expected he would follow. "I never told him."

Yawning, she rubbed her eye, which smudged her makeup. Damnit. She turned on the light above the mirror on the top of her tall dresser.

"You never told him?"

Shrugging, she tilted her face into the light. "He never asked." Using a fingertip, she fixed the smudge at the corner of her eye. "He was caught up with Farrah. It's not like I didn't see him. I think he knows we're not together. We just… never talked about it."

"Why don't you take it off?

Glaring at his reflection for a second, she glanced down at herself. "Take what off? I'm wearing a thong, is that too much for you?"

He smiled and leaned in to whisper in her ear. "Always." The heat of his breath tickled, so she recoiled and laughed while stroking a hand down his chest. "But I meant the makeup."

"It's four o'clock in the morning," she said. "I should probably put more on. I'll look a fucking mess rocking up to his place like this after a full shift at Sizzle and a meeting with your buddy, Hex. I'm all over the place."

"Four in the morning is when you're fucking hottest." She went about fixing her old makeup by covering it with a new layer. Archer kept talking. "This is my favorite time of day with you. Why do you think we were always up so late talking? No one else gets to hang out with you like this. When the whole city was asleep, we were awake, making plans. When you're sleepy and cozy…" Just as she finished her eyeliner a hand appeared on either side of the dresser, trapping her in the arc of his arms. He rubbed his face in her hair. "When you're yawning and stretching and drowsy like this…"

"Mm hmm?" she asked, prompting him to continue. "What? Or are you just listing dwarves?"

His lips curled and he snagged some strands of her hair in his teeth. "You'll tell me fucking anything when you're tired. Your guard is gone. You just talk and talk. I like it."

"I do?"

He nodded before licking the shell of her ear. "You talk in your sleep too. If I touch you just right and wake you up just enough," he said and again held her breast in his hand. This time, with her back to his front, the reflection of his caress in the mirror mesmerized her. "I can kiss you and touch you like this." Crouching, he kissed the back of her jaw. "I ask you any question and you tell me the truth. You never remember in the morning."

When he grinned, she drove an elbow back into his ribs. "And you call me a manipulator?" she asked, using her butt to push him back so she could open the dresser and pull out a bra and a top. "I should really take a shower, I've got the club all over me."

Groaning, she really couldn't be bothered traipsing across the city to Tag's.

"Tell him where to get off. Better yet, give me your fucking phone and I'll do it."

That wouldn't be clever. "Yeah, you've been looking for an excuse to do it for months."

Bending at the waist, she deliberately grinded her ass into his groin as she searched for a skirt.

Archer took her hips and helped her move. "If he didn't care when you got dumped, why should you care when he does?"

"It's what friends do," she said, snagging a skirt and taking her clothes to the bed.

She opened the nightstand to retrieve her hairbrush and pulled the pins from her hair to untangle it as she went.

"You're a better friend than he is."

"Maybe," she said. "But it helps me sleep. If I don't go, I'll just lie here all night thinking about how I should've gone and I'll never get to sleep. And being honest? For the past twenty-four days, I've been willing to do just about anything to distract myself from thinking about you. Now I have a chance to do that. I can't ignore it."

Opening his hands, he moved in front of her. "I'm right here."

She stopped brushing. "Are you staying the night?" she asked, expectant, hopeful, and then resigned to the confirmation that came when his shoulders fell.

He wasn't defeated. "You're not gonna get laid over there either."

"Maybe not, but at least I won't have to sleep alone. You take up a lot of space in a girl's bed, Arch. I'm drowning in those sheets without you."

She stood up and he was instantly against her. "You're gonna sleep with him?"

"I told you before. I sleep in his bed. Doesn't mean I suck his dick."

"You don't have to fuck him to…"

He stopped himself. Maybe because he knew how fucked up it was to ask his ex-girlfriend, who he'd just finished groping, not to lie down and sleep in the same space as another man.

"Are you jealous?" she asked. "Of Tag? Haven't we had this conversation a zillion and one times?"

"I don't like him," he said, opening his arms wide. "I'll never like him."

Nya patted his chest to give herself enough space to squeeze out. "You've made that clear."

She started to dress.

"What if he wants her back?"

"Farrah?" she asked, bending to put her feet in her skirt.

"Yeah, what if he tells you he's willing to do anything to get her back."

She stood up and zipped her skirt, drawing in a grand breath. "Then we'll do anything to get her back."

Archer moved into her field of vision. "Do you think Hex is gonna like that? If his baby sister says the relationship is over and Tag comes sniffing around again?"

Wasn't Archer just the happy, good news fairy?

"Oh, God," she groaned. Sinking down, her head fell into her hands. "We've had this conversation before too. The Farrah girl has a lot to answer for. We just managed to get them together and Hexam to accept the relationship. Now she's playing hard to get?"

"Maybe it's not hard to get," he said, sitting beside her. "Maybe your boy fucked up, ever think of that?"

"Screwed around on her you mean?"

Hmm, she had to concede it was a possibility.

"That or they argued and he got physical."

Bouncing down the bed an inch, she twisted her body

toward him. "Are you saying he hit her? Tag would never do that."

"I'm saying if he did, Hexam's likely to go through him, no matter what Farrah says."

No way. "Tag just wouldn't. He wouldn't. Think about what he did for me. He's never raised his hands to me, and you know how annoying I can be."

"You were never in a relationship with him."

"No," she admitted. "But I've seen it. My dad was a beater, my brother, Damien. I know the signs and Tag doesn't have them."

Proving his trust, Archer accepted that. "Okay. Just make sure he's honest with you."

She'd have to scurry back with the details to keep Archer in the loop. Unless…

While rubbing his thigh, she put her chin on his shoulder. "You could come with me."

He tilted to look at her. "You want me to come to Tag's house at four in the morning?" She dug her chin into his shoulder. "I thought you said he knew we were broken up. Why would we be together at four in the morning?"

Sitting back, she raised her arms in a shrug and let her hands slap onto her thighs. "I don't know, Arch, why are we together at four o'clock in the morning?" His eyes flicked to her bare breasts. She pushed her shoulders back. "Take what you want, I won't stop you."

Now he groaned and covered his eyes. "Is this the way it's always gonna be?" he asked, and his hand fell. "You're just gonna keep telling me you're mine, ready and waiting. You're gonna keep stripping off and flaunting yourself, trying to get me into bed?"

Rolling her eyes to their top corners, she twisted her lips, but didn't think about it for long. "Yeah," she said. "Pretty much."

"You don't want to accept that we're over and move on?"

"Nope," she said, kissing his arm. "Because your reason for dumping me was stupid and now you're just being stubborn. We both know it. You want me. So when you're ready to be a man and fuck me stupid like a good boyfriend should, I'll be ready… If you haven't come to your senses by my birthday, I'll seriously consider getting you drunk and taking advantage."

"I was honest with you so you'd stop flaunting it," he said. "I thought if I was upfront you'd realize what I'm doing makes sense. So you can quit coming round and dressing for me and—"

"Dressing for you?" she asked, amazed at his ego. "I've never dressed for you in my life." It hadn't occurred to her. Huh…? "How would I do that? What would you want me to wear? You've never expressed a preference for any outfit or style or anything except seeing as much of my breasts as you can at any opportunity."

Hence the white tee shirts he always tossed her way.

"I'm not coming to Tag's with you," he said.

Typical that he should avoid the question. "Okay, fine."

Picking up her bra, she put it on and was yawning when she went for her deodorant.

"You're going over there half dead. What use are you gonna be to him?"

"He just needs company. The first night is tough. I only got through it because I was sure you'd forgive me in the morning. I didn't like being wrong about that, by the way."

After spraying, she held out a limp arm for the top she'd left on the bed.

Archer picked it up and threw it to her. "Stay here."

"But I—"

"Just for a minute," he said, rising from the bed.

She was to stay, but he was leaving? What was going on? "Where are you going?"

"Upstairs to get my car key."

"I thought you weren't coming."

"I'm not coming in," he said. "I'll drive you over there, give you an hour, and then I'm bringing you home if I have to haul you out by your hair. You remember how cozy my trunk is, right?"

She blocked the door so he couldn't go through it.

"Why would you do that?"

He held her chin for a second. "Because I don't want you sleeping in his bed."

Lowering to bump his forehead on hers, he ushered her aside to go out. They weren't together. He didn't want them to be. Yet he loved her and was still willing to go to drastic lengths for her.

Archer found out the truth about Hexam. And despite his hatred for Tag, he was still willing to sit alone on a city street with jack squat to do, just so she could console her friend.

Her heart had been broken, their relationship over. Maybe it was her almost coming to terms with it that prompted Archer to change gear. Because, admit it or not, he didn't want to lose her. She had no intention of going anywhere and had to convince him things weren't as over as he thought.

TWENTY-SEVEN

"I THINK WE SHOULD move in together."

Nya stopped mid-chew. "We should what?"

Seated at her bistro table with Tag, he kept shoveling the veggie risotto into his mouth.

Her friend's relationship with Farrah ended just three days ago, yet he was making plans for the future.

"Think about it," Tag said. "You don't want to be here. I'm knocking around that big apartment by myself. We should move in together. It's not like we don't get along. I can watch you if you're at mine."

She speared a pea. "I just moved in here," she said, eyeing the boxes still stacked by her front door.

Optimism was great. Where had it come from?

"Yeah, but it's not like you're settled," he said. "You could pack up again in a day. It might be fun."

"We've lived together before."

He picked up his glass of white wine. "Yeah, but not on purpose. We only stay together when there's some kind of crisis and you need a place to crash. This would be a choice."

Putting her fork on her plate, she clasped her hands over it. Maybe his proactive attitude was a cover for the emotional upheaval.

"I think it's great you've decided not to go after Farrah. I know you're worried about Gio 'cause you haven't heard anything from him for weeks…"

During her conversation on the night of Tag's break-up, she learned Gio had gone on a trip about the same time Tag hooked up with Farrah. So besotted was he that Tag couldn't remember if he'd heard from Gio at all.

Still, he was glib about his friend's safety. "Gio can take care of himself."

"We should try to find out where he is. He might need help. I know you guys sometimes do your own thing, but you usually keep in touch."

Despite thinking of him as a friend, Tag's right-hand man, Gio, hadn't liked it when she hooked up with Archer. One blot of friction on their record wasn't enough to erase her concern for a man who'd been missing for weeks. If he'd been around, maybe Tag wouldn't have been so eager to get embroiled in Hexam's business.

Tag got impatient. "I'm gonna. I want to figure the business out before I look too hard."

Because if Gio came back and saw the mess Tag made of their modest empire, he wouldn't be happy. In the past, she'd never given much weight to Gio's role. All along, he'd been a steadying influence she'd taken for granted.

"I can ask Archer," she said, "find out if anyone's seen anything of Gio recently."

Scowling, Tag scraped the remainder of his food together and tipped his bowl. "No, you need to stay the fuck away from him."

Not liking his judgment, she chose to be obtuse. "From Gio or Archer?"

"From Archer, that's why you should get away from this place. You guys are over. He fucked you up, just like I said he would, and tossed your ass to the curb."

"He paid my rent here," she said, "and he's never asked for a dime."

On the night of the Farrah break-up, after Archer brought her back from Tag's, he'd walked her to her door. She'd tried to kiss him goodnight and invite him in. Of course, he'd ducked that and been adamant about putting her across the threshold and listening to her lock the door. She'd never understood why listening was so important. Not until she lived there. That night she hadn't left her door or even taken off her jacket until she heard Archer slam into his apartment and cross the floor above her.

It had become a habit to wait and listen when she knew he was heading upstairs. She'd gone to bed and had quite a smooth sleep, probably because she was exhausted. And because spending extended time with Archer left her more content.

In that morning's stretch, while thinking about coffee, she'd noticed the cash on the nightstand. Picking it up, it hit her what the bills were, where they'd come from. That was the same scrunched wad of bills she'd given to him for rent. Nestled inside the pile was a Post-it and this one was in Archer's handwriting. It said, "I take care of you."

She'd taken it as a good sign and faced the day with vigor. Tag needed her attention before anything else, then Sizzle issues cropped up. Life got in the way of pursuing her man.

There she was, eating dinner with Tag three days later, still desperate to ask Archer what the Post-it meant.

"You were right about Farrah," he said. "She's too young for me. We should both spend some time by ourselves, focus on our own shit. And if I can get over Farrah, you can for sure get over that bastard."

He nodded upwards, but she hadn't heard anything from Archer all night. The funny thing was, his slamming doors and stomping feet were usually the only sign he was there. He didn't play music and watched the TV on mute with subtitles. Even the coffee machine was too quiet to hear. If he was in the shower at the same time as her, it messed with her water pressure. Working that out took a couple of weeks.

Her situation wasn't the same as Tag's and she had to make that clear. "I'm not sure it is over," she admitted.

Dragging the prongs of her fork through her food, she'd lost her appetite.

"Not sure what's over?" he asked, reaching for a

breadstick.

"Me and Archer."

Biting the stick, Tag crunched and swallowed, then washed it down with wine. "He dumped you, Nya. It doesn't usually take you this long to get the message when a guy's not interested."

"He is interested. Even if he's not, I want to be his friend."

Tag gaped, his limp hand fell to the table. "His friend? Since when do you want to be friends with exes? Careful, Yorkie, you're edging into pathetic."

He eyed the cuff on her wrist. Tag thought she wore it because it signified something special between her and Archer. After being split up for so long it was no surprise her friend thought it strange she'd wear something from her ex. Except he was wrong about her reasons, and it was time to reveal the truth of its purpose to him.

Unfastening the buckle, she shoved her plate away to slap her forearm down on the table, presenting the inside of her wrist to him, revealing the brand and tattoo.

"I wear this to cover the mark," she said. "Because I thought you would freak out if you saw it."

Lowering his gaze, he scrutinized it. "Is that... a burn?"

"Yes," she said. "I told you Archer saved me in Sizzle, and that's true, he did. But I spent the next three days chained up at his mercy. The night after the raid, he gave me this. I've never felt pain like it; I was absolutely terrified of him. But this mark means something to me now. It means I belong to him, and I want that more than anything. I want to belong to him. I will always belong to him."

"He burned you?" Tag asked, surging to his feet. "That bastard, I'm going to—"

She caught his arm. Instead of panic, anger poured into her. "He's not home and even if he was, he'd take you apart. Yeah, Archer dumped me and broke my heart. He did it because I protected him. I risked my life to make sure he wouldn't get hurt."

Grabbing hold of her, Tag twisted her arm to show

her the brand. "After he did this to you?"

The scar didn't make her angry. "You don't understand. He did this to me because he couldn't hurt me in any other way. He couldn't hit me or cut me or make me bleed. After he'd done it, even though he was still trying to scare me into giving you up, he took care of me. He's saved your ass too, Hexam would've killed you ten times by now if it wasn't for him. Wearing this mark…" Nya stood up to present it to him. "Makes me proud of him."

"And the tattoo, did he make you do that after?"

She shook her head. "I did this a couple of weeks ago," she said. "After we broke up when he was bastard enough to tell me I could have my brand removed. That prick thought I might accept his rejection. I don't fucking think so."

"You can't make him be with you. Whatever sick, fucking twisted relationship you got yourself mixed up in, Yorkie. He finished it. Accept that."

Empowered, embracing honesty freed her. "Accept he may never share my bed again? Yes, I might. That doesn't mean I've stopped loving him and I know he loves me too."

"He wouldn't be treating you like this if he did."

"Like what? Putting a roof over my head? Covering my bills even when I've asked him not to? He protects me in ways you can't begin to understand."

"I protect you," Tag said, thrusting his thumb to his chest. "If you need something, you come to me."

Something clicked. So many things Archer said fell into place. "That's the thing about Archer. He doesn't want me to ask. I don't need to. He fixes problems I don't even know I have. Since we've been together, his whole life has become about making mine better."

Archer was better off without her. Every time she went into one of her rants, she came up with a thousand reasons he should run for the hills. Yet he'd said he couldn't lie to her, and he struggled to resist her.

Growing up, Archer had no stability. Ester was a blast to hang with as a friend, but would've made an erratic, unreliable mother. That's why Archer craved responsibility. He had to look after the people he cared about. He needed that structure. Just like his need to keep his apartment in order, to have a process and rules for what he did, rules he was strict about following.

Like telling her they would be through if she protected him. By asking him to come back to her, she was asking him to ignore his own rules. That caused chaos in his psyche.

She and Tag hadn't said anything to each other for a minute. Tag was still angry. Regardless, he could stamp and shout if he wanted, arguing against her declaration wouldn't change her position. Something slid under the door, startling them both. She stared at it for a few seconds before going over to see what it was.

"Be careful," Tag said. "You don't know what it is."

The blue file was the same kind as the one Archer brought to her Sizzle office. It shouldn't be there, it should be in a drawer at the club.

Opening it up, she was still reading when the door slammed in the apartment above and his footsteps crossed the room. Archer was home. That flicker of awareness was vague until she absorbed the words under her eyes.

"Holy fuck," she said.

"What? What is it?"

Tag's shadow obscured the writing. She stepped forward to hold it up into the light.

"It's the Sizzle deeds," she said.

"Why would someone put those under your door?"

"Someone?" she murmured, reading it again.

Obviously, Tag hadn't connected that the folder appeared moments before the clattering above, caused by her former lover. It was too coincidental this shot under her door less than a minute before he got home.

"Let me see," Tag said, taking the file. "What does it say?"

"It's in my name," she muttered the words but couldn't understand them. Someone needed to explain how this could've happened. "Wait here."

Darting out of her apartment, she ran along the hall to the open stairwell, bolted up a floor, and went to hammer on his door. He didn't answer, suggesting he was ignoring her. Good luck, buddy boy. She wouldn't let that fly. Not tonight.

Slapping a palm onto the wood, she let her forehead follow with a light bang. "Fella, I'm gonna stay out here all night 'til you open up. I know you're in there."

That or he was being robbed. Burglars would be quieter.

The door opened and he appeared shirtless, chewing on a power bar.

"I'm getting in the shower," he said from one side of his mouth. "What's up?"

"What's up?"

She wouldn't give him a chance to refuse her entry this time. Pushing against him with all she had, Nya squeezed between his body and the doorframe, bursting into the apartment.

"I have business, Squirm. I don't have time to mess around with you tonight," he said, closing the door and taking another chunk off the bar with his teeth. "Say it quick and get out."

"You know why I'm here. How did you do it? What did you do?"

"I was right," he said, finishing the bar and smiling with satisfaction. "Never get tired of saying that."

Heading for the kitchen, he dumped his wrapper in the trash, and opened the fridge to retrieve a bottle of water. The mineral water she loved; he'd never drunk it before being with her. Either that was a bottle left from the last time she was there, or he'd been keeping a regular stock.

"Right about what?" she asked, too frantic to wait for him to finish drinking.

Lowering the bottle with a full intake of breath, he wiped his mouth on his shoulder. "That gun Hex gave you was a murder weapon. I handed it off to a buddy of mine at the precinct."

Rushing over, she stopped up close. "You got Hexam arrested?" she gasped, touching his abs.

"No, my buddy will sit on it for me. You've gotta give the right evidence to a guy in charge, so I can protect mine.

Hex knows, anything happens to me or my family, my buddy in blue will find the gun by chance in the alley behind Hexam's place." Hexam owned the whole building, the alley behind it was public. "'Nother buddy found a bunch of registration papers for that weapon, turns out Hex has owned it for a while." There were no papers, at least there hadn't been, not until Archer called in a favor, she heard what he was saying. "That could cause him problems, serious problems."

Archer handed her the bottle and tossed the cap in the trash.

"That doesn't explain how you got him to sign Sizzle over to me."

He stroked a hand down her hair. "You working under him was unacceptable. Hex knows how the game is played. I've outmaneuvered him this time. He's not that pissed, but he'll be watching his back. Truth is, I think he's stoked Farrah dumped Tag's ass in the dirt. Your boy's gonna keep out of that muck, isn't he?" She nodded. "Good work, Sweets." He kissed her hairline. "I'm going out."

He passed her.

She looked at the bottle for a second before putting it on the breakfast bar and hurrying after him. "Why did you get him to sign it to me? Why not you?"

"Why do I want a club?" he asked, sitting on his bed to remove his boots. "I wanted Hex out of your life. You can't work for him. And I wasn't gonna give your boy a windfall… forging your signature is easy too."

"I lucked out by process of elimination?" she asked, crossing her arms beneath her breasts.

"That and I know you have big ideas," he said, taking his boots to the closet. "You'll find Sizzle's bank account just got a boost in funds as well. Hex deposited a hefty donation."

He came toward her, wanting to get past, she didn't move.

"Threatening him was a big risk, how do you know he won't come after you?"

"'Cause he likes me. He has a lot of respect for people who outmaneuver him, as long as they show respect. He doesn't like weasels who cheat and scam like your boy. Guys like me who do the legwork to dig up the dirt, who give him a chance to make things right, he has respect for those guys."

Archer could've just put him in jail. Going another way, he'd told Hex how the pieces were positioned and that his ass was safe, as long as Archer's was.

"I don't know what to say," she said, in awe of how far he'd gone to put things right for her, and he'd done it alone.

"I did think about killing him, and if you ever feel at risk, I will."

The man who wouldn't be with her just risked his life for her again.

"I can't believe you fixed it," she said. "I would never have got out of this mess on my own."

If Archer hadn't been in her life, and she'd made it out of the Sizzle raid alive, she'd still have been filled with vengeance. Maybe she'd have crossed paths with Hexam who could've helped her get it. In that scenario, she would either be on one of Hexam's corners or in a jail cell for sure. It never would've occurred to her to check the ME report to confirm how the men really died.

She wouldn't have had the connections to find out if the gun was a murder weapon, or to connect it to Hexam. There was no one she could've trusted to keep it safe in case she needed it either.

"I guess the only motor-mouth we have to worry about now is Tulio," she said. "If he talks to Jonno or his other friend—"

"You didn't hear?" he asked, frowning.

"Hear what?"

"Tulio broke his neck in the shower. Sad," Archer said. "Very sad. Good thing he signed a life insurance policy worth a hundred grand just a few days before the tragic accident. It'll help his wife grieve."

With a grip on her arms, he jolted her aside, then crossed the hall to go into the bathroom. As was becoming the theme, she followed to see him turning on the shower. She closed over the door to open the closet and retrieved a towel for him.

"How do you break someone's neck?" she asked. "Isn't that harder than it looks on TV?"

"I wouldn't know," he said, accepting the towel. He winked before he went to hang it on the shower rail. "Are you gonna stand there and watch or are we done?"

That was a ridiculous offer.

She saucy smiled. "You mean you're giving me the choice?"

Archer didn't rise to the bait.

Propping a hip on the sink, he hooked his thumbs into his belt loops. "You're a legit business owner now, how does it feel?"

"I don't know," she said, staring at his navel. "I can't believe you did this."

Striding forward, he pointed in her face, growing stern. "And you're not allowed to sign it over to your boy. I don't care how much he begs. I'll hurt him until he signs it back and that will be on your head, Squirm."

"Tag." Shit, she'd left her friend downstairs. Wincing in apology, she hoped he wouldn't get mad. "He wants to kill you."

Rather than anger, amusement hit him. "It's about fucking time, we've been broken up for weeks. He should've come at me long ago. Didn't I tell you he was crap at looking after you? I'd have kicked my ass by now." And that was sweet, in its own way. "Is he still downstairs? I can make some time for killing." Something stalled him. "Fuck, why'd I put carpet in your place? It's a bastard to clean up… Can you get him up here?"

"How do you know Tag's in my apartment?"

He didn't respond, just picked up her wrist to graze her brand with his thumb. "If he's in your apartment, you should be wearing your cuff."

"That's why he wants to kill you. I told him the truth. You were right, it does always come out."

"Really?" he asked. "You didn't do it when we were together." She liked that he seemed impressed. "It's about fucking time for that too."

"He wants me to move in with him."

"Sex for rent?"

Shaking her head, she resisted the urge to pinch him. Just like old times, information, that hadn't been requested, spilled out of her.

"No! We're friends."

"You're not fucking going," he said, walking her back until she was in the corner of the bathroom between the two perpendicular doors. "'Cause Farrah's gone, he's lonely. He'll drop you as soon as he's bored."

"That's what he said about you," she said, scraping a fingernail a couple of inches up and down his chest. "And he loves to tell me how right he was about that."

He grumbled. "I bet he feels so smug we didn't make it." She recalled the last time she'd seen Archer standing there. "How many days has it been now?"

"Twenty-eight," she answered and clued him in on her thoughts. "The last time we were standing here was the morning Ester drugged you." He didn't have a sense of humor about that, but she still found it hilarious… Until the truth that bliss would never happen again sank in. "We were happy that morning, Arch."

"You fucking were," he said. "You had wood to play with that didn't go anywhere for hours."

"You chained me to your bed, I was so pissed off. I could never stay mad at you for long. Twenty-eight days later and you're still pissed at me. How do you hold onto it for so long?"

Exhaling, his tone relaxed. "Squirm, I'm not pissed," he said, brushing his palms from the top of her head down her cheeks, capturing her hair against them. "You think I'm happy we're over? I get at you for not letting go, but I'm the guy who follows you home every night, just to make sure you get back safe."

What? She had no idea. Her assumption was he hadn't cared, that he'd fucked off and left her to fend for herself. Finding out she was wrong was a relief.

"Why do you do that?"

"Because I promised your nightmare would never come true and the first time I turned my back, it did. That's on me."

His guilt was strong, but she could alleviate it. "Arch," she said, stroking her hands up his body onto the sides of his neck. "That's not my nightmare anymore. I faced that demon. Hexam didn't mean to, but he did me a favor, I got to close that chapter. I might not have killed that sick bastard, but I proved to myself I was capable of taking control. Putting that knife in that man wasn't just punishment for him, it was punishment for every man who ever hurt me. I stood up to the bully and I won. I know I can do whatever it takes. Doing what I did, it freed me."

"No more nightmares?" he asked, tracing his thumbs over her lips.

"I have a new nightmare; one I don't wake up from. I live it every single day I don't see you. Tag says I'm pathetic for still holding on."

"If you are, sign me up too," he said, crouching to rest his forehead on hers. "I love you, Ny, even though it puts you at risk."

She tipped her head back to speak with her lips against his. "Loving you is my security. I need you, even if you can't bring yourself to ever be with me again. I'm always going to be here. Waiting."

"You can't do that forever."

She kissed him once. "Watch me."

TO BE CONTINUED...

Thank you for reading this tale!
If you can, please take the time to review.

~

Ask your local library for more Scarlett Finn
novels!

~

For all things Scarlett Finn
check out:

www.scarlettfinn.com

BOOK THREE

marked
scarlett finn

OUT NOW!

9 781914 517815